The Parts I Remember

A.K. MILLS

Dark Wolf
Publications

The Parts I Remember is a work of fiction. Names, characters, places and incidents are either products of the author's imagination or are used fictitiously. Any resemblance to actual events or locales or persons, living or dead, is entirely coincidental.

Text copyright © 2013 A.K. Mills

ISBN: 0988903407
ISBN-13: 978-0-9889034-0-1

For Mammy

ACKNOWLEDGMENTS

I would like to take this opportunity to thank everyone who made my dream of publishing this book a reality. First and foremost, I have to thank my sisters for their continued support and dedication in reading each version of the manuscript with the same level of enthusiasm. To my ever-encouraging mother, thank you for reading all of my stories. I am grateful to my personal reading group for offering their critiques not only on the final version, but also the cover design. To Meghan Pinson at My Two Cents Editing, thank you for your expertise in fine-tuning my story. And last but definitely not least, to my wonderful husband whose love and support has made all of my dreams come true. I love you.

The Parts I Remember

PROLOGUE

I remember fireworks, a beautiful display of orange and red sparks flying into the dark sky like sparklers on the Fourth of July, except louder, much louder.

"Ma'am," a voice called out to me. "Ma'am, can you hear me?"

Someone called my name in a faint whisper. "Kelly."

"Unresponsive," the voice called out. "Her eyes were open for a second, but she's out again."

"Sir, it looks like we have an unrestrained driver and a restrained passenger, both unresponsive," another voice was saying. "We need to get this thing opened up."

The smell of exhaust surrounded me as a loud motor was angrily awakened. Then, without warning, the piercing started and the blades screamed their way through the metal of the car. In an instant, I was surrounded by firemen; eight, ten, twenty, even. They hovered, stoic, a swarm of bright yellow jackets, each with the same calcified expression on his face.

"Ma'am," the voice called out louder. "Ma'am, if you can hear me, open your eyes."

I tried to open them.

"She's not—wait!" His stern voice cracked. "They're open—do you know where you are?"

The glare from the light hovering over my head blinded me. Shapes and colors danced in front of my eyes, merging fluidly in and out of each other. Nothing came into focus.

It took too much effort to think, let alone to keep my eyes

open. I couldn't force them. They were operating on their own accord.

"No, no, honey," the voice cried out. "Don't close your eyes on me. Keep 'em open. I know it's hard, but you have to keep them open."

You don't know shit, I thought.

"Open your—"

Fine.

"There we go," he said, relieved. "Now, you just keep looking at me with those beautiful brown eyes, and I'll do my best to get you out of here."

My eyes had never been referred to as beautiful. Big, yes. Telling, yes. Beautiful, no. Was this guy seriously trying to come on to me?

"Kelly." My name was being whispered again. "Kelly. I can't . . . breathe."

"The other one is talking." Another voice had joined the buzzing around me. My head was pounding.

"Kelly," the man's voice said. "Is that your name?"

He didn't allow me to answer. Well, maybe he tried and I just took too long to respond.

"Well, Kelly, my name is Joe, and I am going to do everything I can to get you out of here, okay? If you understand me, can you blink your eyes twice?"

That's when I realized something was wrong.

"Kelly, if you can understand me, I need you to blink your eyes twice."

It wasn't easy, but I blinked, or at least I tried to blink, twice.

"Okay, I'm glad we understand each other." Joe smiled, his face moving closer to mine.

"Kelly." The whisper was back, coming from somewhere to the side of me. It was a soft voice, different from the hard murmurs of the men that encircled me.

"Don't," Joe said when I tried to turn my neck. "Don't move."

"Ma'am." I heard another masculine voice up where the whispering was coming from. "Ma'am, what is your name?"

"M-mm . . . ," the whisper replied.

"It's okay," he said, his voice softer than Joe's, "take your time."

"Meh . . . Meh . . . Meredith."

"All right, Meredith, my name is Troy. I need you to stay awake and keep talking to me, but don't move. Do you think you can do that?"

"Sh . . . sure."

"Perfect," Troy replied.

A voice approached behind Joe. "We have a lone female driver in the other car. It doesn't look good. There was substantial blood loss. She's en route to County General. How's it look here? What do you need?"

"I don't know," Joe said, backing away from me. "She's awake, but her right leg is pinned pretty good."

"And the other one?"

"Not good. Unrestrained, hit the windshield pretty hard. I'm not sure we want to mess around in there too much. We need to get both of them out soon."

What the hell was going on?

"Kelly," the faint voice called out again. "I can't feel anything."

"Meredith," Troy said. "It's all right. Your body is going through a lot right now. Just try to relax. You'll be out of here real soon."

Meredith? Her name clicked in my mind. Meredith? I started to panic. What happened?

"We cut all the way through," a strange voice said. "Let's open it up."

The bitter cold was taking hold of me, enticing me to sleep. Joe wasn't talking and I couldn't keep my eyes open another second.

"Come on, Kelly," he said. "Keep 'em open, please."

I couldn't.

"Joe, are you ready?"

"I need a tarp," Joe replied. "Someone get me a tarp!" he yelled, sounding panicked.

I opened my eyes just as something dark and blue was being pulled over my body. It covered me completely, pressing flat against my face. The voices meshed with the piercing of metal and I could no longer make sense of them. As my eyes fluttered closed, I tried to think of what was going on and how I'd ended up there, wherever that was.

These are the parts I remember.

CHAPTER ONE

I sat as a wide-eyed college freshman in the lecture hall of the Charles Hail School of Business at Haysville University while the dean addressed our incoming class. The late August heat stifled the airflow in the room we were all tightly packed into, eager to be welcomed into college, eager to begin the rest of our lives.

"Take a look at the student on your left," the dean said. I knew where he was headed. "Take a look at the student on your right."

The silent hall rustled with students turning from side to side, making small talk, giggling.

"One of the three of you will not be here in four years."

Silence again filled the room.

It was heavy stuff to think about, but most of the students laughed it off after a minute. I know I did. I was young and I didn't care about who was or wasn't going to make it to graduation. I was going to be there, and that was all that mattered.

The dean concluded his you are no longer children speech by welcoming us one last time to Haysville University, and wished us well as we embarked upon our scholastic endeavors.

We left the hall in one giant mass, some students already friends, some with their roommates, and me alone. Angela, my assigned roommate, had rushed off to a campus ministry meeting at the chapel. She had asked me if I wanted to join her. I'd politely declined. Instead, I walked slowly back to my dorm, taking in the college atmosphere. Part of me still couldn't believe I had finally made it. I was out of high school, and more importantly, out of the house—no longer under the reign of my mom and dad and their rules.

It wasn't as though my parents were strict when I was in high school. In fact, when it came to my mother, I could do no wrong. It was something I knew all too well and had exploited to the best of my ability. But as a college freshman, there was no need to lie or bend the truth. I was going to be living on my own, coming and going as I pleased, eating what I wanted when I wanted. It was all so liberating.

I knew I wasn't going to be one of those kids who went crazy when they got to college, because I drank in high school. Every weekend was a different party at a different house. Most of the time I would stay over at a friend's house, and of course my mom always called to make sure her mother was home to supervise. But Mom didn't realize that she was either talking to one of my friends or that my friends' mothers would lie. There were a couple of moms like that, mothers who wanted to be cool and wanted their kids' approval so badly they would do just about anything to get it. I envied those friends, thinking their mothers were the best.

And at sixteen, they were. But when those mothers brought home boyfriend number six or came home drunk or high, they weren't so amazing. Suddenly my mom, who I knew was home in her sweats reading a book on the couch, became the best mother in the world.

I had fun in high school, and for the most part I stayed out of trouble. Okay, there was the one party I threw my senior year when my parents and Patrick, my younger brother, went to visit our sister Jane at college. Having made up the excuse that I had a group project to work on, I was able to get out of the family trip and was left on my own for two whole nights.

What was I supposed to do? For four years I had gone to numerous parties but never hosted my own. When word got out that my parents were going to be out of town, it didn't stay among the few friends I told in confidence; the party plan evolved. Before I knew it, the entire senior class was asking me what time they should come over.

I went along with it, rationalizing that I would keep it limited to my friends and a couple others. Everyone else I would turn away. Simple enough, right?

Wrong.

The night started off slowly, and I thought everything was going to be okay. I told my friends to park around the block to keep my neighbors from knowing anything was going on, and to come in only a couple at a time. On the inside of the house, music was playing and people were drinking, all having a good time. From the outside, it looked like a quiet night at home. Perfect.

As the night progressed, more and more people showed up. People I didn't know, who didn't even go to my school, were parking in my driveway and in front of my house and knocking on the front door. I didn't answer, and I gave specific instructions that no one was to let anyone else in. But the people we turned away didn't go home. Instead, they congregated on the front lawn, masses of people. It was a mess.

It was only a matter of time before the cops started pounding on the front door. I knew I was in trouble. Any time the cops come when your parents are out of town is never good. On more than one occasion, I'd been among the many who sprinted out the back door. Once I'd walked four miles to get home. But that night I couldn't exactly sprint out my own back door, could I?

When the squad cars pulled up, the crowd on the lawn scattered quicker than cockroaches. Cars peeled off down my street and inside my house, people were running scared, hiding in closets, under beds, anywhere that would keep them from getting caught. I tried to stall, but the knocking just grew more insistent.

I popped a piece of gum into my mouth and opened the front door with a smile.

"Kelly." The officer looked at me and peered over my shoulder into the house. "We have received some complaints about noise and commotion."

I tried my best to play it off. "Really?"

"You wouldn't be having a party this evening, would you?"

I was stuck. The only thing worse than having the police come to your house when your parents are out of town is having the police come to your house when your parents are out of town when your dad is one of the city's finest.

"Officer Fitzpatrick," I had begun when a call came in over his radio.

"We caught a couple of runners out back," his radio buzzed.

"Stay in the house," Officer Fitzpatrick commanded as he turned and ran to the backyard.

The police rounded up as many students as they could and took down the license plate numbers of the cars that were in the driveway and on the street. They gave some people breathalyzers; some knew to refuse, and in turn had to go to the police station. Guys, the same ones who played it so cool all the time, were freaking out. Girls were crying hysterically. I watched from my living room window as the night quickly turned horrendous.

Officer Fitzpatrick never came back. The police took care of the people outside and left. My friends that were in the house waited until I gave them the all clear before resurfacing. The ones that were able to drive home left, offering rides to those who were stranded. My close friends stayed the night and helped me clean.

You'd think that would have scared us straight for the remainder of the evening, but it didn't. We continued to drink, feeling secure because the police had already come and we didn't have to worry about any more random people showing up.

I continued to drink because I knew that when my parents found out, it would be a long time before I enjoyed another weekend.

My mother reprimanded me when they got home. "Do you know what an embarrassment this is, Kelly? Your father has to work with these people."

"It wasn't supposed to get like that," I insisted. "I don't know who those people were. I didn't let them in and they wouldn't leave."

"Do you know what could have happened if someone got hurt?" my father asked. "We could have gotten sued."

"Dad, I didn't mean for it—"

"We could have lost the house, everything we have, just because you didn't mean to have a party," he continued. "I could have lost my job."

How was I supposed to respond to that? My father wasn't one to yell, but I almost wished he would. Instead, he just looked me dead in the face.

"Where did you get the alcohol?" Mom asked. "You don't have one of those fake IDs, do you?"

"Please, Mom," I sighed. "I look like I'm twelve."

"That is fitting of your actions this weekend," she said, and she rose from the table. "I just don't even know what to say to you,

Kelly. I thought we raised you better than this."

She'd switched from anger to guilt, the whole "we must have failed as parents" bit. I waited, knowing it was only a matter of seconds until . . .

"Jane never did anything like this."

There it was, the comparison to my angelic older sister. I had nothing to say. I was a disappointment. I was scum.

Needless to say, my parents weren't happy with me for a while, but they came around. I was seventeen. I'd made a mistake. They forgave me. But that didn't stop my father from bringing home pictures of drunk-driving accidents, overdoses, and just about any other grotesque death he could find at work.

"One stupid decision," he said in his most serious of tones, "and your life, the lives of those who love you, is changed forever."

CHAPTER TWO

The first night in the dorm was weird. It was stuffy in our small un-air-conditioned room and I was, still am, one of those people who need cold air. I hate being hot. Angela, returning from her campus ministry meeting, didn't seem to mind as much. She said the heat was God's way of warming us with his love. When I asked her why He would then freeze us in the winter, she said that she didn't question God and I shouldn't, either. Angela was intense and lacked any sense of humor. Yet I thought, more so hoped, that we would get along. I had my quirks and she had hers. That was apparent almost immediately, the first time we spoke.

Less than twenty-four hours after I opened my housing assignment from the university, the phone in my parents' kitchen rang. As soon as I heard the voice on the other end of the line, I knew it was Angela Harris, my soon-to-be roommate from Hamilton, New Jersey.

While I knew some girls from high school that were going to Haysville University, I'd decided to room with a stranger so I'd be forced to meet new people and get out of my comfort zone. Angela was definitely out of my comfort zone.

"Hi, Kelly, this is Angela Harris," she said excitedly. "I got our housing assignment today. Did you get yours?"

"Yeah," I said. "I got mine today, too." I lied. I didn't want her to think I wasn't as excited as she clearly was.

"Okay, good," she said, then got straight to the point. "I was wondering if you wanted to match our bedding and stuff. I mean, if you didn't already get anything."

"I didn't get anything yet," I said. "Did you have something in mind?"

"Actually, yes," Angela replied. "My favorite color is light purple, well, actually, I like all pastel colors, but I like purple the best. What's your favorite color?"

"Green," I answered.

"Perfect!" she exclaimed. "Do you have a Bed Bath & Beyond by your house?"

"Yes."

"They have a bed-in-a-bag set that's pink, purple, yellow, and green plaid. Maybe you can go look at it, and if you like it, that's what we'll get."

"Sounds good," I said, with the feeling that Angela had probably already purchased hers.

"That's great," she said. "So, tell me a little bit about yourself."

We talked a decent amount that first day. Over the course of an hour I learned that Angela was the oldest of four, and a devote Catholic who looked forward to getting involved with the university's outreach programs and campus ministry. She didn't have a boyfriend and sounded relieved when I told her I didn't either. While she seemed nice, she didn't seem to have many friends. In fact, she claimed that she didn't know one other person who was going to Hay U.

We did the whole matching thing. The comforter set wasn't bad, and to be honest, I couldn't have cared less what our color scheme was. She bought the coordinating rug, throw pillows, and curtains to give our room a homey feel. It was nice for me; by the time I arrived on move-in day, she practically had everything all set up.

"I hope you don't mind the layout," she said. "I figured you wouldn't want bunk beds, so my dad and I arranged the room like this."

I quickly learned that when Angela wanted something, she would claim I didn't want it instead of coming out and saying what she wanted.

My mom loved what Angela had done with the room, and she helped me put my clothes away. My dad and Patrick were relieved that they didn't have to move any furniture around and quickly unloaded the car. Jane just wandered around the room reminiscing about moving into her own dorm room freshman year, how close she and her roommate had become, and how young freshmen now looked to her as a college senior.

When there was nothing else to be done, they left. I walked my family out and hugged my mom, who had started to cry, and told her I would be okay, that I was not that far from home. She smiled and told me to be nice to Angela, emphasizing how two people who are so different can become the best of friends. She was always so optimistic.

That first night, Angela and I talked a lot. We compared class schedules—she was a theology major and I was business undeclared. We didn't have any classes together but agreed to eat lunch together every day.

That lasted less than the first week. Angela was weird.

I immediately made friends, started going to parties, and immersed myself in campus life. Angela stayed home and clipped her toenails. I am not kidding. She would sit at her desk clipping her toenails and then leave the remnants on the corner of the desk for days, weeks. I swear I saw her eat one once. No lie.

Angela's odd habits quickly got old and she got tired of my partying. I asked her to come out with me, telling her it would be good to get out. But she claimed that she didn't want to "partake in the mindless actions of sin," whatever that meant.

She did, however, manage to make one friend, a girl named Theresa Cramer. Having only heard about her, I figured she couldn't be that bad. In my mind, it didn't get much worse than Angela. But it did. Theresa behaved and dressed just as oddly as Angela.

That isn't fair. They didn't dress oddly, just very conservatively. I tried my best not to stare at their short jeans, loose shirts, and sneakers. I certainly didn't appreciate Theresa's scoffing at my tight pants and low-cut shirt, but I didn't really care what she thought.

They were two peas in a pod, and it seemed like Angela got weirder the more they hung out together. I tried, but I just could not be in the same room with them after a while; sober, that is. Coming home from class to find them in my room quickly became unbearable to the point that I had to leave. That was how I met Meredith.

Our dorm room was part of a five-room suite that shared a common area. That common area became my escape. When we moved in, I tried my best to meet and get to know everyone in the suite. I imagine that's what everyone does their first week at college. We all left our doors open and walked freely from room to room. But as the semester progressed, everyone got into their own routines and cliques and the friendly "I love everyone" thing dissolved.

Meredith was one of the girls to whom I'd had a brief introduction the first week of school, but nothing more. That is, until we were ostracized from our own rooms and began spending more time in the common area.

"Roommate?" I asked when I saw her on the couch for the third afternoon in a row.

"Yeah." She shrugged her shoulders. "You too?"

"Yup." I smiled. "Weird friend."

"Boyfriend," Meredith replied. "She locked me out."

"Can she do that?" I asked.

"She did." Meredith managed a smile.

Our brief interactions turned into long conversations, smoke breaks, coffee runs, and eventually weekends out. We used each other to get back at our roommates for excluding us, alternating which one we would annoy. If she knew her roommate was expecting her boyfriend, we would deliberately have a study session—and no, we couldn't do it in the common area, because we needed absolute quiet. Then we would camp out in my room watching, in Angela's opinion, trashy movies until she left in disgust.

I wasn't surprised or offended at the end of the second semester when Angela said she didn't want to room with me the following year. I mean really, did she honestly think I wanted to live with her? I coolly told her that I felt the same and that Meredith and I had already agreed to live together. We've lived together ever since.

That's how the trouble started.

CHAPTER THREE

Freshman year was a year of firsts for me. The first time I slept away from home, the first time I didn't have a curfew, and the first time I had sex.

I was, in my mom's words, a late bloomer. I developed later than the other girls in my class, got my period later, and matured a little later as well. When Jane was thirteen she approached our mother, white as a ghost, and told her something was terribly wrong. Seeing the concerned look on her face, Mom took her into the living room to talk. I waited anxiously outside the door, thinking the worst. Yet when they emerged, my mom had a smile on her face and Jane seemed more at ease.

Somehow, Jane had managed to become a woman overnight. I didn't understand what that meant or how it had happened, but my mom said that we would have a similar talk when I was thirteen. In the meantime, she and Jane were going to lunch and then to the mall. I was so jealous.

So when I was thirteen, we had "the talk" and I waited for my initiation into womanhood. However, it didn't come when I was thirteen. It didn't come when I was fourteen. Finally, it arrived when I was fifteen, on April first. I should have known then that I was destined to one of life's sardonic fates, but instead I reveled in finally being a woman. The blessing, I realized, was more of a curse, and apart from my mother, no one seemed impressed. Still, I got to go to lunch and to the mall.

Being the late developer that I was, boys weren't as interested in me as they were the other girls. Lindsay Prince and her clique were the most popular, best-dressed girls in my class. Lindsay dated Tony Bendetto, the star athlete in soccer, basketball, and baseball. I was left with the likes of Jim Collier and Lance Lewis, the rejects of Lindsay Prince and her girlie gang.

I started dating Jim when we were sophomores in high school and I'd let him go to second base before I realized I didn't really like him. He was kind of cute and really smart, but he just didn't do it for me. He was upset when we broke up but he quickly moved on to Jenny Richardson, a girl further down the ladder than me who quickly gave it up. She got pregnant junior year and dropped out.

After I broke up with Jim, I hooked up with Lance. I asked him to the junior MORP, prom spelled backwards where the girls ask the guys, and we dated briefly after that. We went to third, he wanted more, and when I wouldn't give in, he dumped me.

I wasn't waiting for marriage, but I was waiting for something. I wanted to feel some kind of emotion: passion, excitement, anything. I didn't find it in high school.

It wasn't until late November, freshman year of college, that I felt enough to give up my longstanding membership in the V club. Blake Roberts, the lucky suitor, and I met during orientation and became reacquainted at a party at the beginning of the year. We hooked up all of October and November. And one night when Angela went off on yet another world-saving weekend crusade, I invited Blake to my room and we did it. I knew I wasn't going to be Blake's first, but that didn't really bother me. He was hot and if his kissing was any indication of what he was like in bed, then I was all for it. It sounds shallow, I know. And who has sex for the first time with a guy named Blake? But I wanted to get it over with and I wanted it to be good. Blake, although I had no other references, did not disappoint.

Afterwards, I felt like I had when I first got my period. All that time I had waited to have sex, and when I did, it was nothing special. It was over. I was no different, and no one besides Meredith really cared. Well, that's not entirely true. It turned out that Blake had a girlfriend back home. She cared.

I didn't tell Jane that I'd had sex with Blake for a number of reasons, but primarily it was because I didn't want to let her down. It would have been one thing if I'd had sex with a guy I was dating, who loved me, who I loved. But for me to give myself to a guy who'd had at least one girlfriend I knew about and other previous partners, I would have never heard the end of it.

Blake and I continued to hook up until Christmas break, then sadly, we stopped in the New Year. While Jane can be a bit overbearing at times, she was definitely right about one aspect of losing my virginity: all of a sudden, sleeping with guys became a lot easier to do.

CHAPTER FOUR

The blaring sirens brought me out of whatever state I was in; sleep, unconsciousness, near death. Joe was still by my side, and for the first time, I could see his face. He was cute. He had a strong jaw line lightly spotted with stubble. His cheeks and forehead were smeared with grease mixed with sweat—which was weird, because I wasn't hot at all. In fact, I was pretty cold.

"Well, hello there, sunshine," Joe said when I opened my eyes. "How are you feeling?"

I heard every word he said, but I was unable to respond—or move, for that matter. There was a tube jammed down my throat, my arms were tied down at my sides, and something was securing my head tightly to the board I was lying on.

"That's all right." He smiled a tired smile when I failed to generate any form of response. "You need to save your energy. I'm just happy to see those beautiful brown eyes again."

I tried to make my lips curve upwards. His expression didn't change. Every time we hit a bump, both of us shook and the equipment surrounding us rattled. Trying to think made my brain hurt, which I thought was odd, since I'd had enough hangover headaches to last me a lifetime. None of those, however, came close to the galloping in my head right then. Slowly, the screaming sirens began to fade, my vision blurred, and I closed my eyes again, despite Joe's protests.

CHAPTER FIVE

I can't say that I was expecting my first summer home to be any different from what it turned out to be. Somehow, everyone from high school found themselves back together at Chris Davis's house, drunk, high, and/or hooking up. If it wasn't for the new sense of self-assurance and the modest-to-noticeable weight gain, the freshman fifteen being closer to thirty for some, you would have sworn that we were back in our senior year of high school.

Chris lived in a dream house, complete with gorgeous parents. His father was a man of mystery to us all. I'm not even sure Chris knew exactly what it was that his father did. "He's a businessman," he always said. "And he travels a lot." Chris's mom, a beautiful woman that most of us envied, kept the house in order by turning a blind eye to the parties and substance abuse as long as the crowds were small and no one drove drunk. She flirted with the guys, boys, really, but never took it beyond that. I think she was scared of Chris's dad; I know I was. He was sexy in a Ray Liotta, Goodfellas kind of way. He made you wonder and gave you nice dreams, but those dreams could quickly become nightmares.

I witnessed one such nightmare firsthand when Chris crashed his dad's Mercedes. It took me a good month and a half to go back to his house after that eruption. My father didn't approve of the time I spent with Chris either, knowing more about the Davis family's income than he could share with me.

"Of all of the kids you could spend your time with," he would say. "You have to enjoy his company."

"I'm not going to marry him, Dad," I would always reply. "We're just friends."

And we were. Did we share a mutual attraction? Of course we did. In high school, we didn't realize what that was, but given the time and loss of inhibitions after a year away at college, we quickly gave into that lust. It was everything love wasn't and everything drunken fornication was: sloppy, uncomfortable, and awkward. Whatever. It wasn't serious.

Chris was barely my first, and hardly my last. He swam in a pool of men that meant something to me, but not enough to qualify as any sort of relationship. I was still looking, though not very energetically, for Mr. Right.

I counted down the days of summer, anxiously awaiting my return to life at Hay U. Sure, being off from school and at home with my mom's cooking had its advantages, but it was nothing like being away. Meredith came and stayed with me for a week, then I took the train to Philadelphia to stay with her and her dad. Her mother died of breast cancer when Meredith was only nine. Meredith didn't talk about her mom much, but her picture was by Meredith's bedside everywhere we lived. Her dad is a great man who was never able to let go of the love he had for Meredith's mom and never remarried. Meredith and her father were close. I guess they had to be. All they had was each other.

I loved my time in Philadelphia. We went to South Street, a long road of interesting shops and restaurants that bustled with many different types of people. We had the most fun in a store called the King of Condoms. I couldn't believe it at first, but there was actually a huge store filled with all sorts of things related to sex. From phallus-shaped erasers and lollipops to a whole section in the back that you had to be eighteen just to get into, I was at a loss for words. I'm no prude, but some of the things I saw in there made me blush.

South Street was like nothing I had ever seen before, with such a rich mixture of cultures and expression. And the smells, the smells escaping the open windows of the cheesesteak vendors gripped my stomach and turned on my appetite.

"No," Meredith said when I suggested an early afternoon snack. "If you want an official Philly cheesesteak, you have to go to Pat's."

"Pat's?" I looked around for a sign.

"It's not far from here," she replied. "That is where you get a cheesesteak."

My stomach growled. "Can't we just go to Jim's? They have to be good there. The line is out the door."

"It's your call," she smiled. "But Pat's is better."

Philadelphia cheesesteaks—I had no idea what I was missing. They tasted better than sex; at least, the sex I had been having with Chris Davis.

My week in Philadelphia concluded with a Phillies baseball game. I've never been a big fan of baseball, and I blame my father for that one. When I was little, he used to listen to the games on the radio every time we were in the car. The thought of it still makes me cringe—the crackling static from the AM radio station, the distinct voices of the announcers, and being stuck between Jane and Patrick in the back seat, sticking to the seats on hot summer days. I hated it.

"Phillies games are different," Meredith promised. "My dad and I have been going ever since I was little. Trust me. You'll have a great time."

And I did. We went to a night game, so it wasn't too hot, and the park glistened under the lights. The stadium was packed mostly with Phillies fans, but there were some Mets fans scattered throughout. The Phillies won, the crowd was ecstatic, and I didn't want to leave. Meredith's father took me in like a long-lost daughter. She and I were already practically like sisters. I couldn't wait to move in with her sophomore year.

At the end of freshman year, we were lucky enough to get good lottery numbers for the housing selection for sophomore year and pretty much had our choice of location. Naturally, we chose to live off the main campus and opted for Ashwood Hall. Ashwood was considered to be prime housing because its large apartments each had a kitchen, dining room, living room, and two bedrooms. It was a far cry from the sardine cans the school passed off as freshman dorms. The only downside to choosing Ashwood was that we needed two more roommates. And rather than being assigned two strangers and risk ending up with a pair like Angela and Theresa, we searched for our type of people. We ended up with Molly Brown and Samantha Ashburn.

Meredith had Spanish with Molly second semester freshman year, and Molly quickly turned our twosome into three. Molly was more outgoing and outspoken than Meredith and seemed to have better party connections on campus.

Before we met Molly, Meredith and I were content with the Hay U nightlife, where five dollars bought you all you could drink. But Molly introduced us to Main Street—real bars and real men— where five dollars didn't even cover the cab ride there.

It was Molly who arranged for our fake IDs. She had an acquaintance, a junior, who made them for a hundred bucks apiece. It was the best investment I ever made. I created a new persona for mine: Lexis McBride. Lexi was a sexy and confident twenty-two-year-old (twenty-one seemed too obvious) who liked to party, and possibly an alcoholic. After that, campus parties seemed infantile and boring. Sitting on a gross couch in an apartment, squished amongst drunken frat-boy wannabes, paled in comparison to dancing in a bar and having my drinks bought for me by sexy, successful men. From my first night on Main Street, I was hooked.

Samantha was Molly's assigned roommate freshman year and they'd actually gotten along. Sam didn't join us very often on our weekend outings. She was working her way though Hay U and had little time for anything else. When she did come out with us, though, those were the best nights. Or in some cases, the worst.

CHAPTER SIX

Moving in sophomore year was completely different from freshman year. The anticipation of the year before was replaced with excitement and the unfamiliarity was replaced with a sense of belonging. Unlike freshman year, neither Jane nor Patrick could make the trip. Jane had entered the work force and didn't feel right taking the day off, but she promised to take me to dinner since she was only minutes away. Patrick had soccer tryouts.

I thought back to when I tried out for soccer in high school. Jane, having played varsity as a freshman, had made it seem so easy. "You have to be in shape," she cautioned. "They make you run a lot." I laughed and scoffed at her warnings until I found myself dry heaving on the side of the soccer field with a couple of other girls.

Jane had jogged by us with her senior buddies, laughing hysterically at the cute freshmen. It was hell. Yes, I'd expected to run, but three miles before practice and sprinting up and down the biggest hill on the field afterwards seemed a bit much.

The August sun beat down relentlessly on me that first day, making it nearly impossible to breathe. My heart was racing and just when I felt as though I was going to die, Coach D. blew the whistle and told us she would see us the following morning.

"Race you to the car," Jane laughed as she jogged past me towards the parking lot. Even if I'd wanted to run, my legs would simply not allow it. My body ached as I slid into the car and the thought of going back for more the next day seemed more like self-mutilation than a fun school activity.

"It's always hard the first day," my mom said when I told her how awful it was. "It will get easier."

But I was skeptical. In my mind there was no way it could get easier. Coach D. had said that morning that she was going to take it easy on us because it was the first day. If that was her version of easy, I didn't want to see difficult.

I tried to ignore the alarm the next morning, hitting snooze at the first chirp of sound, and even that movement hurt. My entire body ached and I made my decision. I was not going back. I was not even going to get out of bed. Happy with the thought of lying comfortably in bed all day, I reached over and slid the switch on the alarm from snooze to off and closed my eyes. The tension in my body began to dissipate as I wriggled under the covers and eased back into sleep.

Then Jane stormed into the room screaming, "WE'RE LEAVING IN TWENTY MINUTES!"

"I'm not going." I turned over, wrapping the pillow around my ears.

"What do you mean you're not going?" she huffed.

"It's too much," I said, yawning. "I can't move my body."

"Kelly," she sighed. "You ARE going, so get up! You signed up for the team, so you have to go through with it. What, are you going to quit just because it's a little difficult? What's next? Are you going to drop out of high school because freshman year isn't like grade school? You are not a quitter!"

"God, do you ever shut up?"

"I can go on all day. So either you get up on your own or I'm going to get a pot of water and dump it on you."

"MOM!" I cried out.

"She already left for work. You have five minutes to get out of bed."

"Fine," I groaned.

Maybe I was a quitter. So what? I knew that in Jane's mind, quitting was never an option. Thankfully, I'd never had the same drive to perfection that she did.

I refused to speak to her the entire ride to practice. She sang along happily to Natalie Merchant and the 10,000 Maniacs, tapping her hands to the beat of the music on the steering wheel while I glared at her. It was moments such as those that I utterly despised her.

Jane had not one care in the world. She was strikingly beautiful, with long black hair that never frayed or fell out of place, and calming blue eyes. My hair, when I could get it to grow, stuck straight up at the end of my ponytail and frizzed at the slightest sign of humidity. It wasn't as sleek as Jane's, more of a dirty brown that matched my eyes. The genes that had graced Jane upon her conception were nowhere to be found at the time of mine. It didn't stop with looks, either. The athletic genes also favored her, adorning her with a slender, muscular frame that welcomed the challenge of soccer tryouts, while my scrawny legs were easily beaten and fatigued.

Jane made varsity as a freshman. A freshman! And there I was, struggling to make the freshman squad. Well, technically I didn't have to make anything, because freshmen couldn't get cut. I guess the coaches hoped to eliminate the weak ones like me through the conditioning process to keep the squad small. If it wasn't for Jane, I would have been one of the ones who gladly walked away.

Yet somehow I survived the second day, then the third, then the fourth, and finally I finished the week. I was so excited for Saturday morning. It was the best Saturday I had ever had. I slept in until noon, letting exhaustion take over my body.

When I did wake up, my mom took me to brunch to celebrate my first week of high school life. Jane grumbled that she never got a celebratory lunch and complained that our mother babied me, and that was why I was such a wimp.

"Don't pay her any mind," my mother said, smiling at me.

"I don't," I said, smirking at Jane, who walked off in disgust.

"You are more than welcome to come with us," Mom called to Jane.

"Whatever," Jane replied. And as a parting jab, she looked at me and said, "I'm going for a run."

"Run an extra mile for me," I jabbed right back.

I managed to make it through tryouts and the entire first season. Despite Jane's comments and urges to go out for junior varsity sophomore year, I declined. Without her there to physically force me to go, I wouldn't do it on my own. She was the athlete, not me. I accepted that.

It was hot moving into Ashwood. Although there were many upgrades in the apartment from freshman year, there was still no air conditioning. Luckily, Meredith and her dad had arrived first, and he had already put fans in the bedroom window and the living room. The fans didn't do much in terms of cooling, but at least they helped circulate the stuffy air.

I unpacked my clothes and put them in the dresser while my mom made my bed with the same awful sheets and plaid comforter from the year before. Meredith and I joked about matching our comforters for sophomore year. I told her she could get the same set I'd shared with Angela. She laughed and suggested that instead I offer Theresa my comforter and sheets for a discounted price.

I thought about it and made the offer, solely in jest, to Theresa on the last day of finals freshman year when she came by to help Angela move her stuff out.

"You can't be serious," she said, widening her eyes in shock at the mere suggestion.

"Why not?" I said. "Angie (she hated when I called her that) already has the set, and I thought it would be nice if you guys could match as well. We got so many compliments on our bedroom this year."

Angela blushed. Theresa, unimpressed, turned to me and said, "Thank you for the offer, but I wouldn't feel right sleeping on those sheets."

"What do you mean 'those sheets'?" I asked.

"Well," she replied, putting her hands on her hips. "You had a lot of company this year and I wouldn't feel comfortable sleeping where so many men slept."

"So many men?"

"I don't think we want to have this conversation right now," Angela interrupted.

"What conversation is that?" I asked.

"Angela told me all about you and your men."

"Me and my men?"

"Yes, she told me how you had S-E-X in the room while she was sleeping. She even showed me the condom," Theresa said sternly.

"The condom . . ." I couldn't believe what I was hearing. "You took it out of the trash?"

"I didn't believe that you would be so brazen as to subject her to your immoral actions," Theresa replied. "But Angela told me that she had proof."

I turned, aghast, and looked at Angela. "Is she telling the truth? Did you really go through my trash?"

"It was our trash, actually, and yes, I did," Angela said meekly. "You put me in a very uncomfortable position. You know that condoms are considered birth control and they go against the Christian way of life."

"Is that where that speech came from?" I asked, remembering a lecture about the Church's view on birth control one morning while I was struggling to combat a particularly bad hangover.

"I have tried to guide you in the path of righteousness," Angela sighed, "but I don't think you are ready to make the changes that are necessary to live a life of Christ."

Let me say for the record that I was not the lady of the night Angela made me out to be. I'd only had sex with her in the room once, and I was extremely drunk. In my defense, I didn't know she was in the room, honest. The night she was talking about was when Meredith and I were at a party at the Crew House, and I ended up talking to this guy Luke, a hot guy from my math class that I was infatuated with. As with most college hookups, we started talking waiting in line for the keg and were making out a couple of cups later. He offered to walk me home and I graciously accepted. He was really hot.

Anyway, I could have sworn Angela had said she was going away on some kind of Bible study retreat and would be gone all weekend.

Luke and I stumbled into my room and disrobed each other in the dark. I may have heard the slightest noise coming from Angela's side of the room, but I was focused on Luke, whose solid body consumed me as we fell onto the bed, completely naked and unrestrained. We moved in unison like we'd been together many times before. Our rhythm was undeniable and the sex was incredible. By that point, even if I'd known that Angela was in the room, I wouldn't have stopped. It was that good.

We both passed out when it was over. I was hoping for a repeat performance the following morning, but when Luke and I awoke to the sound of Angela clipping her toenails, I knew there was no chance. She paused when she heard us stir and turned and glared at us like the sinners that we were.

"Morning," Luke smiled, exposing his dimples.

Angela turned back around and continued clipping.

"Okay," he said, turning to me with a smirk. "Well, good morning to you." He kissed my neck.

"Good morning," I smiled, running my hands down his bare back.

Suddenly we both became aware of how naked he was.

"Angela," I asked. "Are you going to get some breakfast?"

"I already did," she replied without looking at me. It was obvious that she had no plans of leaving.

Luke sighed and rolled onto his back. "I should . . ."

"Yeah . . ." I returned the same regretful sigh, wanting more of him and hating Angela for preventing me from getting it.

I got out of bed naked to gather our clothes that were strewn about the floor. Angela made some kind of noise to protest but I ignored her. "But that's how God created us," I'd said the first time she made a big deal about me walking around the room naked. "Wasn't it when Adam ate the forbidden fruit that he became ashamed of his bare body?"

My knowledge of the Bible shocked her, but it didn't stop her from believing I was any less immoral.

I gathered Luke's clothes and sadly passed them over to him. You would think that Angela would have given us at least a minute or two of privacy so we could say goodbye, but she remained in her seat, crouched over her disgusting feet.

He got dressed and left. I dropped back into bed and suddenly realized how sick I felt.

"I don't think you want to have premarital sex like that," Angela began to rant. "It will only lead to emptiness."

I rolled over and went back to sleep.

Because of that one oversight, Theresa pegged me and my bedding as dirty. It didn't bother me, though. I was more than content to keep the sheets for sophomore year.

Molly's parents were the first to leave once we were settled into our new apartment. After saying goodbye to her mom and dad, she went to work planning our first night back.

My parents were the next to go. Mom wanted to get back to see how Patrick's first day of tryouts had gone. I walked them down to their car and thanked them for their help. Mom's eyes welled with tears, but she didn't cry as much as she had the year before. I didn't take it personally. Dad gave me a tight hug and a kiss on the forehead before getting behind the wheel. "Be good," they said in unison, and drove off.

Samantha's mom, Carol, seemed to take a liking to Bob, Meredith's dad, and she stayed back while he finished putting together our entertainment center. Bob seemed to pay her no mind. I guess he was good-looking, in an older, handyman kind of way. I felt bad for Carol because she seemed so desperate for male affection. If you ask me, she was out of Bob's league. She continued to linger, despite's Sam's attempts to get her to leave. But as soon as Bob packed up his toolbox and kissed Meredith goodbye, Carol grabbed her bag and made for the door so they would go out together. "Goodbye to you, too," Sam sighed as her mom waved and blew a kiss from the elevator. When the doors closed, we burst into hysterical laughter.

"What if your dad and your mom . . . ," I said, looking from Meredith to Sam.

"Don't," Meredith laughed.

"Please," Samantha begged.

"You guys would be stepsisters," I concluded. "How sweet."

We laughed, but I could tell Sam was a little more concerned than she was letting on.

"Let's get this year off to the perfect start," Molly said, entering the living room from the kitchen with the bottle of vodka and four shot glasses she'd kept hidden from our parents in her stuffed bear.

And so began our second year of college, four friends and a bottle of vodka. Life didn't get any better than that.

CHAPTER SEVEN

Sophomore year was quickly labeled The Year of the Blackout. In my naivety, I thought that when a person blacked out it meant they got so drunk that they passed out and were unable to remember anything from the night before. According to that definition, I blacked out a lot freshman year. Isn't that what all freshmen did? Well, all freshmen with the exception of Angela and Theresa.

Meredith and I had an acquaintance named Jodi Kinwall who, by the end of first semester freshman year, was better known as Jodi "Can and Will." She brought home all types of guys on a consistent basis. If guys weren't leaving her room first thing in the morning, she was stumbling back, often with less than what she went out with. One morning she came home without a shoe. I can understand coming home without a sock, underwear maybe, but a shoe? How do you lose a shoe? Then again, the guys' rooms were pretty nasty. The smell that leaked from under their doors was a combination of musty, dirty clothes and body odor. On second thought, maybe losing a shoe wasn't that hard to do.

Jodi "Can and Will" and her walk of shame, though she referred to it as the stride of pride, defined blackout to me.

I blacked out often freshman year and would usually awake to Angela glaring at me from her bed, ready to berate me for lashing out at her in my drunken state. "I don't think you realize how nasty you get when you are drunk," she would say. I couldn't reply because I would have no recollection of what had transpired.

There was one night that I brought a guy home, Phil, no, Bill, something like that, and I'm not quite sure what happened. When he got out of my bed the next morning sporting nothing but an erection, Angela just about had a heart attack.

"I don't think you mean to be so loose," she counseled me after he left. "I blame the alcohol."

I was barely able to hear her over the pounding in my head.

"There's a support group on campus," she continued. "I'll go with you if you want."

"I'm good, thanks." I yawned and got out of bed with the same lack of attire as Bill, Phil, whoever.

Angela blushed and turned away.

"You can't tell me you don't walk around naked," I said, noticing that my nudity set her ill at ease.

"What?" she asked with her nose stuck in a book.

"Clearly you are not comfortable with the naked female form," I replied.

"I believe in privacy, modesty," she answered.

"You should try walking around naked. It's very liberating."

She snorted. "I am not like you, Kelly. I prefer to keep my clothes on."

"Don't knock it until you've tried it, Angie."

"I don't even know what that means," she said in disgust. "And don't call me Angie."

There was a lot that Angela didn't know and would never understand. And when it came to blackout drinking, there was a lot I didn't know but would quickly come to understand. And it all began harmlessly with a game of Never Have I Ever.

The game itself was simple enough; we sat around in a circle and each took turns saying things we had never done. If anyone had done what was said, they had to drink. Since it was Meredith's idea to play the game, she went first.

"Never have I ever . . . had sex at the movies."

Molly, Sam, and I all looked at each other and laughed.

"Come on," Meredith said. "I know one of you whores has."

Sam was next. "Never have I ever . . . hooked up with two guys on the same night."

Meredith and I looked at each other and took a shot of beer. We'd actually hooked up with the same two guys on the same night. We were that close.

I didn't know what to say when it was my turn. It was hard to think of something I had never done that all the other girls would have. "Never have I ever . . . hooked up with my sister's boyfriend."

"No fair," Meredith protested. "I don't have a sister."

"A family member's boyfriend, then," I offered.

"Oh." Meredith smiled mischievously. "Well, that changes everything."

She and Molly clanked their shot glasses in a toast and threw back their shots.

Molly continued the game. "Never have I ever . . . gotten blackout drunk."

"Liar," Sam cried out. "You have gotten blackout drunk. You're the one who taught me how to get blackout drunk."

"I think we all have been blackout drunk," I said, filling everyone's shot glass.

"Not pass-out drunk, Kel," Meredith said, "blackout drunk. And you, Miss Liar," she said, turning to Molly, "you know what the consequence is for lying in this game."

Molly smiled and chugged her beer happily while we all took our shots.

"I hardly remember second semester last year," I said to Meredith.

"Yeah," she replied. "That's because you passed out almost every night that we went out."

"I don't understand," I said.

"Let me," Molly said, "being as I am the one who introduced you to the concept."

I sat attentively, eager to learn what I had been missing.

"Blackout drinking," she began, "is when you get so drunk that you have no idea what's going on around you, yet you appear to be completely fine."

"How is that any different from regular drinking?" I asked. "You still don't remember much the next day."

"It's hard to explain," she said. "It's easier to show you. Let's do it tonight."

"I don't know how to."

"I'll take care of it," she said. "Now let's all do a shot for Kelly getting blackout drunk."

We all took a shot, dispersed from our circle, and prepared for our night out. We were in and out of each other's closets, mixing and matching tops, bottoms, and shoes. The four of us had no problem interchanging our wardrobes to achieve the perfect look.

Being my first B.O.D. (blackout drunk) experience, Molly wanted to keep things under control, so we stayed on campus.

"The trick," she said, sauntering in my room in skinny jeans and a black lace bra, "is to not drink too much too fast. You need to let the alcohol get absorbed."

I was already well on my way to intoxication, as evidenced by my struggle to zip up my knee-high boots.

Dressed in our best party attire, which consisted of dark, tight, and slightly revealing clothing, we hit the shuttle stop for our favorite destination, the Crew House. The Crew House sheltered the upper-class crew members and catered to underclassmen wanting to get drunk. The shuttle was filled to normal Saturday-night capacity when we got on and reeked of perfume, cologne, alcohol, and cigarettes.

We could hear the music from half a block away as we walked toward the Crew House. I was ready for my night to begin.

"Molly!" a husky junior at the door said. "Where have you been?"

"You know how I feel about keg parties," she said, kissing him on the cheek and accepting four free cups.

We squeezed through the crowd in the foyer and made our way to the keg in the kitchen. My boots stuck with each step I took across the beer-spattered linoleum floor. Thankfully a window was open, allowing for some fresh air. The cologne of eager freshmen males was enough to choke anyone daring the keg line.

Molly looked at me. "Remember to pace yourself," she said.

"Doesn't that defeat the purpose?" I asked.

"Trust me," she replied.

I did trust her.

It was warm in the Crew House. The smoke from the cigarettes and whatever else was circulating had meshed into a cloud above our heads. The beats from the techno music blaring pulsated through my body as I drank my beer, maintaining a steady pace.

Meredith bounced up to me with a joint in her hand. "How are you feeling?"

"Feeling good," I smiled, reaching for her hand.

"No, no, no," she pulled back. "Not tonight."

"Come on," I pleaded. "Just one drag."

Meredith didn't say no to anyone, especially me. She looked around cautiously before offering me her hand.

I inhaled long and deep, feeling the smoke burn its way to my lungs. It was a great feeling.

Molly came up behind me. "How ya feeling?"

"Great," I replied. Though truth be told, I couldn't feel much of anything. I was floating through the party.

"Hey, Kel," I heard from behind me. I felt a hand grab my waist and spin me around.

I needed time to adjust from my quick turn and when my eyes focused, my heart jumped. Standing in front of me was Luke Rymes, the best sex I'd ever had.

"Luke," I said, and my entire body began to tingle. I wanted to eat him. "How are you?"

"Good," he smiled, his dimples exposing themselves on his flawless face.

My body quivered under his gaze even though I knew it probably had more to do with my alcohol consumption than the sexual attraction mounting between us.

"Where are you headed after this?" he asked.

"Oh, no," Molly cut in. "She's coming home with us tonight."

Luke smiled at her and turned to me, sliding his fingers between mine. My heart lurched and my head filled with a sudden rush of excitement.

"Why don't we let Kelly decide who she goes home with?"

"Yeah," I said, "why don't we let Kelly decide?"

"We can't do that," Molly replied, "because Kelly is in no shape to go home with anyone other than her friends."

"She looks more than okay to me," Luke replied. "And besides, Kelly and I are good friends."

"Well, looks can be deceiving, there, lover boy," Molly said with a hint of aggravation. She obviously was in no mood to discuss my situation any further. "We are leaving in half an hour."

She smiled curtly at Luke and walked off.

"I don't think she likes me very much," Luke said, frowning.

"That's okay." I leaned in to kiss him. "Because I'll like you enough for the both of us."

I woke up in my bed the next morning. Meredith was sleeping soundly across the room from me, curled up under her pink comforter. I lifted my comforter to see what, if any, clothing I was wearing. Much to my surprise, I was in my pajamas, a pair of boxers and a T-shirt from Victoria's Secret. It wasn't often that I woke up the morning after a night out completely clothed. Most nights when I stumbled in drunk, I would grab whatever I could find and throw it on, inside out or backwards, clean or not. Yet somehow I found my way home, got dressed, and went to bed. I wondered how that happened. The last thing I could remember was Molly preventing me from an amazing night with Luke.

I got out of bed, slid my slippers on, and shuffled into the living room. The apartment was still. The building, for that matter, was quiet. It, along with my roommates, had not yet woken up. I put on a pot of coffee and sat by the kitchen window while it brewed. A few cars passed on the street below, but there was no movement in or out of Ashwood. It was only nine thirty in the morning, which in college time is closer to dawn than noon.

When the coffee was done, I poured myself a cup and put the pot back with the warmer on, even though I knew Meredith would brew a fresh pot when she eventually woke up. I walked over to Molly's jacket and borrowed her lighter and a cigarette, trying my best to piece together the night before.

Usually, little bits and pieces were fuzzy, like a picture taken out of focus, but I couldn't think of one thing that happened after Luke. Luke. I got the warm fuzzies at just the thought of him and his lips and his body and his . . . I had to stop myself. What happened? Molly . . . me and Luke . . . then nothing. I contemplated going back to sleep, knowing it would be at least two more hours before anyone else woke up. Instead, I decided to get some fresh air. So I called Jane.

"What are you doing up so early?" she asked when she answered.

"I don't know," I said, and pulled on my cigarette. "I woke up and couldn't go back to sleep."

She sighed when I exhaled. "Are you smoking? Jesus, Kelly. It's not even ten."

"I know, I know," I replied. "Do you want to get some breakfast?"

"Umm . . ." She took some time answering what I thought was a simple question.

"If you can't, don't worry about it," I said.

"No, no," she quickly replied. "It's just that . . . I'm not . . . do you mind if I bring someone with me?"

"Uh-oh." I smiled. "Are you not alone? Did you have company last night? Did I interrupt a little morning time?"

"Kelly," she interrupted before I got graphic, "breakfast sounds great. I would really like you to meet someone. We'll be there in half an hour."

Jane had a night guest? I couldn't believe it. Miss Holier than Thou had someone spend the night and I was going to have the honor of meeting him? At least I hoped it was a him.

I threw on my favorite distressed jeans, a grey and black Hay U hoodie, and black Uggs. In true Jane fashion, she pulled into the parking lot exactly thirty minutes later. I stubbed out my cigarette (another one of Molly's; I would have to buy her a pack), and left the apartment. I was quickly reminded that fall had moved in almost overnight as I exited the building and was hit with brisk morning air. I should have thrown on a jacket.

Jane smiled at me and waved as I approached the car and did a quick take at the stranger beside her in the passenger seat.

"Hey, Kel," she said, looking in the rearview mirror as I slid into the back seat.

"Hi," I replied, my stomach turning a little awkwardly. It was warm in the car, very warm, and the smell from the vanilla air freshener attacked my nostrils.

"This is Pete," she continued. "Pete, this is my sister, Kelly."

Pete turned around and shook my hand with a warm, albeit fake, smile. "Hi, Kelly," he said. "I have heard a lot about you."

"That's funny," I said with a smile, "because I have heard nothing about you."

"Kelly," Jane reprimanded quickly.

"I'm just playing around," I sighed, suddenly queasy.

Pete laughed off my comment. "You were right," he said to Jane, and he patted her right hand.

"Right about what?" I asked, fighting the nausea that was gripping my stomach.

"I told him all about you, Kel, so don't try anything funny."

Try anything funny? I swear, you come on to your sister's boyfriend once as a joke to see what he would do, and you never live it down. Was it really my fault he'd tried to take the bait?

Jane put the car in reverse and just as we were leaving the

parking lot, I asked her to stop.

"What did you forget?" she asked. "We are not stopping so you can go back for your cigarettes."

"I don't have cigarettes," I replied. Technically, I never did, because I refused to purchase my own pack. "I need you to stop the car for a second, please."

As soon as the car stopped I opened the door, bent halfway out, and threw up.

"Jesus, Kelly," Jane exclaimed.

"Rough night last night?" Pete joked.

"She didn't tell you, did she," I said somberly, sitting back up.

"Tell me what?" Pete asked, suddenly uncomfortable.

"That I'm pregnant." I wiped my mouth with my sleeve and closed the door. "Let's go. I'm fine now."

"I'm sorry, Kelly," Pete said. "I had no idea."

"She's not pregnant," Jane sighed, and then paused. "Are you?"

"No." I rolled my eyes. "I'm not pregnant."

I could have convinced them that I was and continued with the story through breakfast, but that would have been too easy. Jane rolled her eyes at me in the rearview mirror and turned to Pete. "Don't listen to anything she ever tells you."

Normally I would have taken it a little easier on Pete, being that it was the first time that we'd met, but there was something about him I didn't like, and I wasn't exactly feeling great, either.

Jane controlled the conversation the remainder of the way to the diner. Although I commented on everything, Pete said as little as possible. Maybe the whole pregnancy thing had taken it a bit too far, but I didn't appreciate being judged, and that was exactly what Pete was doing. Even when he wasn't looking at me, he was judging me. I could feel it.

My stomach was still sour when it came time to order, so I played it safe with a cup of hot chocolate and a blueberry muffin. Jane was in love; it was so obvious in the way she looked at Pete. If his hand was on the table, she would rest hers on top of his. If it wasn't, she would place her hand on his thigh. The whole thing was rather nauseating.

"It makes you look like you're giving him a hand job when you do that," I commented when she moved her hand below the table.

Jane rolled her eyes and Pete pretended as though he didn't hear me.

"So," I began in an attempt to create real conversation, "how did you meet? How long have you been dating?"

"We met through a friend," Jane beamed, "and we've been dating for about a month."

"A month?" I sipped my whipped-cream-topped hot chocolate. "Sounds serious. Has he met Mom and Dad yet?"

"Soon," Jane replied. "We're not rushing into anything too quickly."

"Why buy the cow, right?" I laughed.

"Seriously," Jane reprimanded. "Can you go even five minutes without a smartass comment?"

Obviously Pete was as square as Jane had become, so I decided to tone it down a little.

By keeping my mouth shut, I actually learned a decent amount about Pete. For instance, he, like Jane, had graduated valedictorian from high school and magna cum laude from college, and was currently managing a very promising accounting career at a well-known firm in the city.

He didn't seem surprised when I told him I was still undeclared and didn't have the slightest idea what I wanted to do.

"Kelly wants to get paid to have fun for the rest of her life," Jane quipped.

"Nothing wrong with that," I replied with a wink.

"Except that it's not possible," Pete added.

"Really?" I asked. "Do you really think there aren't people out there who get paid to have fun?"

"People get paid to do all sorts of things," he replied, taking the bait, "though some of it may not be legal."

"Are you saying that I want to be a prostitute?" I shot Jane a hurt look.

"I'm sure that's not what Pete meant," Jane said, and rubbed his thigh. "He was just—"

"Hand job," I interrupted, to get her to stop her groping.

"I was just saying that respectable careers require respectable work," Pete said.

"I know exactly what you were saying." I winked at Pete. "Don't worry. It would take a lot more than calling me a prostitute to offend me."

"That I believe," he replied, and finished his coffee. "The exhibit starts at one." He glanced at his watch. "Are you ladies finished?"

"Exhibit?" I asked with forced interest.

"There's a new exhibit on the human brain at the Institute. Do you want to go with us?"

"Ye-ah." I took a second to seem as though I was considering it. "I actually have some work I have to get done today, but thanks."

The drive back to Ashwood from the diner was awkward at best. I was starting to feel sick again and had to talk myself into keeping my breakfast down. When we pulled into the parking lot, I leaned into the front seat, gave Jane a kiss on the cheek, thanked Pete for treating, and escaped the hot, vanilla-infused car.

"Oh, thank God," Meredith said when I walked in the door. She was sitting on the couch with a steaming cup of coffee watching Dirty Dancing. "Where have you been?"

"I went to breakfast with Jane and her new boyfriend."

"New boyfriend?" She smiled, ready for gossip. "What's he like? Is he cute?"

"He looks like a rapist," I replied.

"A rapist?"

"Yeah, he was dressed head-to-toe in black and had these black wire-framed glasses. He gave me the creeps."

"So he's not nice," Meredith concluded.

"I didn't say that, but he definitely does not approve of me."

"Fuck him, then."

"No thanks, he's not my type."

"So he's no Luke." Meredith smiled.

"What is that supposed to mean?"

"You know exactly what I mean."

"No idea," I replied, my mind flashing with images of Luke.

"You can't be serious," she said.

"What? I remember seeing him last night and Molly refusing to let me leave with him."

"And after that?"

"And after that nothing."

"This is great," Meredith giggled. "Molly! Get in here!"

Molly came into the living room brushing her teeth and lit up the instant she saw me. She muttered something excitedly and ran out of the room. When she returned ten seconds later she was minty fresh. "So the whore has come home?"

"Whore?" I asked.

"I'm just kidding," she said. "Where have you been? Didn't get enough last night? Did you have to go back for more?"

"Get enough last night? Go back for more? What are you talking about?"

"It seems as though Miss Blackout doesn't remember much of last night," Meredith explained.

"Really?" Molly laughed.

"Well, I remember you running interference with Luke." I glared at her. "So thanks for that."

"That's the last thing you remember?" she asked.

"Yes."

"You don't remember anything else?"

"Nothing."

"Interesting," Molly replied.

I tried to remember what happened after Molly stopped me from leaving with Luke. I remembered his touch, remembered the want, the need to go with him. And I remembered the utter disappointment I'd felt when Molly ran interference. After that, it was like someone had flipped a switch in my mind. Luke . . . excitement . . . nothing.

"So it worked," Molly said. "You got blackout drunk."

"Does that mean I passed out at the party?"

"You did anything but pass out at the party."

Molly and Meredith looked at each other and laughed.

"What is so funny? Can someone please tell me what happened?"

"Fine," Molly sighed. "I could tell that you were feeling pretty good when I talked to you and Luke, so I decided to make it an early night."

"I remember that." I wanted her to speed up and get to the missing part.

"So after about a half an hour, Mer, Sam, and I were ready to leave, but you were gone."

"Gone?"

"Yeah," Meredith said, "you disappeared."

"I thought maybe you had left with Luke," Molly said, "and we almost left without you."

"Whatever happened to 'Arrive together, leave together'?" I asked, referring to the pact we made freshman year. Leave no one behind was our mantra.

"That's why we didn't leave," Molly answered. "Then Meredith suggested that we look in the bedrooms."

"Bedrooms?" My pulse began to quicken.

"Well, after Molly told you we were going to leave soon," Meredith cut in, "you got all sad and turned and said something to Luke. I couldn't hear what you said, but he smiled and leaned in and kissed you."

"He kissed me." I felt a rush of excitement. Damn, why couldn't I remember that?

"Yeah, and not just a little one. It made me really uncomfortable. So I left you two going at it and went to find Molly and Sam."

"And when we came back, you were gone," Molly added.

"Where did you find me?" I asked, racking my brain.

"In one of the bedrooms," Meredith giggled, "half-naked."

"No," I gasped.

"Yes," Molly laughed.

"What was I doing?"

Meredith's laughter joined Molly's. "It's not what you were doing, it's what was being done to you."

"What? What did Luke do . . . what did I do?"

"There's only so much you can be doing when you're naked."

"Naked." I was blurting out one-word responses.

"So when we barged in—wait . . . I have a picture."

"A picture?"

"I forgot about that," Meredith giggled.

"Let me see it," I demanded.

Molly ran into her bedroom and came back with her phone. After a little scrolling and tapping on the screen, she smiled and said, "Voilà." On the tiny screen before me, in full color and great quality, was Luke standing, naked, his mouth open in surprise, and me on the bed.

"They say a picture's worth a thousand words," Meredith said. "What does this one say to you?"

"Whore," Molly laughed.

"You have to delete that," I cried out.

"How much is it worth to you?" Molly taunted, dancing the phone in front of me.

I grabbed the phone from her and deleted the picture. It never happened if there's no proof, right? I wish that really could be the case. Unfortunately, I've come to learn that in life, there is no Delete button.

CHAPTER EIGHT

We were the queens of the fifth floor sophomore year and loving every minute of it. Robin, the RA living on the first floor, left us alone provided that we didn't smoke in the apartment (which we did) or flaunt our drinking (did that, too). She was wonderful compared to George, our RA from freshman year.

George, who we named Captain Catholic, had lived to enforce dorm rules. He routinely walked the common area to ensure that we weren't doing anything we weren't supposed to. We could feel his presence when he entered our suite, as all fun would be sucked out of the room. He always waddled in with the same bland grin on his face, trying to be pleasant but just coming off weird.

"Hello, girls," he would say, his voice as bland as his grin.

"Hi, George," we sang with dry enthusiasm.

"You aren't up to any mischief, are you?"

It was bad enough that he looked forty-five, but to speak that way was so unnecessary. We laughed at his prepubescent voice and Meredith did her best to get it to crack. But no matter what her advances, he never seemed interested. He knew she was mocking him and he brushed her off as though she was beneath him. It was no shock that he got along with Angela. Truth be told, I think he had a crush on her. Either that or he was gay.

Despite his constant patrols, he never wrote us up for much. The only time he really came down on us was when we set off the smoke detectors in the common area and the fire department had to come. But even then he couldn't do much, because he didn't know who'd actually set the alarm off. Angela tried to get it out of me, showing her softer side, but when I suggested that she and Theresa were the culprits, she walked off muttering something about liars being the devil's preachers.

After that afternoon, we kept a two-liter bottle of Diet Coke on the table as a place to stash our cigarettes should George stop by for a surprise visit. He did get suspicious once, but as he walked over to inspect the bottle, Molly grabbed it and took a nice long swig. He left, content, and Molly practically vomited on all of us.

We had to be careful, though, because although we tried our best to not get caught, I believe Angela called George whenever she saw us out there.

"I don't think you really want to smoke, Kelly," Angela would tell me when we were alone. "Just because Meredith and that other girl are on the wrong path doesn't mean you have to follow."

"Wrong path?" I laughed. "For someone with such high beliefs, you certainly do a lot of judging. Jesus didn't judge."

"What do you know about Jesus?" she scoffed.

"You're not the only one who believes in God."

The discussions Angela and I had on religion almost always turned into a holy war. She claimed that my lifestyle went against the teachings of Christ. I told her she knew nothing about my lifestyle. She replied by telling me she had witnessed plenty of my aberrant actions (whatever that meant) and that if I believed I was leading anything other than a corrupt life, I was sadly mistaken. I told her she didn't have to worry about my soul, that JC and I were tight. She screamed and stormed out.

I won.

Needless to say, I didn't miss Angela at all during sophomore year. She stayed on campus with Theresa and far away from me. When our paths crossed from time to time, she would look right through me as though we hadn't shared a living space for nine months. Theresa was always good for a smirk or a glare, but Angela didn't even dignify my presence. I could tell everyone about you, you toenail eater, I thought defensively every time I saw her.

I made it a point to wear my crucifix around Angela, letting it fall comfortably into my cleavage. She called it sacrilege, I called it faith.

I do pray to God. I talk to Him a lot, actually. Anymore, He's the only one who will listen.

CHAPTER NINE

I was rattled awake by the rough movement of my body being transported. Joe's voice was joined by at least three others as they discussed pulse rates, oxygen rates, blood pressure, and a slew of medical terms I had never heard before. I opened my eyes briefly to see what was going on but a blinding light hit me and I shut them instantly. I don't think anyone saw me open my eyes; they were too busy discussing me to notice. I heard new voices chattering nearby and intermittent beeps. In the distance, I could hear a television on, The Simpsons, I think.

"Ready on three . . . ," Joe said aloud, "two . . . one."

On his count, I was slid and dumped onto another flat surface. Joe said something again, and then I felt a hand on my shoulder. "Stay with us, Kelly," he said. I tried to open my eyes for him, but I was too tired. I tried to move my hand but nothing was working. The pain in my head was blurring my vision, causing Joe's face to morph into two. It was too much.

Something globbed onto my stomach and was followed by something hard and cold. The wand, or whatever it was, moved around my stomach and up my chest.

"BP is ninety-three over fifty," someone called out.

Who were all of these people speaking to?

"I've got something here," another one said. "Looks like a hemorrhage. Is there an OR open?"

I was on the move within seconds, opening my eyes to a wave of people clad in blue and white rushing me somewhere. We traveled quickly down narrow halls past dozens of people before entering the light. The light was the most magnificent thing I had ever seen. Even with my eyes closed I could feel its intensity.

I began to panic because I figured I had to be dead at that point. Everyone talks about the light and how to go into it willingly. But I didn't choose to go into the light. I was rolled into it, and rather briskly, at that. I wasn't in control anymore. I expected to feel my pulse quicken and my heart begin to pound, but I felt nothing in my body, nothing in my chest. Had my heart stopped beating? Was this the end?

CHAPTER TEN

Jane called me when she got home that afternoon from the museum with Pete. "So what do you think?"

"I think he could be a rapist," I replied honestly.

"Kelly," she said in a hurt tone.

"What? You asked me what I thought."

"Do you really think that?"

"No," I sighed, "but he does look like one."

"That's not very nice."

"Well, he wasn't all that cordial to me."

"What do you mean?"

"He practically called me a whore."

"He did not," she shot back defensively. Her desire for me to like him made it obvious how much he meant to her.

"Don't you remember the whole prostitution thing?"

"Come on, Kel," she laughed, "he was kidding. Besides, you weren't being the most angelic person yourself."

"I was being me," I replied.

"I really like Pete," she said.

"I can tell."

"Do you think Mom and Dad will like him?"

"Of course they will. Have they ever not liked any of the guys you've brought home?"

Jane's taste in men was about as boring as a Sunday afternoon in a brain museum. She always brought home "nice" boys, as my mom emphasized. "We never have to worry about Jane," she would say. "She has such great taste." By saying that, she meant to imply that I did not have great taste, and that I could learn a thing or two from my sister.

But like I said, I didn't date a lot in high school. Jane, on the other hand, was a serial dater, though she didn't go through a lot of guys. She just always seemed to have a boyfriend.

I had to ask. "What did Pete think of me?"

"He thought you were interesting," she replied.

"Is that the word he used, or is it your censored version?"

"I'd told him you would probably give him a hard time, so I don't think he was all that surprised by some of the things that came out of your mouth. The pregnancy thing was good, though. I'll give you that."

And that right there is what I loved so much about Jane. Despite our differences, she could enjoy me for who I was. No matter how free my spirit was and how conformed to society she was, I was her sister, and at the end of the day, that was all that mattered.

"I think I'm going to bring him home next weekend for dinner. Are you free?"

"What day?"

"Probably Sunday. I couldn't interfere with your weekend plans now, could I?"

She was smart enough to realize there was no way I would allow Pete's introduction to my family to conflict with my social life.

"Can Meredith come?"

"I couldn't imagine her not coming. I'll pick you guys up at four."

Once they'd learned what happened to Meredith's mother, my entire family had taken Meredith in as an extension of me. Meredith gladly welcomed the acceptance. When I told her about dinner, she couldn't wait. She loved going to my house.

Jane and Pete picked us up promptly at four on Sunday afternoon. In true pre-game fashion, Meredith and I each did two shots of vodka in the apartment to take the edge off, then took a bottle of water and another water bottle full of vodka for the road.

Meredith climbed into the back seat of Jane's car first, commenting on its vanilla scent. I followed behind and shut the door, the vodka tingling through my limbs.

"You're right about the rapist thing," Meredith whispered not-so-subtly after Jane proudly made the introductions.

"What was that?" Jane asked.

"She said Pete is hot," I replied, loud and clear.

Jane rolled her eyes, Meredith and I laughed, and Pete seemed to let the whole thing go without giving it any thought.

"Behave, girls," Jane said, gently rubbing Pete's thigh as if to reassure him.

I couldn't help but wonder on occasions like that whether or not Jane knew I was buzzed. If she did, she never let on. It's not that I gave her any reason to suspect anything. I never acted out of control, just a little more fun and a little less inhibited. But that didn't really differ from when I hadn't been drinking. I lived my life and enjoyed every second, never afraid to get a little silly.

"So, Pete," I asked when silence had taken over the car, "are you excited to meet the family?"

"I am." He smiled at Jane.

"You know that their dad's a cop, right?" Meredith asked.

"I do," he replied.

"Did he do his regulatory background check?" she taunted.

"I told you," Jane said to Pete, shaking her head at us in the rearview mirror. "Frick and Frack."

Meredith leaned forward and patted Pete's shoulders. He jumped and she laughed. "You need to relax, Petey. We're just having a little bit of fun with you."

I can't say he was pleased with the nickname, but he maintained his composure and said nothing. Meredith's phone beeped with a new message and we temporarily lost interest in Pete and our mission to make him feel uncomfortable.

"Sam's coming out tonight," Meredith announced. "She says she needs a good night."

Meredith looked at me and I looked at her and in unison we both said, "Tonic."

"Isn't that a bar?" Jane asked.

"Yes," I replied.

"Don't you have to be twenty-one to get into bars?"

"And your point would be what, exactly?" I asked.

"You're not twenty-one."

"And?"

"So how do you get in?"

"Lexi McBride."

"Who is Lexi McBride?"

"A good friend." I laughed and took a swig of vodka from the water bottle.

People say vodka doesn't smell, but it does, and I was shocked that neither Pete nor Jane could smell it as Meredith and I passed the bottle back and forth.

To say that I was drunk by the time we got to my house was an understatement. After a year at college, however, I had gotten pretty good at appearing normal in my most intoxicated of states. Meredith and I both popped a piece of gum into our mouths and walked in behind Jane and the guest of honor.

Excited to meet the guy that Jane had described as being "the one," our mother had gone to extreme measures in preparing for what should have been a simple Sunday dinner. For starters, we were eating in the dining room. The table was set with the china that made an appearance only on holidays, and the tablecloth was newly washed and ironed.

"Is this dinner or a betrothal?" I asked.

My mom waved me off as she hurried around the kitchen stirring pots on the stove and checking the chicken in the oven.

Jane made the introductions and my parents welcomed Pete. Patrick sat in front of the television in the living room catching glances here and there, more interested in what was for dinner than in Jane's new boyfriend. Meredith and I went up to my room before dinner to plan out the night and finish the vodka.

While Pete did little to impress me, he appeared to be saying and doing all he could to impress my parents. The compliments to my mother about the house and the food were nonstop and the interest with which he listened to my father speak was sickening. He tried to lure Patrick in with some comment about soccer, to which Patrick shrugged his shoulders and mumbled something. Patrick's indifference to Pete was great.

Jane offered a sarcastic objection when I slid a glass over to my mom when she opened a bottle of wine. "Since when do we condone underage drinking?"

"Well, it is a special occasion." I smiled and waited for Mom to fill my glass, then handed her Meredith's. "It's not every day that we meet a special friend of yours. Meeting the family is a big deal." I smiled at Pete and raised my glass. "To Pete. Here's to buying the cow."

"Kelly," Jane growled.

"Buying the cow?" Mom gave me a warning look.

"Yeah," I laughed, a mere host to the vodka, which had invaded and taken over my body. "You know . . ."

"To Pete," Jane interrupted. "I hope you can come to tolerate my sister and her outbursts just as we all have."

Patrick laughed and my parents smiled. We tapped our glasses lightly against each other's and began to eat.

We had just finished the salad and were starting the roasted chicken and potatoes when Meredith's stomach started growling. Her once-blushed cheeks had drained of color and were now whitish-grey. It was a look I knew all too well; it only meant trouble.

Meredith quietly excused herself from the table and ran to the bathroom. A few seconds later we heard her retching into the toilet. My mother's pleasantry morphed into concern and she rose from the table. I followed her.

In the bathroom we found a cool and clammy Meredith hugging the toilet with her head resting on her forearm on the seat.

"I'm so sorry," she said to my mom. "I had a chicken sandwich for lunch that didn't taste right and I guess when I had the wine it just . . ."

She couldn't finish the sentence without turning her face back over the toilet and vomiting again. I told my mom to go back and enjoy dinner and that I would sit with Meredith until she felt better. At first she objected, but I insisted, telling her that Pete deserved her undivided attention.

"Poor thing," I heard Mom say from the dining room. "She had some bad chicken for lunch."

I closed the bathroom door and laughed at Meredith, who had repositioned herself against the wall. "Too much wine?" I asked.

"I'm sorry, Kel." She wiped her mouth with a wad of toilet paper.

I smiled. "Don't be. Dinner was pretty boring. And anyway, when did you become such a lightweight?"

"Maybe I skipped lunch today," she replied with a weak smile.

Meredith spent the remainder of the evening in my bed, sleeping off her "food poisoning," and I returned to the table for the rest of dinner and dessert.

I had to promise Jane when it was time to go that Meredith

would be okay in the car. Even then, she made me bring a plastic bag and a roll of paper towels.

The ride back was mild compared to the fun we'd had on the way to dinner. The color had returned to Meredith's face and she was talking about what we were going to do when we got back to school. Jane laughed when Meredith brought up going to Tonic, saying that she would be down for the count if she had thrown up as much as Meredith did.

"Make sure you stay hydrated," Pete advised, looking at me in the back seat.

"Always do." Meredith shook her water bottle.

"I noticed," he replied, staring me down in the rearview mirror.

What had he noticed? His response was so direct and so cold that it sent a shiver down my spine. Did he know I was drunk? Did he really know we were drinking in the car? Was he going to tell Jane?

I kept my mouth shut the rest of the way back to school, taking Pete's observation as a warning not to harass him or annoy Jane. Meredith, clueless as ever, didn't pick up on anything and continued to happily type messages into her phone. I kept a close watch on Pete. He was going to be a problem for me. That I could tell.

CHAPTER ELEVEN

I didn't have the pleasure of seeing Pete again until the night before Thanksgiving. Well, actually it was early Thanksgiving morning. My mom had invited Meredith and her dad to dinner, and Meredith came in the day before so we could go out. Too scared to use our fake IDs close to home, I brought Meredith to Chris's house. As always, he was hosting a party with all the usual suspects. I asked Jane, who was home to help Mom make the desserts, if she would mind driving us, as I knew Meredith and I would be in no condition to drive home.

"I don't understand why you can't drive," she said loudly in front of our parents.

"Yeah, honey, you can take my car if you want," Mom offered.

I shot Jane a death glare before making up an excuse about how the Davises didn't like it when their driveway and street were taken over by cars. My father mumbled something about the Davises and how they thought they owned the world.

"We'll walk," I bluffed.

"No," my mom objected, "I'll take you girls."

"I'll take them," Jane sighed, and she rolled her eyes. "I'd like to see them try to walk in those boots."

Hooker heels is how Jane referred to them. Stylish is how I liked to describe them. But she was right about one thing: they hurt, and there was no way I could walk around the block, let alone to the party. Jane grabbed her keys, Meredith and I armed ourselves with our two-water-bottle combo, and we set out for a fun night.

I remember walking up the Davises' long, circular driveway in the brisk November air. I exhaled slowly and watched as my breath made a cloud against the dark sky before disappearing.

Sonia, Chris's mom, answered the door with the same welcoming smile as always. Dressed to perfection, she took our coats and asked how I was doing. She led us to the patio out back where everyone was crowded around three large kerosene space heaters.

It seemed as though the conversation picked up where it had left off the summer before, and everyone fell back into the same routines. Hank Roberts was funneling beer with Scott Kendall next to the keg, and in the corner of the patio Rose Douglas was sharing a joint with Nancy Rogers.

I'd described everyone to Meredith as acquaintances, because they were good to hang out with when I was home, but that was about it. They never came to visit me at Hay U and I had no interest in their lives. While it was the same cast of characters in attendance, a few were missing from the summer. In fact, every time we got together fewer people came. Were they too cool for high school reunions? Did they move on? Should I have moved on?

Just like at campus parties, Meredith and I found ourselves quickly bored. When someone suggested going to a local dive bar, we were in. Kelly Rockport and Meredith Short went home and Lexi McBride and Carin Lewis came out. Were we a little eccentric with the names on our fake IDs? Maybe, but we had fun with it. We had fun with everything we did.

After passing Sonia's sobriety test, Meredith and I left with Jake McIntyre and Kevin Wilford. Chris wanted me to stay and have a little fun of our own. I wasn't interested.

I had some reservations about diverting from our plan to avoid the local bars and was nervous to venture out as Lexi McBride so close to home. The bars at home were stricter than the ones at school and I couldn't bear the thought of losing my ID.

Jake's Jeep shook as it maneuvered the gravel parking lot of Puss N' Boots Tavern. Judging from the number of cars already in the lot, the night before Thanksgiving was a popular night out. Meredith and I followed Kevin and Jake as quickly as we could in our boots, shivering in the cold but allowing them to go through the door first. If they passed without a problem, we would enter confidently; if not, we would find an exit strategy. To our pleasant surprise, there was no bouncer at the door and the four of us entered freely.

The bar was dark and hazy and smelled of alcohol. It definitely was not Tonic, but it would suffice for the evening. We found an abandoned table towards the back that hadn't been cleared of its dirty ashtray and empty glasses. Unconcerned about the clutter, we slid onto the stools while Kevin went to get our first round. The bar was crowded with what appeared to be mostly middle- to lower-class men above the age of thirty. There were a few young, attractive women mixed in with a bunch who were clearly past their prime. An uneasy feeling began to form in the pit of my stomach.

"Sweet place." Meredith lit a cigarette and graciously accepted a beer from Kevin.

"It's cool," he said, pulling a stool close to her. It was obvious where they were headed.

By default, I got Jake. He was all right and not that bad-looking; I just wasn't in the mood to hook up. I wanted to drink, dance, and then go home.

Puss N' Boots definitely got shadier as the night progressed. The few young girls, and by young I mean early thirties, had left and when they did the unease in my stomach grew in intensity.

Meredith and Kevin disappeared for a good twenty minutes, and when they returned they sat face to face, lips on lips, while Jake and I continued to talk uncomfortably.

"It doesn't count when I'm Carin," Meredith had told me one night at Tonic after hooking up with a random guy.

At first I laughed, but then I realized that that reasoning would make it a lot easier for us to enjoy ourselves. If I wasn't responsible for the things Lexi did, then she could do whatever she wanted. Unfortunately, she did.

Last call is normally one of my favorite parts of the night. At Tonic, they ring a bell and everyone goes crazy. No matter how drunk we are or how sick we may already feel, when that bell chimes, it's tequila time. A night is not properly ended without it.

But there was no bell at Puss N' Boots and no tequila. Instead, we did a shot of vodka, settled the bar tab, and began to walk out. I could feel the refreshing cold air confronting the smoke-filled room as we approached the front door and my unease began to subside. We were two steps from the door when a guy barged in with a baseball bat yelling for somebody named Tony.

We all jumped back in horror.

"Where's Tony?" he demanded again.

We tried to maneuver around him, but when he saw us move, he made it clear with the bat that we weren't going anywhere.

"Nobody's leaving 'til I see Tony."

The feeling in my stomach exploded into panic. It had been ticking like a bomb in my subconscious all evening, and when our exit was blocked, it detonated.

"Tony's not here, Roy," the bartender sighed, as though a baseball-bat-wielding lunatic was nothing new.

"I saw his pickup outside, Gina," he replied. "Stop covering for that motherfucker and tell me where he is."

"We need to get out of here," I whispered to Meredith, who was trembling.

We made another small movement forward, which angered Roy even more. He swung violently at a table full of glasses. Wet shards of glass went flying into the air and we all ducked. Before we knew what was going on, a guy behind us lurched forward and tackled Roy. The bar erupted in chaos and fury. Meredith, Jake, Kevin, and I bolted for the door. The bitter air welcomed us to freedom as we escaped the mayhem inside—only to find three police cars flying into the parking lot and blocking the entrance.

Kevin didn't want to abandon his car, but he wasn't thrilled with being caught drinking underage with the intent to drive.

"We need to run," I said, and took off down the street.

I begged my boots to be more forgiving and to carry me painlessly from the chaos, but they didn't listen. They revolted. It felt like they tightened with each stride I took. Every pebble dug into the bottom of my feet as they hit the pavement. But there was no time to stop or slow down. We needed to get a safe distance from the bar.

We came to an empty field and collapsed onto the cold, wet grass, and watched as the lights from the cop cars flashed beacons of red and blue into the early Thanksgiving morning sky.

My lungs burned when I breathed and pins and needles pricked through my body as my heart rate regulated. I hadn't run that far or that fast since my high school soccer days. Panting, I reached into my clutch, grabbed my phone, and dialed. Jane answered on the second ring.

"I need you." I couldn't breathe.

"Kelly?"

"I need you to come and get us now."

"I thought you said you would get a ride."

"I can't explain right now," I huffed. "Please, can you come get us?"

"Fine," she yawned. "I'll be there in ten minutes."

"We're not at the party anymore."

"What?"

I told her where we were but didn't get into why. I asked her to hurry because it was freezing. Twenty minutes later, Jane's car drove slowly up the street. Jake, Kevin, Meredith, and I broke from our huddle and walked out to where she could see us. She was not alone. Poised beside her, glaring through the window, was Pete.

"I don't even want to know," she said as we drove off, leaving the excitement behind us. "But Puss N' Boots? What were you thinking? Do you know what kind of people hang around there? Do you know what Daddy would do if he found out you were hanging out there? I swear, Kelly. Sometimes you just don't think."

The heat in Jane's car burned my frozen limbs as they defrosted. Meredith, Jake, and Kevin watched quietly like three nervous children as I was scolded. After that, we drove in silence, Kevin and Jake only speaking to give Jane directions to their houses.

The house was dark and quiet when Jane, Pete, Meredith, and I returned home. I thanked Jane again and Meredith and I scampered off to my room. I thought it best not to speak to Pete. I changed into sweats, Meredith into her pajamas, and we climbed into my bed, curled up under the covers, and passed out. Overall, it wasn't a bad night.

CHAPTER TWELVE

The aromas of Thanksgiving made their way from the kitchen to my bedroom and I awoke to the sweet smell of pumpkin pie. With Meredith still passed out, I crept out of bed and went downstairs. My mom was carefully mixing ingredients for apple pie at the kitchen island with her apron on. Dad was reading the paper at the kitchen table.

"Happy Thanksgiving," Mom smiled as I pulled out a stool in front of the island and sat down.

"Happy Thanksgiving," I replied.

"Do you want some breakfast?" she asked.

"I'll wait until Meredith gets up."

"You guys were sleeping pretty soundly when I looked in on you this morning. What time did you get in last night?"

"Two thirty," Jane said, walking into the kitchen.

"No wonder you slept in," Mom smiled.

"How's your frostbite?" Jane asked.

"Frostbite?" My mother's smile faded. My father looked up from his paper.

"It was cold last night." I shot Jane a dirty look.

"It was," Mom agreed. "I could hear the wind howling outside all night."

"I'm going to make pancakes," I said, and walked over to the pantry. "Who wants some?"

"That would be great," Dad said, going back to the news.

Jane sighed and sat on my vacated stool. While I knew she

would never do anything to cause real tension between our parents and me, she did like to stir the pot every once in a while. However, more often than not, she wouldn't succeed and would be left objecting with her self-pitying sigh.

The dining room glowed under the golden chandelier that day. The food seemed to stretch for miles across the long white tablecloth, their scents mixing in the air. Mashed potatoes steamed next to wiggling cranberry sauce and a bountiful green salad. We gladly took our seats.

Dad sat at the head of the table with Mom and Meredith's dad on either side of him. I sat next to Mom and Meredith sat next to her father across from me. Patrick took the seat opposite our father at the other end of the table, leaving Jane and Pete to sit across from each other. Pete seemed unsure as to whether it was safer to sit next to me or Meredith. I wasn't surprised when he chose Meredith.

I winked at him as he sat down. "I don't bite."

Pete smiled uncomfortably as all the attention shifted to him. In the presence of my parents, he was less likely to react to my comments.

Dinner began with a short prayer and a toast in honor of our guests made by my mother. Then, in true Rockport family tradition, we went around the table and announced what we were thankful for.

We all were thankful for family, friends, and our health. Yada yada yada. I was thankful that we'd escaped Puss 'N Boots unscathed and without running into the police, but I couldn't exactly say that in front of my parents.

Pete said he was thankful for my family's hospitality and my mother's fabulous cooking. He was such a suck-up.

"I bet you're thankful for Jane and her hospitality, too," I added. I couldn't help it. His insincerity was making me sick.

"I am truly thankful for Jane," he said, smiling at her. "And I bet you are thankful for her, too. You are really lucky to have a sister who's always there to get you out of a jam."

"I am very thankful for my family," I replied sharply, kicking Jane's foot under the table to get him to stop.

Mom smiled approvingly in our direction. "Jane has always been there for Kelly."

"So I've noticed," Pete replied.

"Can I have the potatoes?" Patrick interrupted.

"I can't believe him," I whispered to Jane frantically as we cleared the table for dessert. "What is his problem?"

"He doesn't like that I put myself in jeopardy to bail you out. He wasn't going to say anything. He was just messing around. What's the big deal?"

"The big deal is that he has something against me and I don't trust him."

"Kelly," she sighed.

"Jane, I'm serious. Why did he find it necessary to bring up you always being there to get me out of a jam? What else have you told him?"

"Nothing," she replied.

"Are you sure?"

"I don't remember everything I've told him about you. When we talk about our families, things just come out."

"What kind of things?"

Our mother came up behind us in the kitchen. "What are you girls whispering about?"

"Nothing," I smiled. "Just girl talk."

"Please limit what you tell him," I said as soon as Mom walked back into the dining room.

"How about you try to stay out of trouble?" Jane replied. "And then I won't have to say anything about you."

I rolled my eyes and walked away.

As I always do on Thanksgiving, I ate too much and felt sick by the end of the night. After coffee and dessert, Meredith's dad thanked us all and he and Meredith left. Jane and Pete stayed a while longer before calling it a night and leaving with leftovers. Patrick retreated to the basement to play video games and Mom put on a movie. I fell asleep on the couch, thankful that all was right with my world.

CHAPTER THIRTEEN

In a word, finals sucked. But the reward was well worth the agony of studying.

"You're the only person I know who studies just so they can party harder after," Jane said when I spoke of my post-finals plans. "Don't you want to retain any of the information you learn instead of drinking it away?"

"I'm on the dean's list," I replied. "What more do you want?"

Jane had voiced her concerns about my excessive drinking and partying numerous times, warning that my grades would suffer. They didn't. So in turn, I didn't listen to her. I knew for a fact that she drank in college. She may not have gotten blackout drunk, but she drank. She didn't become lame until she graduated. Then it was like she was abducted by aliens and replaced with a robot that looked and sounded exactly like her. I pulled at the skin on her arm once to see if she was real. She said she could do the same for me, but was scared she might cut me and I would bleed alcohol.

Jane's concern and interest in my alcohol consumption had increased drastically one night freshman year after I called her when I was drunk. It was all downhill after that. At the time, Jane's number was stored in my phone as Sis. One night, Meredith and I were waiting for Sam to meet us out at Tonic and when she was late we decided to call her. In my inebriation, I confused Sam for Sis and dialed Jane. When she answered the phone, I got confused and asked her who she was. She said that it was Jane, and I said I hadn't called a Jane. I asked her where Sam was and she asked me who Sam was. I asked her who she was and why she wouldn't let me talk to Sam. She told me again that it was Jane, but her name and voice didn't click. So I called her a bitch and hung up.

Sam showed up a couple minutes later and I forgot about the conversation. Jane didn't. She called me the following afternoon (I was still sleeping) and said we needed to talk.

"It concerns me that you were so drunk you didn't recognize your own sister's voice," she said. "Even when I told you it was me."

I apologized. She didn't buy it.

"Do you always get that drunk? Where were you?"

She was upset, I got that. I would be upset too if my sister didn't recognize my voice and called me a bitch on top of it.

"You were so hostile," she said.

I apologized over and over and explained that I was just confused. She accepted my apology, but she didn't sound convinced.

Angela was eavesdropping on my conversation and as soon as I hung up she said, "When your alcohol intake begins to affect your relationships, it may be time to cut back."

I ignored Angela, changed Jane's name in my phone from Sis to Jane, and went back to sleep. The benefit of being away at school was that it was a while before I saw Jane again, and by then the phone incident was a thing of the past.

Fresh from our last finals, Meredith, Molly, Sam, and I met back at our apartment and commenced our three-phase celebration with a round of shots. From there we went to the Crew House, phase two. Though beer pong was beneath Molly, Meredith and I enjoyed a good game. That and flip cup. Truth be told, however, I was hoping to run into Luke one last time. I wanted to wish him a very Merry Christmas in a very special way.

The Crew House was hot and crowded, yet merry. Christmas lights were haphazardly strung throughout the first floor and in the living room three large plastic candy canes were duct-taped to the wall. One of the housemates was dressed in a Santa suit, and John, the guy at the door with the cups, was wearing a Santa hat with mistletoe hanging from the top. We all kissed him on the cheek as we took our cups and walked in.

"I wonder how many stupid freshmen have kissed him

tonight," I said.

"With him at the door," Molly said, "they aren't going to make a lot of money."

The mood at the party was much more relaxed than usual. The stress of the week had been lifted and everyone was enjoying their freedom. We stayed long enough and drank just enough to get us ready for phase three: Tonic. Unfortunately, I didn't see Luke.

The third bar from the corner of Main Street and Lexington Avenue, Tonic lit up the dark December sky with its blue neon sign. As people entered and left, the music pumped through the doorway, infiltrating our bodies and causing us to bop to the beats as we approached. The four of us couldn't dance, but together we had a drunken rhythm.

The bouncer smiled when he saw us and let us through without an ID inspection or a cover charge. We entered graciously, eager to officially begin the night.

The side bar was crowded with men ogling Jen, the blonde bartender whose outfit consisted of a glorified bra and short black shorts. Max, the owner, was poised behind the main bar in the back. He smiled and waved us over when he saw us.

"Looks like the bomb squad is in full action tonight," he said when we were within earshot.

"Hi, Max," we sang in unison.

"What are we celebrating tonight, ladies?"

"Freedom," Meredith answered.

"Finals over already?"

"Yes, sir," I smiled.

"Well, let me start you off right."

Max pulled four shot glasses from under the bar and poured us each a generous shot of vodka.

He'd known we weren't twenty-one since the first time we went to Tonic second semester freshman year. I was nervous to try out my new ID and shocked that it worked to get me in. Actually, all of our IDs worked. Meredith, Molly, and I had happily found a table and sat down, and I'd offered to get the first round. I approached the bar anxiously and ordered three rum and Cokes. Max took one look at me and smiled. He asked me what my name was and if it was the first time I'd been to Tonic. I smiled back and introduced myself as Lexi, and said yes, it was my first time in Tonic.

He shook his head and asked me what my real name was.

Scared that I had been caught, I took out my ID and presented it to him as confidently as one could with trembling hands.

"Your other one," he said. "I want to see the real one."

I knew better than to carry both IDs on me at once, especially if I was going to a bar. So I lowered my head and told him to forget the drinks, and I turned to walk away.

"Wait," he called out. "I'm Max, the manager."

"Well, Max, the manager," I said, turning back, "I'm Lexi and I'm leaving."

"Look," he said. "It's obvious you're not twenty-one. But you have an ID that says you are, so I'm okay with that. And if you and your friends want to drink here, there are some ground rules."

I cautiously approached the bar, falling under the gaze and scrutiny of his blue eyes.

"Number one, if the cops show up, you're on your own and I don't know anything about you. Number two, you don't get out of control. Number three, you tell me your real names."

I could live with those rules, and I felt a lot better not having to lie about who I was. It kept things easier.

"I'm Kelly."

"It's nice to meet you, Kelly," he said with a smirk. "Let me get you something to drink."

We went to Tonic almost every weekend after that. Soon our casual greetings with Max evolved into casual conversations, which morphed into personal conversations, and after a while, Meredith and I considered Max a friend. The girls joked that Max and I were bound to have sex, that he flirted with me as much as I played around with him, but I didn't listen to them.

I would be lying if I said I wasn't attracted to him. Max was hot. His crystal-clear blue eyes seemed to glow under his long, dark eyelashes and his amber hair fell into place perfectly around his face. He was twenty-seven, nine years my senior, but that made him even more appealing. He was comfortable with his strong physique, not arrogant like the guys who walked around on campus like they had a hanger stuck in their shirt. But Max didn't look at me that way. I think he saw me more as his little sister than an eighteen-year-old adult.

To continue with our post-finals celebration, the four of us did a shot of vodka, followed fittingly by a Mind Eraser. We danced.

We laughed. We were having a great time. Sam paired up with a guy named Chris, Molly entertained his friend James, and Meredith and I just hung out at the bar and let men try to pick us up all night.

Max stood back and observed, as he always did. He enjoyed watching men fail miserably at seducing us. Sure, we played along. We accepted their drinks, danced with them, sometimes let them cop a feel. We let them think they had a chance so they'd keep the drinks flowing.

One guy that night actually did have potential; Shawn Lancer from Haysville told me he was in law school studying torts. He was cute, with curly brown hair and dark-green eyes. He dressed well and smelled amazing. I am a sucker for good cologne.

I, of course, introduced myself as Lexi McBride, a senior at Haysville University. Shawn droned on about torts and negligence and how sticky it could all be, trying to impress me with his legal knowledge. He went into detail about a case he was studying in which a guy, Mr. Jones, hired a handyman to renovate his home office. The handyman left his nail gun behind one afternoon when he finished for the day, and Mr. Jones's son found it and ended up nailing himself in the foot. I opened my eyes wide and nodded my head as Shawn told the story, making sure to keep my glass full at his expense. He concluded with a question.

"So, who was at fault? Was the handyman negligent for leaving the nail gun, or was the father negligent in watching his son?"

I was at fault for allowing myself to get pulled into such a boring conversation. The free drinks were definitely not worth the agonizing law session. Thankfully his friends decided to leave, sparing me from coming up with a way to escape him. He asked for my number. I made one up and pretended to store his in my phone.

As soon as Shawn left, Meredith and I went for a refill at the bar.

"I'm glad you didn't go home with that guy," Max said, pouring my drink.

"Are you jealous?" I taunted with a drunken grin.

"Let's just say I've heard things about that guy," he replied.

"What kinds of things are those?"

"Things that innocent girls like you should stay away from."

"Trust me, Max," Meredith said, reaching for her jacket, "this girl is anything but innocent."

"Yeah." I winked at him. "Why don't you let me show you just how not innocent I am?"

"Just stay away from him," Max cautioned. "The guy is contagious."

"Who isn't?" I laughed off his warning and pecked him on the cheek goodbye.

Max didn't find anything about the situation funny. He looked out for me, and I got that. Maybe Shawn was bad news, maybe he was contagious. I wasn't going to marry him, just have a little bit of fun.

"Hey," Sam said as she sauntered up to Meredith and me with her new friend Chris. "How's it going?"

Chris was wasted, and Sam, it appeared, wasn't too far behind.

"We're going to have a little party in the bathroom, if you know what I mean," she whispered before we could respond. "Do you want to come?"

Meredith looked at me and I looked back at her. She didn't say anything, but her eyes said everything. She didn't want to go and didn't want me to go, either. She wanted me to say no, but I was intrigued.

I now know why curiosity killed the cat.

CHAPTER FOURTEEN

Cocaine, coke, toot, snow, blow, whatever you call it, it's all the same thing. My personal favorite is nose candy. Though it isn't sweet; it actually stings. Now I have never and would never dare to inject anything into my body. I am not a drug addict or a crack whore. Sniffing something, however, didn't seem that serious.

Meredith helplessly tagged along behind me as I followed Sam and Chris to the bathroom. Molly was more headstrong and independent and stayed back to talk with James. "I don't mess with that shit," she said. "And you're stupid if you do."

Sam checked the girl's bathroom and quickly ushered Chris into one of the stalls when it was all clear. Meredith and I followed and locked the stall door. My heart began beating out of my chest when Chris removed the small bag of powder from his jacket. He was calm, as though he had handled cocaine many times before. I watched him closely, his dark eyelashes covering even darker eyes. He appeared harmless enough, and he passed Sam's test. If she trusted him, so could I, or should I say Lexi.

"Are you sure about this?" Meredith asked.

"You don't have to do it if you don't want to," I replied. "Why don't you go find Molly? We'll be out in a minute."

Meredith thought for a minute and shook her head. "No," she said. "I want to stay."

Before that moment, I had never seen cocaine up close. My knowledge had come strictly from movies and television. Chris opened Sam's hand and emptied what seemed to be the tiniest bit of white powder into her palm, arranging it nicely into a long, thin line. Then he took a dollar bill, rolled it tightly, inserted it into his right nostril, plugged his left, and snorted the line from Sam's hand.

I watched, eyes wide open. His eyes bugged out for a second, he sniffed twice, and then he smiled. "Who's next?"

Sam quickly volunteered. Chris opened my palm just as he had with Sam's and lined up a smaller amount of cocaine. He handed Sam the dollar bill and told her to take a deep breath and relax.

Sam trustfully took the dollar and just as Chris had done, plugged up her nostril and inhaled. In a matter of two seconds, the line disappeared from my palm. Sam's reaction was not as graceful as Chris's. She immediately brought her hand to her nose and coughed.

"Relax," Chris smiled. "Take a deep breath."

Sam's eyes were watery, but she looked all right.

"Lexi?" Chris looked at me, prepping a line in Sam's hand. "Are you ready?"

I took one last look at Sam to make sure she was still breathing and that her nose wasn't falling off before I took the rolled dollar from her. I was experiencing a rush I'd never had before, and that was even before I did the coke. I was nervous, excited, and petrified. Before I could chicken out, I placed one finger over my left nostril, inserted the dollar bill into my right, and inhaled deeply.

The powder shot up the dollar into my nose and stung a path down the back of my throat. My nose went numb and all of a sudden I felt like gagging. You know when you go to bed with a bad head cold and the mucus just drips down the back of your throat and there is nothing you can do about it? That's exactly how I felt, except the taste was worse than mucus and it was continuous.

"Is that normal?" I asked Chris.

"You'll get used to it," he said. "Just relax. All right, Carin." He turned to Meredith. "Your turn."

Meredith turned white as a ghost and looked as though she was going to pass out. The main bathroom door opened and I started to panic. Was it Max—or worse, the police? Were they coming to bust us? What would my father say? What was happening to me?

I began to feel extremely claustrophobic. My heart was practically leaping from my chest and I felt as though it was going to explode. I needed air.

After my sudden reaction, Meredith declined Chris's offer and suggested we go get some fresh air. Chris and Sam stayed behind in the stall, preparing another line. Sam seemed to be coping with her high better than I was.

"I think I'm going to die," I said with a shiver when Meredith and I emerged from the bar into the cold December air.

"You're fine," she replied, but her face betrayed her panic. "Do you want a cigarette? Maybe that will make you feel better."

"That sounds good," I answered. Anything at that point sounded good. I needed something to calm me down and get me back to normal.

Meredith bummed a cigarette from a couple of girls huddled together by the door and brought it over to me. It was the best cigarette I'd ever had. The smoke combated the dripping in the back of my throat and I began to feel less panicked and more aware.

With my heart still racing and my senses heightened, we went back into Tonic. Max stopped us at the door and asked if everything was okay. "Sure," I said. "I'm fine. Everything is fine. Why wouldn't everything be fine?" My mind started to race as quickly as my heart and I couldn't say all the things I wanted to say. My lips couldn't move fast enough. Suddenly I wanted to tell Max everything. Unicorns popped into my head. Did he like unicorns? Did he believe in unicorns? They can exist. They're nothing more than horses with horns. "Horns, that's a funny word. Horns. Say it slower and it's even funnier." Why didn't he think that was funny?

Max grabbed my arm and escorted me into his office. Meredith followed closely behind.

"Rule number four," he said harshly, closing the door behind us and sitting me down in a chair in front of his desk. "No drugs."

"Drugs?" I laughed. "What are you talking about?"

"Unicorns?" he asked. "You ask me about unicorns and then say you're not on anything. What did you take?"

"What side of the bed did you get up on today, Max?"

"Kelly," he cautioned.

"Max." I sang his name.

Max looked at Meredith. "What is she on?"

Meredith looked from me to Max and back to me.

"Cocaine," she replied. "This is the first time she's done it. Is this normal? I don't know if something is wrong or not. She freaked out at first and now she's all chatty and talking about horns."

Max looked at me. "She'll be fine," he said. "It just needs to wear off. Where did she get it?"

I loved how they were talking about me as though I wasn't in the room with them. Again Meredith paused.

"I'll find out one way or the other," Max said.

"It was Chris," I said.

"Chris who?" Max asked.

"The guy with Sam," I replied. "It's in his jacket."

"Stay here," Max instructed, and he stormed out of his office. I jumped out of my seat and followed him out the door, grabbing Meredith along with me.

Max radioed the bouncer on his way to confront Chris. By the time Meredith and I caught up with Max, he had a tight grip on Chris's arm and was reaching into his jacket. It didn't take long for him to find the tiny plastic bag. When he did, he released Chris's arm and shoved him towards the bouncer, who wasted no time in escorting him out. James gave Molly a quick kiss on the cheek and ran after Chris.

"What the hell was that about?" Sam asked.

"He knew about the coke," Meredith replied.

"He knew or he was told?" Sam snapped back.

Meredith didn't answer. She turned to me and shrugged her shoulders. Sam glowered at me. "You're unbelievable. You couldn't handle your high so you had to go tell your boyfriend."

"What are you talking about?" It was so unlike Sam to be confrontational and mean.

"Why don't you guys just fuck already and get it over with."

Before I could say anything else, Max approached us and asked all four of us back to his office.

"You can come with me or you can leave the bar," Max said when Sam refused.

"Fine," she huffed, and begrudgingly walked into the back with us.

Max's office was more along the lines of a linen closet than a working space. There were three chairs and a file cabinet, and his desk swallowed up the majority of the room. Once we were all in, he closed the door and sat behind his desk. The four of us stood. No one wanted to take a seat.

"I let you girls drink here and have your fun," he began. "I don't give you a hard time or monitor what you drink. But what you allowed to happen tonight is inexcusable."

Sam rolled her eyes and Meredith shifted uncomfortably on her feet.

"Do you realize what kind of position you put me in? Say one of you overdosed. Then I have to call an ambulance and the police. Then I have to explain why it is that an underage girl is passed out or dead in my bar. I would get fired. Tonic would be liable for what happened, and what for? Because you wanted be cool and do a little coke?"

I hadn't thought about it that way.

"I think you should take a break from coming here." He said it firmly, but there was a hint of sorrow in his eyes.

"Max . . . ," I started, but didn't know exactly what I wanted to say.

"Fine by me," Sam said. She turned and stormed out of his office. Molly followed her without saying a word.

"Can you give us a minute, Mer?" I asked once Molly was gone.

Meredith left and I closed the door and sat in the seat in front of Max.

"What is this all about?" I asked. "We made a mistake, Max. Are you really going to ban us from the bar for this?" I was still a little jittery, and that annoying drip thing was still going on in the back of my throat, but I was trying to be serious.

"I didn't like seeing you like that," Max said. 'I thought you were smarter than that."

"You mean to tell me you've never done coke?" I asked.

I looked into Max's eyes. God, they were beautiful. I began to lose focus on what I was talking about and became oddly fixated on him. I got up from my seat and walked over to him and sat against his desk. He was close to me, very close. He didn't wear cologne, but I could smell his shampoo.

"I've tried it," he said. "But that stuff is no good for you. Trust me."

"I trust you," I replied, inching closer to him.

"What are you doing?" he asked, though he didn't move.

"I don't know," I smiled.

I was outside my body at that point. I had lost all control, and with it, all sense of what I was doing. I inched farther along the desk until my knees brushed gently against Max's leg. When he didn't move, I slid into his lap and pressed my lips against his. He hesitated for a fraction of a second before kissing me back. It was rough and hard at first, and then gentle and sweet. He gripped my waist firmly with both of his hands, picked me up, and leaned me against the desk. It was the most exciting kiss I had ever had. And then, abruptly, it ended.

Max stood back and shook his head. "No. This is a mistake."

"What are you talking about?" I wanted more.

"Kelly, you're high."

"No, I'm not," I lied. "I know exactly what is going on." I stood back up and walked towards him. His back was against the wall and he had nowhere to go. I gently placed my hand on the back of his head and ran it down his neck. "I know exactly what is going on," I whispered in his ear before biting it softly.

Max exhaled loudly, grabbed my waist again, and pushed me back. "I think you should go," he said, and sank back down in his seat.

The moment was gone. I felt like shit, and on top of it, embarrassed. I walked out of Max's office and Tonic without saying a word.

CHAPTER FIFTEEN

I couldn't escape the disappointment I felt with how the start of winter break had gone at Tonic. Sam and I had never even had a disagreement before that night, and I couldn't understand where the hostility came from. Meredith told me not to worry and that things would be fine when we met back up for New Year's. I agreed that some time apart probably would do everyone some good.

When she asked what happened with Max in the office, I told her that I'd asked him to change his mind, but that he refused to. I left out my failed attempt at seduction. I felt bad lying to Meredith; we normally told each other everything, embarrassing or not. And when I say everything, I mean everything.

There was one night when she came into our room after taking a shower, all freaked out. She stood in front of me, dripping wet with a towel wrapped loosely around her body. "I think I have an STD," she said, her face as white as her towel.

"I found a bump," she said, "down there."

"Does it hurt?"

"Yeah."

"How big is it?"

"Like the tip of an eraser."

"And you just felt it now?"

"It's been sore there for a couple of days, but the bump is new."

"Do you want to go to the infirmary?"

"No." She shook her head vehemently. "Can you look at it?"

"Sure," I replied without thinking twice.

Meredith leaned back on her bed and unwrapped the towel. I walked over and stood above her.

"Can you imagine what people would say if they walked in on us right now?" I joked.

"Nothing they haven't thought already," she smiled.

It was true. People thought we were lesbians. So we kissed a couple of times when we were drunk. It meant nothing.

I looked where Meredith was pointing, and sure enough, there was a round, brown bump on the outside of her labia.

"Do you see it?"

"Yeah."

"What does it look like?"

"It's round and brown."

"Is it big?"

"It's not huge, but I would definitely get it looked at." I had no problem looking at it and describing it to her, but I wasn't about to touch it or get in any closer.

Meredith made an appointment with her gynecologist for the following week, as did I. Nothing can make you more paranoid about STDs than a friend who might have one. It wasn't that we weren't careful in our sexual endeavors; we were. But there were those few times when things had gotten a little intense rather quickly, and I may not have always been on top of protection.

In preparation for our appointments, Meredith scheduled two bikini waxes at the salon down the street from Hay U. She wanted the doctor to have a clear view and was against the idea of shaving. Bibi Salon and Spa was considered one of the best in town, which meant they were one of the cleanest; a big thing for both of us.

Dorri, the wax specialist, came into the waiting area and called me back first. She was a stout woman, short to the ground and more square than round, yet very soft-spoken. She asked me how I was doing and how school was going. She was very pleasant, even as she was ripping the wax off my sensitive skin. Like always, it was over before it started and my reddened skin began to tingle less. Dorri thanked me for coming in and walked out as I got dressed.

Meredith was sitting in the waiting area reading a magazine when I returned. "How bad was it?" she asked. She always asked me how bad it was, as though she had never had it done before. I told her it was the same as every other time. She smiled uncomfortably at me when Dorri called her back. "Wish me luck," she whispered, and handed me her magazine.

From the waiting room I could hear Meredith yelp in pain. Although she was the one who always suggested getting waxed, she hated getting it done, referring to it as a necessary evil. Within minutes, she reemerged with a big smile on her face, a departure from her usual battered and beaten look, and she appeared almost refreshed.

"I love Dorri," she said, walking towards the cashier.

"What?"

"I don't have to go to the doctor's anymore," she whispered. "I don't have an STD."

"Dorri told you that?"

"Yes."

"I like Dorri and all," I said, "but I wouldn't trust her medical advice."

"It's gone," Meredith said.

"It's gone?"

"She popped it."

"She popped it?"

"Yeah, I asked her to be careful down there, she asked me why, and I told her. She took one look at it and said, 'Is no problem,' and popped it."

I gagged. "She popped it? Just like that?"

"Yeah," Meredith smiled, "and it hurt. It was pretty gross. Dorri said it was just an ingrown hair."

"That's disgusting."

"I feel so much better now."

"I'm just glad I went before you."

"The hair was like a foot long," she continued.

I begged her to stop.

The thought of Dorri willingly popping Meredith's ingrown hair and draining it of all the puss and gunk made me want to vomit. But that's how close Meredith and I were. No topic was off-limits.

Meredith canceled her doctor's appointment and I canceled mine. I had my checkup in the summer when I was home and everything looked all right. The nurse asked me if I wanted to get tested for STDs, but I declined. I was careful enough that I didn't find it necessary, and to be honest, I didn't want to know.

CHAPTER SIXTEEN

"I'm engaged!!!" Jane came screaming into the kitchen at my parents' house Christmas afternoon with her left hand outstretched.

Mom was in the midst of holiday dinner preparations, tied tightly into a red and green apron, and Dad was sitting in the family room by the fireplace watching the Celtics-Lakers Christmas Day game.

"What?" Mom shrieked, running over to hug my sister. "That's so wonderful."

Jane embraced Mom but kept her arm straight. Apparently, her ring would fall off her hand if it was not extended. I congratulated her and asked to see the ring. It was beautiful.

"One point four carats," she boasted, "set in white gold." The diamond solitaire sparkled, perched in its high setting.

"Ray," Mom called out to Dad, "you have to come and see this thing."

Dad rose from his seat, muted the television, and joined us in the kitchen. "Congratulations, sweetheart," he smiled, taking Jane's left hand in his for inspection. "That certainly is some rock."

Jane was beaming as brightly as her ring. She was beyond elated and I was happy for her. "Don't act surprised," she sighed at our father. "I know you knew, Daddy."

"Ra-ay," my mother said, almost whining his name into two syllables. "You knew and you didn't tell me?"

"I wanted it to be a surprise for Jane," he smiled.

She gave him a dirty look and went back to cooking. "When did he ask you?"

"Thanksgiving," Dad replied dryly.

"Uh-huh," Mom replied. Dad was in trouble and we all knew it. My mom doesn't like secrets, especially when they're kept from her and pertain to her children.

Jane's engagement brightened everyone's spirits. I don't remember seeing her lower her arm at all for the rest of the day. Everyone that walked through the front door got a good look at her ring, whether they wanted to or not.

When Pete arrived, Mom ran over and hugged him, welcoming him to the family. At dinner, Dad made a toast and everyone applauded the newly engaged couple. It was beginning to get rather nauseating.

"So, how did she trick you into this one?" I asked Pete during dessert.

"Your sister has captivated me with her beauty," he replied, "and enamored me with her love." Everyone oohed and ahhed. I threw up in my mouth.

"She took away the milk, didn't she?"

Jane sighed. "Why do you always have to go there?"

"I'm just kidding." I smiled weakly. "I am really happy for the two of you. Congratulations."

I finished my dessert, excused myself from the table, and went to call Meredith. I needed to vent and she was the only one I trusted with my true emotions.

"Merry Christmas," she said when she answered the phone. "I have good news."

"Merry Christmas," I sighed. "I hope so."

"Why so glum?"

"Jane and Pete are engaged."

"Why is that a bad thing?"

"It's not. She's really happy, but he is so annoying and I don't trust him at all."

"Yeah, I know. I'm sorry about that."

"So, what's your good news?" I asked.

"I talked to Molly and she said everything was all cleared up with Max. We're good to go there for New Year's!"

"Really?" I asked, truly surprised.

"Yeah, she and Sam went back to Tonic to apologize to Max,

and they worked everything out. He even asked how you were."

"Seriously?" My surprise was replaced by a strange surge of happiness.

"Yep," she said. "He said everything is good, but no drugs. That's his thing, and he won't make any exceptions. He also said that if we're around for New Year's, we definitely should come in."

That was a good sign. That meant things weren't awkward, which meant he wasn't embarrassed or angered by what transpired between the two of us, and we were cool. Maybe, I went as far as to think, he wanted to see me because he was interested in me. Instantly, my mind began to envision many fantastic possibilities of what the New Year would bring. They all, of course, started with me and Max in his office with the door locked. The locked part was optional in some of the scenarios, which added to the fantasy. Either way, I was going to ring in the New Year with Max.

That was the plan. But in keeping with the misfortunes of my life, I woke up at noon on New Year's Eve with a hundred-and-two-degree fever and a horrible sore throat.

"Looks like you'll be celebrating the New Year right here with us," my mom said, smiling after feeling my forehead with her palm. She was more than relieved that I wasn't going out.

"This is one of the worst nights of the year for kids your age," my dad added. "It's just like prom night, but with more alcohol."

My mom nodded her head in agreement. I started to cry.

"What's this all about?" she asked.

"I had plans for tonight," I sniffled.

"You're probably just not feeling good," she said. "Why don't you take some Tylenol and go back to bed."

Sadly, I accepted the medicine she offered, swallowed it down with a large glass of water, and went back up to bed. I felt awful. Every muscle in my body ached and the idea of speaking seemed impossible. I cried myself to sleep as my night of fun and romance turned into an acetaminophen-induced haze.

I tossed and turned until my fever broke and I awoke drenched in sweat with my hair stuck to the back of my neck. I had a missed call from Meredith at midnight and a text from her right afterwards wishing me a Happy New Year. It was three o'clock in the morning, and while there was a very good chance that she was still awake, my throat was on fire and I couldn't talk to anyone. I sighed and went back to sleep.

I made no resolutions for the New Year because I was happy with my life. For me, resolutions were for old and unhappy people. I was neither.

CHAPTER SEVENTEEN

I'd missed out on New Year's, and Meredith, Molly, and Sam refused to let me live it down.

"It was awesome," Meredith said. "There were so many people there."

"And Max had a party afterwards back at his place," Molly added. "So we crashed there."

My heart sank. "Max had a party?"

"Yeah," Molly said, "it was crazy. He was disappointed you were sick. He asked us if you really were sick or if you were still mad about the whole coke thing."

"What did you tell him?"

"I told him he was kind of a prick about the whole thing, but you really were sick."

"What did he say?" Was he really interested in me? Did I have a chance?

"Nothing," Meredith said. "He was distracted by this blonde girl who kept trying to talk to him all night."

"Did she go to his party?"

"She sure did."

"What is that supposed to mean?"

"Let's just say that no one saw much of her and Max after three a.m."

They left it at that and I understood exactly what they meant. Max, the man whore, was too good for me but not for some skank who wandered into Tonic on New Year's Eve. Whatever, it was fine. There were plenty of other guys at Hay U who would be lucky to have my interest.

Bored at home planning Jane's wedding, I went back to Philadelphia and spent a couple of days with Meredith and her dad during winter break. Jane and Pete had decided to get married in the fall because she'd always wanted an autumn wedding. I asked her what the rush was for and if she was pregnant. She rolled her eyes and ignored me. It was definitely time to get out.

Meredith's winter break consisted of going to bed around two in the morning, waking up at noon, and watching television all day. "It's called break for a reason," she explained. I was all for it. We went out with people she knew from high school, hung out at a few parties, and hooked up with a couple of guys.

I knew I hadn't lost my touch. I knew Max was the one with the problem. But I couldn't get him out of my mind. I had been turned down by guys before. Not many, but enough to know how it felt. While the initial rejection always stung, it never hung on for weeks. Was it that I had real feelings for Max? Whatever it was, I temporarily forgot about it with a guy named Del, short for Delaware.

Del and Meredith had known each other since grade school. They went to high school together and as it turned out, he was the first boy she ever kissed. I didn't mind that so much. It happened when they were like twelve. It's not as though they still hooked up, though that wouldn't have bothered me much, either. Neither Meredith nor I were serious with any guy, and sharing was always fun. If there was ever a guy who was off-limits, say, Luke, we just had to make it clear from the beginning. Other than that, whatever happened happened. And with Del, it happened.

He was shorter than I preferred, under six foot, with an all-American smile. His body was cut and his smell fantastic. I didn't plan on sleeping with him, it just sort of happened. I was really drunk and he was really hot. Meredith was off with one of his friends from college, so it just kind of worked out that way. Though I hadn't made any resolutions, I did want to limit the number of guys I had sex with in the new year. Surprisingly, Lexi didn't participate in random sexual acts nearly as much as Kelly did. She may have kissed more men, but when it came down to doing the deed, Kelly was the closer. And although she was selective concerning the guys she slept with, always knowing and having some kind of rapport with them prior to disrobing, Kelly still didn't discriminate as much as she should have.

"Did you sleep with him?" Meredith whispered to me when we left Del's house.

I smiled and said nothing.

"I knew it," she said. "How was it?"

"Six," I replied, being kind.

"That's it? I thought he would be at least an eight."

Meredith and I rated the guys we slept with on a scale of one to ten. One meant the guy had no idea what he was doing and ten meant he did everything just right and more. Luke was a ten, definitely a ten. Chris Davis, a four. And if I hadn't been so intoxicated during our encounters, I probably would have stopped him halfway through. Most guys fell between five and seven, and scores of three or lower didn't count in our tally. We reasoned that it shouldn't be counted if we didn't enjoy it.

"What about you?" I asked. "How was Glenn?"

"Didn't do it," she replied.

"What? You were in the back room for a while."

"I didn't say we didn't do anything," she smiled. "We did everything but."

Then she got quiet.

"You can't get an STD from swallowing, can you?"

"I don't think so," I said, though I wasn't sure. "I think there's something in your saliva that protects you."

Meredith and I met up with Del and Glenn one more time before I went back home. Unimpressed by the night of passion we'd shared, I told Del I had my period when he started to grope me again. He backed off and put the television on while Glenn and Meredith disappeared for twenty minutes.

"How was it?" I asked when we left.

"It didn't happen."

"What?"

"He put it in for like a second and I changed my mind and told him to stop. So it didn't count."

"Why did you change your mind?"

"I didn't feel like doing it. I don't really know him, and it wasn't as fun as it was the other night."

"You're such a tease," I joked.

She rolled her eyes. "Whatever. He should be happy with the

action he got."

I returned home well rested and eager to get back to school. Spending time with Meredith always made me miss the freedom and independence we had at Hay U. I was ready to live on my own.

Things quickly got back to normal once we all returned to school. I was worried that things with Sam would be a little awkward at first, but they weren't at all. We did a toast our first Friday back in celebration of the New Year and the beginning of a new semester. Molly suggested we go to Tonic to kick the weekend off right. Sam and Meredith quickly agreed. I did not, for two reasons.

The first was that Jane had sent me a text message earlier in the day asking me to not drink too much and to get some sleep, because we were going shopping for bridesmaids' dresses the following morning and she needed me awake and in a good mood. She had originally wanted to go at ten in the morning; I told her to pick me up at noon.

The second and main reason I didn't want to go to Tonic was that I wasn't ready to see Max. I didn't know what I was going to say to him. I mean, technically, he hadn't done anything wrong. In fact, he'd treated me with nothing but respect. He could have done anything he wanted to do to me that night in his office, but he chose to send me home. How many guys in his situation would do that?

But after much begging by Meredith, I agreed to go with them. I let Meredith do my hair and makeup—it looked amazing—and selected my hottest outfit. I went with a low-cut glittery tank top, a pair of skinny jeans, and my hooker boots. If I had to go, I was going to show Max exactly what he gave up in December.

Chris P., my favorite bouncer, was working the door when the cab dropped us off in front of the bar. His eyes lit up when he saw us approach and he opened the door to let us in. I leaned in and gave him an unexpected kiss on the cheek. My mission that night was simple: to flirt with every single guy in sight except for Max.

Max welcomed us with a smile. "I've been waiting for you girls to come in. I haven't seen you since New Year's Eve."

My stomach turned at the thought of me at home sick in bed and him in bed with some blonde.

"Yeah," Molly said, "you were pretty occupied that night."

"Yeah." Max looked uncomfortably at me. "So what do you

want to start off with tonight?"

"What was the shot you gave us on New Year's Eve?" Meredith asked. "That was so good."

I became more angry every time the words New and Year were spoken together. They rang the year in together, I got it. I didn't need to be reminded that I'd missed out on the party, the inside jokes, and the new drinks.

"The Year Eraser?" he asked with a mischievous grin.

"Yes!" Meredith replied emphatically. "Kel, you have got to try this. You are going to love it."

I smiled weakly but didn't say anything. I turned away from the bar and scanned the crowd. I needed to find a prop. I needed to find a man.

Max lined up four shot glasses and filled them with a mixture of alcohol and juice, dropping a cherry in for aesthetics. We raised our glasses, clinked them together saying cheers, and threw them back. Meredith was right. The shot tasted great, but I couldn't give Max the satisfaction of knowing I enjoyed it. I casually put my glass down and once again turned from the bar.

"Rich Girl" by Gwen Stefani started to play, and Sam pulled Molly onto the dance floor. It was Sam's favorite song. Molly pulled Meredith, and Meredith motioned for me to come after them. As I started to walk away from the bar, Max put his hand on mine to stop me. My heart skipped a beat and a weird sensation ran through my body.

"Can we talk?" he asked.

"About what?" My heart began to race.

"You know what."

"About the girl you hooked up with on New Year's?"

He rolled his eyes.

"I get it, Max," I said. "You flirt with us and give us shots, but that's it. I made a mistake in thinking it was anything else."

"Can we go to my office and talk about this?"

"I don't think there's anything else to talk about."

"Please, Kelly."

I loved how he said my name and hated it all at the same time. He was looking into my eyes, bearing deep into my soul.

"Fine."

The bass from the speakers vibrated off the walls in the hall leading back to his office. Behind the closed door, the music was muffled but the beats could still be felt.

"I like you, Kelly," he said when we were seated. "I always have. But you are nineteen."

I crossed my arms and leaned forward, resting my elbows on my knees. I looked at him, really looked at him, without saying a word. I wanted to say something sharp and witty, but my mind wasn't cooperating.

"If you were twenty-one . . . ," he began.

"Really?" I sighed. "Is this what you called me back in here to talk about? If I were one and a half years older, would it really make that much of a difference? I can tell you feel bad, but don't. I'm a big girl and I can handle the rejection. It's fine. Everything is fine. Let's just pretend it never happened."

"I'm not sure I want to," he replied.

"I don't think you know what you want," I said, standing up, "but when you told me to go home, you made your decision. So live with it."

My blood was pumping feverishly through my veins. I'd had the last word, and I was ready to storm out of his office and slam the door behind me for dramatic effect. But as I reached for the handle, it opened. A petite blonde stood in front of me, average-looking in my opinion, with a perplexed look on her face.

"Jen said you were in the office," she said, giving me a once-over. "Hi, I'm Alicia."

"Hi," I smiled smugly, "I'm Lexi."

"Kel . . . uh . . . Lexi was just applying for a job as a bartender," Max said, walking around his desk. "I'll let you know if anything opens up."

"Yeah," I replied, "you do that."

Who did he think he was playing? I mimicked his voice in my head. What if I can't? I couldn't believe it. Operation Scorn Max was now on, in full effect.

"Where did you go?" Meredith asked when I joined my friends on the dance floor.

"Max wanted to make sure everything was cool since I didn't come on New Year's."

"Oh." She giggled at Molly and Sam, who were holding back smiles.

"What?" I asked.

"Nothing," she replied, and broke out into hysterical laughter.

"No, there is something, so tell me."

"We just think that you lu-uv him." They all were laughing.

"Trust me," I said. "There is no love there. Can we please do some shots?"

We returned to the bar and sat down, hoping to find someone to pay for our drinks. We knew the routine well; patience was key. All we had to do was wait for a while until a couple of guys came calling. They always did.

Sal and Mike were the first suppliers. They bought us a round as we introduced ourselves and then another one before we hit the dance floor. Sal was hot and available, so I decided to use him. He was a little more touchy-feely than I would have liked him to be, but it worked to my advantage in my ploy against Max.

I felt Max's eyes burning holes through my clothing as I danced with Sal. Max was standing behind the bar and Alicia was on a stool in front of him with her back to me. I purposefully turned around, placed my back against Sal's chest, and slowly moved up and down, keeping my eyes fixed on Max. Max was staring right back at me. Sal's hands wandered from my thighs up my sides, then back down to my thighs before returning to my waist and spinning me back to face him. My eyes hadn't yet focused from my quick twirl before he lodged his big and slimy tongue in my mouth. He didn't know what the hell he was doing, but I went along with it.

The longer we kissed, the more intense and insistent Sal got. I was hoping for some kind of relief, something to calm him down a little, but nothing came. Out of the corner of my eye I saw Meredith dancing with Mike. Mike appeared a lot tamer than his friend.

"Let's go to the bathroom," Sal said, letting up for air.

I gulped the stale bar air as though we were out in the wide-open country. My mouth hurt and my lips were numb. I was afraid that if I went to the bathroom with him I wouldn't come out alive. Not to mention the fact that I wasn't really a sex-in-the-bathroom kind of girl.

"The bathroom?" I made a repulsed face. "Why?"

"I want you," he replied, forcefully pulling me into him by my waist.

I didn't know what to say, but my gut was screaming Danger, Danger. Sal was breathing heavy in my face. His eyes had turned darker than they were before and his face had hardened. I desperately looked for Meredith, but she was gone. I wondered if Mike had taken her to the bathroom. I wondered if she went. Was that their thing? Molly and Sam had disappeared, too. I began to feel sick. I'd thought I was so clever in picking Sal for my prop, when all along he'd picked me for his prey.

"You're not one of those stupid bitches who lets a guy buy her drinks without giving anything back, are you?" His voice had no pleasantness to it. Sal had made up his mind about what he wanted, and he wasn't going to take no for an answer.

I took a step back to increase the space between us, but he grabbed my wrist and pulled me back.

"You're hurting me," I said.

"Listen, you tease," he growled, "you and me are going to go to the bathroom and have some fun."

"I'm not going anywhere with you." I tried to wriggle my wrist free but his grip tightened. "Please let go of me."

I looked back at the bar. Both Max and Alicia were gone. He wasn't watching anymore. No one was watching. I began to tremble. I felt really sick, really dizzy. Suddenly I had trouble focusing on Sal, on anything.

"What did you do to me?"

"So now you want to play innocent?" Sal pulled me in tightly to his chest and began to drag me to the back of the bar where the bathrooms were. "We'll see just how innocent you are."

My entire body shook with fear. I could not believe what was happening to me. I couldn't believe that no one was helping me. I had lost control of my limbs and my speech. Sal was in complete control.

"Everything okay, bro?" A guy stopped us towards the back of the bar.

I was outside of my body and unable to respond.

"Yeah," Sal smiled pleasantly. "My girl had a little too much tonight. She said she's going to throw up."

The guy smiled and shook his head. "Gotcha."

"Yeah," Sal smiled back, "but thanks."

No, I screamed in my head as the nice stranger walked away.

Sal's hold on me didn't loosen until we were in a stall with the door locked. Meredith and Mike weren't in the bathroom. All hope was gone. Sal viciously tore at my top and my jeans, clawing at the stubborn material. His hot, sour breath panted on my neck.

"No," I cried out. "Please, no."

CHAPTER EIGHTEEN

My clothes were being ripped off of my body. My shoes and socks were gone. I knew that because my feet were cold. My legs were exposed, then my stomach, then my chest. My bra was cut in the middle and opened like a book. My breasts perked at the change in temperature. My entire body was on display.

For extra credit in my sociology class freshman year, I attended a speech by a woman who was date-raped in college. I sat for almost two hours and listened as Jessica Cooper detailed her experience. As she spoke, Jessica tried her best to make eye contact with everyone in the audience. She was soft-spoken and petite. I saw her as the adorable captain of the cheerleading squad in high school who had gone off to college with wide eyes and the world in the palm of her hand.

"I was raped," she'd said, standing behind the podium in the lecture hall. "It took me a while to be able to say that, admit that it happened. My counselor—I prefer that term over shrink—said that being able to admit that it happened was the only way I could move past it. I was raped.

"For weeks, my mind refused to form those three words into a sentence. I could say the word rape, though it made me want to vomit, but I couldn't use it when talking about myself.

"He was gorgeous," she said in a steady voice, "and I couldn't believe he had an interest in me. He was popular with both the guys and girls on campus and I couldn't wait for our date."

The room was silent as she recounted how her excitement quickly turned to fear when he took hold of her wrists and threw her down onto the bed. Her fear turned to horror as he ripped her clothes off and undid his pants. And the horror morphed into shame when he got up, told her that it never happened, and left her on the bed, cold, bruised, bleeding, and alone.

"I had two drinks that night," she said, "but I wasn't drunk. I knew not to drink too much. I knew not to accept drinks from strangers. I didn't dress provocatively. I never put myself out there. Those were all things that went through my mind while I tried to figure out why it happened to me. But then I realized that none of that matters, because a woman never deserves to be raped. It doesn't matter what she wears or how she acts. It should never happen. But sadly, it does. One out of four women will be sexually assaulted in their lifetime, one out of four.

"One out of four," she repeated again. "Those four words actually ran through my mind when I became the one, when I became the statistic. Those four words actually helped me to get through it all. One out of four meant that I was not alone.

"I didn't call the police when it happened, and I didn't tell anyone except for my best friend, and eventually my counselor. I didn't speak about it for a while after that first night because I'd convinced myself that it didn't happen to me. It happened to someone else. My counselor said it wasn't healthy to think that way, that often people who have had a violent act committed against them do separate the action from their own reality. She said I needed to admit what happened to me: I was raped."

Even though I was scared, I opened my eyes big and wide, then squinted at the bright light above my head. A man hovered above me and murmured something behind a mask. A second masked person appeared, a woman with soft eyes.

"There's been an accident," she said. "You're going to be okay. Try to relax and close your eyes. I'm going to give you something to make you feel better." I continued to stare at her. "You are going to be okay," she said.

CHAPTER NINETEEN

I awoke alone in a strange place, in a strange bed. The flannel sheet wrapped around me was soft and smelled familiar. Sunlight poured in through the window to my left like a vast waterfall. The bedroom itself was small and cluttered. Clothes, men's clothes, were strewn about. I sat up.

My head felt like it had split into two different pieces and I was extremely nauseous. I looked under the sheet to see what, if anything, I was wearing. In place of my normal pajamas was an extra-large T-shirt. I cautiously slid the shirt up to my thigh and was relieved to see my pink thong still in place. Where was I?

A television was on somewhere and I could hear movement in another room. I was unable to remember anything from the night before. My head ached so badly that it was hindering my thought process, and fear began to take over. I was going to be sick.

I got out of bed and ran to the door. Left or right, left or right, I only had two options but I was almost paralyzed by fear. I heard footsteps approaching from the left so I ran to the right. Thankfully I ended up in the bathroom. I sat on the cold tile in front of the toilet; the lid and seat were both up. It had to be a guy's apartment. Within seconds, I was heaving the contents of my stomach with immense and violent force into the toilet.

Someone tapped on the door. "Are you all right?"

I froze. I had forgotten to lock the door. I grabbed the cold ceramic bowl in fear and watched as the doorknob turned. I was sick and scared and had no idea where I was.

The click of the latch releasing from the jamb sent a chill down my shaking body. Slowly, the door opened. I looked around for a weapon—the closest thing was a toilet brush. It was hopeless. I leaned over the bowl and vomited again.

"You really know how to get a guy's attention," said a masculine voice behind me.

My grip on the toilet released and I looked up, relieved. Smiling down at me with no judgment on his face was Max.

"Good morning," he said.

"What happened?" I asked.

"We can talk about that later," he replied. "How are you feeling?"

"Like shit." I wiped my mouth with the back of my hand. "Did we . . . ?"

Max laughed, setting me at ease. It's not that I would have been upset if he had told me yes. I would have been more disappointed than anything else. If and when it did happen with us, I wanted to remember.

"How did I end up here?" I asked.

"You got sick at the bar and the girls were in no shape to get you home."

"So they left me behind with you?"

"I didn't really give them a choice," he answered. "Meredith came back and helped me get you to bed. She told me to tell you to call her when you got up and that she would come back and get you."

"What time is it?"

"Almost one thirty."

"Wow." Though throwing up seemed to quell the turning of my stomach, it had done little to ease the pounding in my head. "How much did I drink last night?"

"It's not what you drank," Max replied. "Are you finished in here or do you have to puke some more?"

"I think I'm good for now." I pulled on the handle and watched as the contents of the toilet were replaced with fresh water.

"Do you want something to eat or drink?"

My stomach gurgled loudly. "Please don't mention food," I said. "Do you have a cigarette?"

"Yeah," he said, helping me to my feet. "Let's go into the living room, unless you just want to go back to bed."

Max walked me slowly to the living room and sat me on the couch. His apartment was cute, and not that dirty for a bachelor pad. The small kitchen was tucked into a corner in the back. A breakfast bar opened up to the dining room that shared the same open space as the living room. He rummaged through a jacket hanging on the back of a dining room chair and produced two cigarettes. He placed them both between his lips and lit them one by one with a lighter, then drew a breath in to get them started and handed me one, exhaling a large cloud of smoke. He'd never looked hotter.

If it wasn't for the fact that my head felt like it was going to burst at any second, I may have acted on my impulse to seduce him on his couch, or at least try.

"So, are you going to tell me what happened last night and why I ended up in your bed?"

"How much do you remember?"

Seriously, was he trying to turn me on? His white T-shirt hugged his body as he reclined on the couch, outlining almost every muscle in his stomach. Every time he pulled in on his cigarette, his bicep flexed just enough to show its form and I wished it was me that was pressing up against his lips.

I tried to think about the night before, but my brain seemed to swell at the task.

"I remember coming into Tonic," I finally said. "I didn't want to go, but the girls wanted to so I went."

"Why didn't you want to go?" he asked.

"Because I was mad at you."

"Do you remember talking to me?"

Again, I asked my brain to think. It wasn't cooperating. "Nope."

"What next?"

The next part was a blur, a series of indiscernible flashes, then dancing.

"I was dancing."

"You remember dancing."

"Yes."

"Do you remember who you were dancing with?"

I tried to piece together the fragments floating around in my head.

"A guy," I said.

Max rolled his gorgeous eyes. "Thank you for the clarification. Do you remember what his name was or what he looked like?"

My stomach tightened and a chill ran from my head to the tips of my toes.

"What's the matter?" Max asked.

"I don't know," I replied, becoming very emotional. "Max, what happened to me?"

Max got up and sat right next to me. He put his arm around my shoulder, pulled me into his chest, and kissed the top of my head.

"The guy you were dancing with was an asshole," he began. "He slipped something into the drink he bought you."

"Oh my God." Vivid flashbacks were storming my head. They still formed an incomplete picture, but I got the gist. "Did he rape me?" I began to cry.

"No," Max whispered, "he didn't."

"So how do you know he put something in my drink? Did you see him do it?"

"I wish I did."

"Then how do you know he did?"

"Meredith couldn't find you and started to panic, so she came and got me. She said that you and this guy, Sal, just disappeared. I didn't think it was that serious, but when Molly and Sam said they saw you heading to the back with that guy, I got a little worried. They said you looked pretty wasted. They just thought he was taking you to sit on one of the couches."

"Is that where we were?"

"No, Meredith said she'd already checked there. So the only other place at the back of the bar was . . ."

"He took me into the bathroom?" I shuddered at the thought of the men's bathroom—the smell, the urinal cakes. It was enough to make me want to vomit again.

"Yeah, he locked the two of you in a stall."

"What was he doing when you found us?"

"He hadn't gotten started yet," Max said. "Let's just leave it at that."

I sat in silence and smoked the rest of my cigarette. When it was finished, I asked Max for another one. He sat on the couch holding me while I smoked four straight.

"You asked me if I remembered talking to you?" I said when I had enough of myself together to speak. "When did we talk?"

"That's not important," he replied. "I'll tell you later."

"Was it before or after?" I asked.

"Before, though you did tell me a lot after."

"What did I say?"

"That you loved me."

"I did not." I hit his stomach. Rock hard, as I had suspected.

"No, you didn't," he said. "But after saving your ass last night, you should."

I didn't say anything back. Instead I enjoyed the moment of being safe, being held, and feeling cared about.

CHAPTER TWENTY

Jane had left me a voicemail at ten thirty. "Where are you? I want to make sure you're awake and ready to go. Call me when you get this."

She left another one at eleven.

"Kelly, this isn't funny. We have an appointment for twelve thirty. If we don't make it today, I'll have to reschedule for two weeks. Call me."

Again at eleven fifteen.

"I have to leave in ten minutes to come and get you," she barked. "I am not going to waste the trip out there if you aren't going to answer your phone or come down. Kelly, where the hell are you?"

Again at eleven thirty.

"Obviously today was not important enough for you to remember or stay sober for. I'm leaving now to go to the bridal shop. The address is 1125 North Broad Street. The shop is called An Elegant Affair. The appointment is at twelve thirty. You have all the information. Hopefully I'll see you there."

The last message came at one fifteen.

"Mom and I just left the shop. I told her you forgot about a paper that was due on Monday and that you had to work on it all weekend. I covered for you because I didn't want Mom to worry." The hurt and agitation were clear in her voice.

I had another message from my mom. "Hi, honey," she sang pleasantly. "I just wanted to call and say hello. We missed you this afternoon. Jane told me you have a paper due on Monday. Give me a call when you want to take a break. I love you."

It was nice to see I had messages waiting for me on my phone, but I would be lying if I said it didn't bother me that no one seemed concerned that I was MIA.

When I got back to the apartment, Meredith apologized a million times for leaving me alone with Sal and kept asking me how I was feeling. To say that I felt like I was hit by a car didn't even begin to describe the aching of my body. I once saw a guy on the news that was hit by an eighteen-wheeler and lived to describe his ordeal. That was a more apt description of my pain.

I did my best to try and forget Sal and the whole night. It wasn't hard, being that I didn't remember much of it to begin with. And the thought of tracking him down and pressing charges didn't even cross my mind. First of all, I had no actual proof that he did slip me anything. Secondly, I didn't want to go through the hassle. I'd escaped, luckily, unscathed. I could deal with the headache and the queasiness. I would take that every day over being raped.

I called Jane back at seven o'clock that night. I was pretty exhausted and ready for bed but wanted to call her before the night was over. When she didn't answer her cell phone, I tried her apartment. Pete answered.

"Hey, Pete." I tried to sound enthused to hear his voice. "Is Jane there?"

"Yes."

"Can I talk to her?"

"You know, you really upset her today," he said.

"Yeah, well that's something I want to talk to her about," I replied with less patience than usual.

"I don't like seeing her that upset."

"Can I talk to her or not?"

He paused, and I really thought he wasn't going to let me talk to her.

"It's Kelly," he said. He had pulled the phone away from his mouth. "She wants to talk to you."

I heard Jane say something back, but I couldn't understand it.

"She's really tired," he said, coming back on the line. "She said she'll give you a call tomorrow."

"I need to talk to her," I barked. "It's really important."

"So was this afternoon for her," he said, and he hung up.

I couldn't believe it. I realized she was upset and didn't expect her to be thrilled to talk to me, but I really wanted to talk to her. She was my sister. I had been attacked. She was supposed to be there for me. Fucking Pete! Who was he to get involved? It had absolutely nothing to do with him.

I went to bed at eight thirty and slept until noon on Sunday, and was surprised that I still felt exhausted when I woke up. I contemplated going to the infirmary on campus, but I didn't want to tell the nurse I had been roofied. I didn't know what the school's protocol on that type of thing was. I was over eighteen, so I guessed they wouldn't call my parents; or would they? I didn't want to take the chance.

I lounged around the apartment all afternoon in my pajamas, which consisted of Max's shirt and my boxers. Ah, Max. He had been so good to me. It was almost as though he felt guilty, but what did he have to be guilty for?

My mom called around four thirty to check in because I hadn't called her back the day before. I apologized for worrying her and assured her that I was fine, even though she said she knew something was wrong. She said she could hear it in my voice. I told her I was just tired, that I'd stayed up late to work on my paper.

When I asked her how the dress shopping went, she got all choked up and rambled on about how she couldn't believe Jane was getting married, that she looked so beautiful in every dress, that it would only be a matter of time until I was getting married. I told her not to get ahead of herself. I asked if Jane was mad that I didn't go, and she said, "Of course not." I could tell she was bending the truth. I then played out how horrible I felt while emphasizing the importance of getting the paper done. My mom concurred, and let me go so I could finish it.

Jane called about an hour later.

"I don't know how you've managed to get Mom so wrapped around your finger, but it's disgusting," she hissed into the phone.

"Hello to you, too," I replied.

"Cut the crap, Kelly. I'm not Mom. I'm not going to buy any of your lies."

"I'm sorry about yesterday," I cut in.

"Are you? Because you must have had a pretty good time Friday night to blow your only sister off. I thought you said you were going to take it easy."

"I was, but then everyone wanted to go to Tonic and I told them I couldn't go . . . but they made me."

"So this is your friends' fault? Why am I not surprised?"

"If you would listen to me, I'll tell you what happened." I was beginning to get angry. She wasn't even giving me a chance to explain. She was so angry, no doubt fueled by Pete.

"Let me guess," she barked. "You didn't realize how much you drank and then you passed out and didn't wake up until after noon, and by then it was too late so you went back to bed and figured you would just call and smooth everything over with an 'I'm sorry.'"

"You know what," I snapped, "just forget it. You obviously have it made up in your mind what happened, so don't worry about it. I could have been dead somewhere or something really bad could have happened to me, and you would have had no clue. Did it not bother you or worry you at all when I didn't answer any of your calls?"

"At first, yeah," she admitted. "But before you go and play the martyr that we all know you're so good at playing, you should know that I did call your apartment, three times. Meredith finally answered and told me you were at Max's and to call you on your cell. So yes, I was concerned. But when I heard that you opted to spend the night with some guy, I didn't worry as much. So how was it? Was it worth skipping out on dress shopping?"

"Do you even care?" I asked.

"Yes, I do, because I want to know what is going on inside of your head."

I had been holding back my tears almost the entire conversation. I was fighting all emotion with the exception of anger. That was the only real thing I felt.

"I was almost raped last night," I blurted out, unleashing the tears.

"What?" Jane shot back, sounding uncertain of whether I was telling the truth.

"I was almost raped," I repeated in a calmer voice, tears flowing from my eyes. "The reason I didn't answer my phone was because I was drugged. Some guy slipped something in my drink and it knocked me out."

"You better not be making this up," she said wearily.

I hung up on her. She didn't have to believe me. She had every right to be angry with me, but after explaining to her what happened, if she thought I was making something like that up, then I had no desire to talk to her.

When she didn't call back, I took that as her response. I went to bed. Twenty-five minutes later, she walked into my bedroom.

"Tell me everything," she said.

I started to cry all over again.

I sat up in bed and recounted the entire story from start to finish. She sat across from me on Meredith's bed with teary eyes and a sad face. When I finished, she got up, sat next to me, and hugged me. "I'm sorry," she sniffled. "I am so sorry. I'm just glad you're okay."

Jane didn't condone my underage drinking or naivety when it came to accepting drinks from strangers. She just sat on the bed and held me. I was hit with overwhelming guilt. If I had been a better sister, I wouldn't have gone to Tonic and the whole mess would have been avoided. I apologized for letting her down. She shushed me, said that it was over, that she hadn't found her dress and there was plenty more shopping to do.

After we were both cried out, she offered to take me out to dinner, but I wasn't hungry. I was still feeling pretty lousy and the only thing I wanted to do was sleep. She said she understood.

"Well, I was going to ask you this yesterday," she said with a half smile, "but I guess today is just as good. How do you feel about being my maid of honor?"

I was shocked. "Really?"

Maybe that's why she was as angry as she was. When she got engaged I'd naturally assumed that Mary, her best friend, was going to fill that role.

"Really," she said. "I couldn't imagine it being anyone other than you."

CHAPTER TWENTY-ONE

It would be encouraging to see, and would definitely show maturity, if I had taken a step back from Tonic after my experience with Sal, but I didn't. In fact, I felt more in control after that night, vowing to myself that it would never EVER happen again.

Max was wary the first night I returned to the bar, and he kept a close eye on me the entire time. I did a couple of shots, had one martini, and stopped after that. I kept myself controlled and showed no interest in any men. Even when they approached, I just brushed them off. It was weird, because I actually ended up enjoying the night more than any of the other million times that we had gone there. Meredith and I danced. I flirted with Max. We were safe.

After I told her what happened, Jane wanted to know how it was that I was able to get into a bar when I was only nineteen. Whenever she'd asked me that before, I would say that Lexi McBride got me in and leave it at that. I finally explained to her who Lexi McBride was.

"Lexi? What kind of name is Lexi?" she sighed while looking at my fake ID.

I shrugged my shoulders and told her that it got the job done.

"It doesn't even look real." She flipped it from front to back. "I can't see how this would work."

"It doesn't have to when you know the manager."

"I don't know." She shook her head. "I understand that he did a great thing for you this weekend, but just be careful, Kel. There's something about a grown man hanging around college girls that I don't trust."

I could hear the concern in her voice and knew she didn't want to come down hard on me, considering what had happened. But at the same time, she still felt it necessary to voice her opinion. According to Jane, anyone older than her (twenty-four) was a grown man, and dating or being involved with a man in said age group was not acceptable. It was just another instance of her imposing her opinion on me whether I wanted to hear it or not.

When we were kids, it was about what I should wear or how my hair should be styled. In high school she felt it necessary to advise me on my extracurricular activities and which colleges I should apply to. Hay U wasn't at the top of her list. I always listened to what Jane had to say—it was the only way to get her to stop talking. But in the end, I almost always made my own decisions. As the older sister, she had the right to give me her opinion. As the younger sister, I had the right to ignore her.

I was more of a free spirit, and unlike her, I wasn't one to test the waters. I just dove right in. I didn't dip my feet in first to feel the temperature. I always jumped in headfirst with a smile and never looked back.

I asked Jane not to tell our parents or Pete about what happened. "It's a private matter," I said, "and I would like to keep it between us."

She wasn't happy about keeping things from Pete, but she agreed.

The following two weekends were consumed with Jane's search for the perfect wedding dress. Mom was right; Jane looked gorgeous in every dress she tried on. During our second outing, she found exactly what she was looking for: an empire-waist dress with a beaded corset top. When Jane tried it on, the smile on her face was bright enough to light up the boutique.

"This is it," she smiled, smoothing the dress over her hips. "This is it."

Joy was radiating from my sister's entire body. She was happy in every sense of the word, and for those couple of minutes, I put my feelings about Pete aside and reveled in her happiness.

Jane chose candy-apple red and gold as the palette for her autumn wedding. She envisioned tall vases filled with apples and gold beads. Encircling the vases would be red and gold votive candles. The tables would be draped in white and the chairs would be adorned with red satin bows.

"Just don't adorn me in any bows," I joked.

Thankfully, she didn't. For her bridesmaids, she chose a high-necked sleeveless dress with a trapeze skirt. "Breezy" was the only word I could think of as I twirled in front of the mirror and the skirt moved freely with me. Any color other than gold would have been better for me, but Jane's mind was made up.

Mom sobbed continually as we tried on dresses and discussed the details of the wedding. Jane and I did our best not to make fun of her and the faces she was making as she tried to hide her emotions. But she was emotional, in a good way.

It was nice spending time with Mom and Jane like that. Since Jane got her apartment and I went to college, the only time we seemed to come together was on holidays, and things were always so hectic then.

Jane carried a wedding binder filled with pictures, papers, and swatches of color. Among the mass of papers was a checklist for each of the remaining eight months leading up to the wedding. She informed me that traditionally, checklists start twelve months prior to the wedding, but since she and Pete wanted to get married within the year, she was forced to cram several months' worth of tasks together. The list was rather cumbersome, but Jane didn't seem overwhelmed. She was more than happy to tackle each task with a smile.

"It says this is the time to file for a prenup," I read from her list. "Is that something you and Pete need to discuss?" I knew Jane didn't have a lot of money going into their union, but judging by her engagement ring, Pete wasn't strapped for cash.

"Half of nothing is nothing, so what would be the point? Besides," she said. "I don't believe in prenuptial agreements. I'm marrying Pete because I want to spend the rest of my life with him. I'm not marrying him on the hope that it will work out."

"Excuse me while I gag." I mimicked the motion.

"I'm serious," she said, and I knew then that I had opened the door for one of her preachings. "Marriage is a serious thing. Love is a serious thing. You know, the divorce rate wouldn't be so high in this country if people were more selective in choosing their mates."

I shut my ears off while she continued. When she finished, I nodded in agreement, having no idea what she had said.

CHAPTER TWENTY-TWO

Matt Stevens sat next to me in Macroeconomics. He wasn't what I would label as hot, but he wasn't ugly, either. He was all right. What he was, however, was a really nice guy. He introduced himself to me the second week of class after I failed miserably at answering one of the professor's questions aloud.

"Don't worry," Matt whispered when Professor Klein gave up on me and sought out another victim. "It was a really hard question."

I smiled at him and asked him if he knew the answer. He proudly admitted that he did, thus igniting our friendship. No matter how hard I tried, I could not get a good grasp on economics. I read the textbook and looked over my notes, but it never made sense. On the rare occasions when I did think I got it, my test scores reflected otherwise. But it came easily to Matt, and he came easily to me.

After I bombed the second pop quiz of the semester, Matt offered to tutor me. I think he felt bad because he knew his scores were the ones that were throwing off the curve. We agreed to meet for lunch on Tuesdays and Thursdays before class to go over our notes together.

Meredith and Molly teased me about my new boyfriend and asked if I was going to ditch them on the weekend for the debate team. It only got worse when I defended Matt, which they took as a sign that I was in love with him.

"What is it?" Meredith asked after spotting me with Matt in the cafeteria. "He has a big penis, doesn't he?"

"How would I know that?" I asked in revulsion.

"You haven't seen it yet? All that time you guys spend together, and he hasn't whipped it out?"

"You're disgusting," I said to her.

Did I think Matt was attracted to me? Yes. Did I share his attraction? Absolutely not. Do I admit to flirting with him anyway? Yes. A little flirting never hurt anyone. Besides, it kept things pleasant.

If you described his traits on paper, Matt was the perfect guy. My mother would have done cartwheels if I brought him home and Jane would finally be happy with my selection. He was a gentleman in every sense of the word. His patience for my stupidity was exemplary, and above everything else, he respected me. He always greeted me with a smile and his eyes never left my face, not that I had much to gawk at.

And despite my hopes that it wouldn't happen, it did. It always does.

We were prepping for another class in the cafeteria one Thursday towards the end of February. I had just finished my chicken Caesar wrap when he looked at me. The look in his eyes was different than usual. He was serious, nervous, even.

"Kelly," he started off, almost choking on his soda.

I looked away, giving him a chance to catch his breath and wipe his mouth. His cheeks were flushed and I picked up on a slight tremor in his body.

I smiled to reassure him that all was well. "What's up?"

"I was thinking maybe I could take you out to dinner this weekend or sometime when you're free."

I smiled again. I didn't know what else to do. I wasn't attracted to Matt. I wished I was, but there was just nothing there. But he had been so nice to me and helped me so much that I found it hard to say no. So I accepted.

Matt came to my apartment that Saturday night in a long-sleeved Polo shirt and crisp jeans, smelling of Axe body spray—not my favorite. Meredith oohed and ahhed when he gave me a single sunflower, my favorite.

He took me to dinner at a local Mexican restaurant; he remembered me telling him how much I liked Mexican food. He remembered almost everything I'd ever told him. I didn't think we'd talked about so many personal things, but he seemed to know a lot about me, and sadly, I knew almost nothing about him. He opened the door at the restaurant for me and at the café we went to afterwards for coffee and dessert.

My phone vibrated constantly throughout our date. I knew it was Meredith; she was a texting freak. It was, however, partly my fault, because I'd told her that if things got weird I would need her to save me.

After dinner, Matt suggested we go to Ali's Place, a popular café that had fresh pastries and free Wi-Fi and was open until midnight, which made it the perfect place to study and write papers. I think he wanted to go there just to be seen with me.

We chose a comfortable seat by the large window that looked out onto Main Street. It was weird to be downtown on a Saturday night and not en route to Tonic, which was just three blocks away. While Matt talked, I watched cabs drive by and couples walk past tightly bundled up against the cold February air. I watched him as he spoke and wondered why it was that I was not attracted to him. He was so nice and interesting, but there was just nothing there.

He had just asked me about my family when my phone vibrated against the table for the third time within two minutes.

"Excuse me," I said. "She'll keep calling if I don't answer."

"No problem," he smiled.

I'm pretty sure I could have talked to Meredith for an hour straight and he wouldn't have minded. That's how nice of a guy he was.

I answered the phone. "What?"

"Date going that well, huh?"

"It's actually going great." I smiled at Matt. "What's the emergency?"

"Nothing," she sighed. "Just wanted to see how things were going. We're out at the Crew House."

"We're at Ali's Place," I said. "I'll see you when I get back."

"OK. Hold on just one sec."

Meredith's voice was replaced with a ruffling noise, and an instant later a male voice came on. "Hey, Kel."

My heart stopped. It was Luke, sweet, handsome, sensual Luke. "Where are you?"

"Out with a friend." I felt my face flush.

"Are you coming here after?"

"Maybe." I hate to admit it, but I was flirting with him. I was on a date with one guy and flirting with another. "Are you still going to be there?"

"Maybe." He was playing with me. "You'll have to come and find out."

He hung up and I was left practically panting. As far as I was concerned, my date with Matt was over and it was time to go.

"Who was that?" he asked.

"Meredith. She's at the Crew House."

"I've been there a couple of times. Do you go there a lot?"

"It depends. We drop in every once in a while." I finished the last of my cake and slurped up the bottom of my coffee. "I've never seen you there before."

"I've seen you," he said with a creepy grin. "But that was before we met."

"Oh." Things were beginning to get awkward. I wanted to go and he was trying to prolong the date.

"Do you want to go there?"

"Now?"

"Yeah, we can go together if you want."

Together is a funny word. Depending on the circumstance, it can mean a lot of different things. For instance, Matt and I were out together, but we were not together. If we went to the Crew House together, chances were we wouldn't leave together, because Luke and I would be leaving together, or at the very least disappearing together. But in Matt's mind, if we showed up at the Crew House together, we would be together and leave together. I couldn't let that happen.

I didn't want to hurt his feelings, but I didn't want to go with him. But I wanted to go. I had no idea what to say. He was sitting there staring at me with yearning, hopeful eyes. I began to resent him.

I quickly came up with a plan. "That's not a bad idea," I said. "That way I can go home with my roommates and you won't have to worry about getting me back to Ashwood."

"I wouldn't mind," he replied.

"Yeah, but it'll be easier that way."

By stating my thoughts on how the rest of the evening was going to play out, I alleviated the awkwardness of the end of the night drop-off. I really didn't want to kiss Matt, and it was almost guaranteed that he would try.

Things were in full swing when we arrived at the Crew House. John stood at the door with the cups and eyed Matt and me as we approached. He grinned when Matt pulled out his wallet and paid for the both of us. I shook my head and John laughed. Matt was oblivious.

The hot, stifling air circulating through the party was a welcome relief to the frigid cold outside. Meredith and Molly usually congregated in the far left corner of the living room, so I made a quick line in that direction to find them.

Meredith's eyes lit up when she saw me, but the happiness quickly dissolved when she saw Matt trailing behind me. Her insincere greeting was welcomed with a genuine smile from Matt. I introduced him to Molly, who gave him a quick acknowledgment before going off to speak to someone else. Molly didn't bullshit. She either knew you and would talk to you or she didn't and would not. After ten seconds of awkward silence, Matt offered to fill up our cups.

"Oh, thank God," Meredith said when he disappeared into the kitchen. "Is he just going to hang around us all night?"

"I don't know. Maybe he'll run into someone he knows in the kitchen and forget about us."

"Unlikely," she sighed.

"Maybe he'll find a friend for you," I suggested.

"Seriously," she laughed. "If I were you, I would ditch the geek and find you know who. He was looking pretty good tonight."

"When's the last time you saw him?"

"I'm not sure. He walked through a while ago and asked if you were here yet."

"No, he didn't. Are you serious?"

"I think it would break his heart if he saw you with your boyfriend."

"He's not my boyfriend," I laughed. "Do you have a cigarette?"

I scanned the crowd for Luke so intently that I was startled when Matt came up behind me.

"I didn't know you smoked," he said, frowning as he handed me a cup.

"Just on the weekends." I pulled on the cigarette.

"Oh. Okay. So what do you usually do here? Do you want to dance?"

Meredith just about choked on her beer she started laughing so hard. I shot her a nasty look.

"No," I smiled at Matt, "I don't really dance. But you can if you want to."

"No." He shrugged his shoulders. "I was just wondering."

I felt bad for turning him down, but no one with the exception of stupid freshmen ever danced at the Crew House. I began to regret bringing him to the party. I knew it wasn't going to work, but I'd convinced myself to go along with it because I wanted to see Luke. Luke, the reason I was at the party. I needed to get rid of Matt and find Luke.

I chugged my beer as fast and inconspicuously as I could and asked Matt to get me a refill. Clearly my smoking made him uncomfortable, and apparently so did my quick disposal of alcohol.

I pleaded with Meredith as soon as he was out of earshot. "You have got to help me get rid of him. Please."

"Sure," she laughed. "Do you want me to dance with him?"

"This isn't funny. I need him to go."

A soft whisper blew on my neck. "Now this is what I like to see," I heard. My knees almost gave out.

"Luke." I turned with a smile.

"You've been difficult to track down lately," he said. "Have you been avoiding me?"

"Never." I felt weak in his presence.

Meredith's eyes opened wide, which could only mean one thing: Matt was fast approaching.

"Come with me." I grabbed Luke's hand and fled through the mass of students.

"I like this," he panted behind me. "Where are we going?"

"Upstairs," I said, leading the way. As I reached the third step, I peered over the crowd and saw Meredith gesturing something to Matt. Judging from her charades, she was telling him that I got sick. I smiled as Luke and I disappeared into one of the bedrooms.

When I reemerged into the party a little while later, Matt was gone and Meredith was trashed and hooking up with a random on the couch. Randoms, as we referred to them, were fun. They were the guys we may have seen on campus or at parties but knew nothing about, not even their names. And most of the time we didn't know their names even after we had hooked up with them. The random Meredith was with was cute, but the fact that she was keeping it on the couch meant he had no chance of going further. When it was time to go, Molly and I detangled the lip-locked couple and exited the party.

Once back in the apartment, we dropped a barely coherent Meredith on the couch where she passed out while Molly and I smoked one last cigarette at the dining room table. The last cigarette of the night always tasted the best. It was soothing and relaxing and made me ready for bed. It was my version of warm milk.

"Did you get your fill tonight?" Molly asked from across the table.

"I could see him every night and never get full."

"So why don't you guys go out on a real date?"

"Because it would ruin it. I don't want to date him. I just want to fuck him."

"Isn't that romantic."

"We both know what we want." I shrugged. "It keeps it from getting complicated. Emotions just get in the way."

Molly laughed and stubbed out her cigarette.

I smiled. For the first time since before Christmas, things were finally back to normal. I was back to normal.

CHAPTER TWENTY-THREE

The second time I did coke was right before finals. The sweet spring air was being muscled out by the beginning of summer and we were all getting restless. Luke and I had continued our late-night hookups and Crew House getaways throughout the semester, and Meredith began to do the same with his roommate, Kenny.

After I ditched him at the Crew House, Matt stopped meeting me before Econ, claiming that he had to work on another project during that time. He also switched his seat in the classroom. I guess he'd only helped me because he wanted to date me. If that was the case, he was no different than any other guy. In fact, he was worse. I respect the guys who come out and say what they want more than the ones who pretend all they want is a friend, when they want the exact same thing as the scumbags who try to pick you up. Thankfully, by then something had clicked in Economics and my grades stayed respectable. I didn't need Matt and his false pretenses.

Meredith and I were hanging out in the apartment watching Dirty Dancing for the millionth time when Luke and Kenny stopped by. They often came over when they were bored and needed entertainment. We never turned them away.

Once we were settled in the living room with a couple of drinks, Luke asked if we wanted to party. We, of course, happily said yes.

"No," Luke grinned, "really party."

Kenny pulled out a small plastic bag and my mind flashed back to Tonic, to Chris, and to me on Max's desk.

Meredith looked at me. "I don't know." She was uncomfortable and I didn't blame her. She was probably suffering from flashbacks similar to mine.

"It's clean," Luke said, sitting up while Kenny prepared the lines. "I know the guy who cuts it."

"Are you sure?" I asked. "Because the last time some guy said that, some really bad stuff happened to me."

"Well, I am not some guy," Luke smiled, his dimple making an appearance just for me. "Do you trust me?"

"Of course," I said, and walked over to where he was sitting.

"Are you sure?" Meredith asked. She drank like a fish and smoked pot like a chimney, but cocaine made her nervous. Hell, it made me nervous.

Kenny was the first to go, followed by Luke, then me. A line remained on the table for Meredith in case she wanted it. No one was pressuring her. Luke walked over and grabbed my hand and brought me back to my bedroom. The dreadful drip had returned to the back of my throat, but other than that, I was feeling good.

"My teeth feel fuzzy," I said as Luke pulled my shirt over my head. He didn't respond. Instead, he continued to disrobe me, piece by piece, until I was lying naked on my bed. Together we rode the powdered wave until it crashed on the shore. Sweaty, tired, and completely satisfied, we passed out. I had never had an experience like that, and I wanted to do it again and again.

When I awoke, I ran my tongue over my front top teeth. Just as I had suspected, the rush was gone. I left Luke sleeping in my bed, threw my clothes back on, and went to see how Meredith and Kenny were making out.

The apartment was quiet as I walked down the hallway to the living room. Just as I made it to the entryway, Meredith let out an enormous moan. I froze with one foot in the hall and the other in the living room. The fourth line was gone, as were Meredith and Kenny's clothes. She was straddling him on the couch and oblivious to my presence. I did an about-face and went back to my room.

"That was awesome," Meredith said after the guys left. "I had no idea. We have to do that again."

I one hundred percent agreed. I had never felt so free, so open, so orgasmic before. Things with Luke just kept getting better and I began to wonder if I should claim him for my own.

But Meredith and I weren't about boyfriends and commitment. We were about flings and fun. What harm was there in that?

CHAPTER TWENTY-FOUR

My eyes opened to faces, to people saying my name over and over. What were they saying? There were noises, too. Why couldn't I keep my eyes open? They were so heavy. It was dark and I was so tired.

". . . have to keep you moving . . ." Someone was pulling at me. I heard beeping.

What was happening?

I finally woke up on a Sunday morning. The brilliant sun was shining in through my window and I heard some priest singing Jesus' praises. Who was watching TV? Or was that the radio? What happened? Where was I?

I tried to turn my head, but couldn't. Something was holding it down. My arms were tied down as well and my side began to throb. I started to panic. I tried to scream but nothing came out. There was a tube in my mouth. I began twisting and turning to free myself. I was too tired to fight.

"Monday morning workout," someone said in a pleasant voice, massaging my arms. "Hey, she's awake!"

A commotion ensued and my mom's face appeared. She looked like an angel. I knew I was safe. I relaxed and closed my eyes.

The next time I woke up, my mom was asleep next to me. My side still hurt, but my hands were free. I gingerly picked my hands up to look at them. My right shoulder was bandaged and it hurt when I touched it, but it could still move. My mom stirred, but didn't wake up.

I continued the exploration of my body and touched my side, which was bandaged from my hip to my chest. My right leg was in a cast from my knee to my toes. I wiggled them to make sure they still had movement. My left leg seemed okay.

I reached out and touched my mom, who awoke instantly.

"Oh, Kel," she smiled. "It's all right. I'm here. You're okay."

"We're both here," my dad said, coming into view. "You're okay. You're in the hospital. There was an accident."

Accident?

I tried to think, but I couldn't remember anything. Accident. I tried to mouth the word.

"Just rest now. Everything's okay." My mom had tears streaming down her face. I started to cry.

"What's the matter, Kelly?" she asked, sounding panicked. "Are you in pain? Nurse . . . nurse!"

My dad joined in, hysterically yelling for the nurse. I tried to shake my head to signal that I wasn't in any pain, but it was still restrained. I closed my eyes. I felt no pain.

"She's awake again," I heard. My dad was hovering above me.

My head was free. I could talk. It was Wednesday morning.

"Kelly," my dad said, sitting on the side of the bed. "How are you feeling?"

My throat felt like I had swallowed a piece of barbed wire and thrown it back up again. I was uncertain as to whether or not I should try to talk. I decided not to.

"That's okay," he said, and leaned in and kissed me on the forehead. "Get your rest."

CHAPTER TWENTY-FIVE

Partying after spring finals always felt so rewarding, so deserved. For two weeks straight, I'd crammed everything I'd learned into my brain. Meredith and I made sure to take study breaks, some alone, some with friends. We cleared our minds, relaxed our bodies, and did some cramming up our nose. Sam joined us a couple of times. Molly held her ground about us being stupid for messing with the stuff. Our cocaine use would end with the semester, Meredith and I both agreed.

Finals ended on Friday at twelve noon. We were doing shots by twelve thirty-five. Molly, Sam, Meredith, and I packed up our apartment while we drank; we had to move out by Saturday afternoon. I had used Jane to help gradually transport some of my stuff home for summer over the prior couple of weeks. Every time she went home for wedding planning, I asked her to pick me up and was able to empty our apartment little by little. It stunk having to bring everything home when Meredith and I would be moving into our new off-campus apartment less than two months later.

We'd enjoyed living with Molly and Sam, and at first we looked for a two-bedroom apartment for the four of us to share again. But after talking, we realized it would be nice for everyone to have her own room, and there weren't many four-bedroom apartments within our price range.

Our search began around Hay U's main campus. We wanted to be outside the rules and regulations of the university but close enough to get to class without a lot of hassle. We looked everywhere but were unable to find anything we liked. Then one night we were at Tonic and about to get in a cab when Meredith said how awesome it would be if we found a place off Main Street. Then we could walk to Tonic and all the bars and not have to worry about cabs anymore.

"But how would we get to class?" I asked.

"We could take a bus," she offered.

I didn't like that. "It would be so much easier if we had a car."

"So let's get one," she replied.

"What?"

"Let's buy a car, together. I can get my dad to sign the lease and we'll both make the payments."

I loved the idea.

"Absolutely not," my father said when I called him that night to ask what he and my mother thought.

"Why not?" I demanded, annoyed. I'd called more for a donation to my cause than an opinion.

"Because you don't buy a car with someone unless you're going to spend the rest of your life with that person. So unless there's something else you want to tell me about your relationship with Meredith, the answer is no. You can take the bus like everyone else does."

I was clearly going nowhere with him. "Can I talk to Mommy?" I asked.

"Your mother and I are in agreement on this, Kelly."

"I'm going to be a junior," I said. "Do you know how many of the freshmen have cars? What if I want to get a job? How will I be able to get to work?"

My father sighed, but it was a good sigh. It meant he was thinking about it. Maybe he wasn't closed to the idea of me getting a car, just me getting one with Meredith.

"Let your mother and me talk some more," he said. I was happy with that result.

As it turned out, Meredith's dad wasn't keen on the co-ownership idea, either. He too, however, didn't throw the whole idea of a car out. In fact, he agreed to buy Meredith a car with the provision that she pay the insurance. He told her she had to have some kind of vested interest in it or she wouldn't truly appreciate it.

My parents agreed to help me buy my own car, as well. They thought it would be a good way to mark my journey into adulthood. I would, of course, have to make the payments, but they would co-sign for me.

It worked out great. Meredith and I had gone into the situation with nothing and emerged with both of our parents offering to help us get a car of our own.

But after a while, although the thought of having my own car was really cool, I decided I didn't want to be locked into making payments on my own. And I wasn't going to buy a clunker just to keep the payments down. So we agreed to let Meredith's dad buy her a car. I would chip in for the insurance and we both would drive it. It really was the best solution.

Once we knew we were going to have a mode of transportation other than the bus, we looked at apartments in downtown Haysville, starting with Lexington Avenue. We knew several other students who lived off Lexington Ave on the Hill, the neighborhood behind Main Street. More often than not, parties were either on campus or on the Hill. The Hill parties, however, were usually for upperclassmen only. We'd gone to one before hitting up Tonic one night and had found it to be rather boring.

Meredith and I were lucky enough to find an apartment four blocks from Main Street. It was perfect. On the smaller side, with an outdated kitchen and a tiny living room, the apartment was just what we needed. We were used to cramped quarters from living in the dorm, so the petite bedrooms didn't bother us. The only downside was that it had street parking instead of a parking lot or a garage, but that wasn't enough of a deterrent to keep us from renting it. Both of our fathers insisted on meeting with the landlord, who was obviously used to dealing with parents of Hay U students, and we signed the lease.

Walking distance door-to-door from our place to Tonic was less than a mile and took us about ten minutes; we imagined fifteen in heels. It was liberating to know we could walk to and from the bars with ease and never have to worry about driving. While I believed it was the responsible thing to do, Jane compared it to a drug addict getting a job in a pharmacy. According to her, I was "enabling my addiction."

I was surprised by her reaction, but not caught completely off guard. Her wedding was quickly approaching and she was feeling the pressure and taking it out on me. As her maid of honor, I got the pleasure of keeping up with her checklists and demands. Pete seemed to be doing nothing.

Whatever her mood, however, I didn't let it detract from my happiness about finding an apartment. Meredith and I had asked if we could move in earlier than August, but the landlord said the current tenants were staying until the lease was up. So we were left to pack our stuff up from Ashwood and move it home, only to turn around two and a half months later and move it back.

It was bittersweet to leave Ashwood. We'd had a great time there and I was scared to move on without Molly and Sam. It wasn't like we weren't ever going to see them again, but they decided to stay closer to campus and got an apartment in a place called Haysville Court.

When we finished packing, we changed and got ready one last time. With the Barenaked Ladies blaring in the background, we got dressed, danced, did a couple more shots, and left as we always did: as a group.

We went to bid a final farewell to the Crew House for the summer. It was a good place to go for freshmen and sophomores, but definitely not for juniors. We made our rounds there; I caught up with Luke and we disappeared together one last time; Meredith did the same with Kenny. When that was over, we went to Tonic to say goodbye to Max.

The scene at Tonic was the same as it always was. Businessmen unwinding at the bar, desperate women eyeing up the exhausted suits for a weekend romance, and Meredith, Molly, Sam, and me drinking as many two-dollar cocktails as we could manage.

Max was in higher spirits than usual and was elated to see us. Due to finals and the partying we'd been doing on campus, our visits to Tonic had been less and less frequent.

"We're going to be neighbors," I told Max excitedly. "We're two blocks over."

"You just want to be close to me, don't you?" he replied.

"You had your chance," I said with a smirk.

"What is that supposed to mean?"

"I'm just saying that I practically threw myself at you and you wanted no part of me. Well, you did, but then you passed. So I've moved on."

"Is that so?"

"That's so. Now, can you give me and my girls here a shot?"

"We'll see about that." He grinned and set four shot glasses on the bar.

I danced freely with a couple guys that night, the weight of the school year off my shoulders, making it a point not to get too close, but just close enough. Max stood back and watched.

The four of us captivated the crowd as we moved rhythmically together in our tiny dresses and high heels. Guys stared, women stared. We let everything that happened all year go as we moved; the catty fights, the failed tests, the hard classes, everything.

Our celebration was interrupted by a bachelorette party bursting through the crowd. Five girls wearing pink T-shirts that read "Bachelorette Party in Progress" on the front and "Tonight Doesn't Count" on the back screeched and laughed their way to the bar with the bride-to-be, who was wearing a veil and a white T-shirt that read "Last Chance for Romance."

They all flirted with Max and he sucked up the attention. Each of the girls wore a penis-shaped pendant around her neck that swayed back forth as they did shots of tequila. The bride-to-be sported the same necklace but had to lick salt off a stranger's neck before each shot. I couldn't believe it when she brought out a checklist for her bachelorette party. I swore in that moment that I would never, ever have a checklist for any part of my wedding. That is, if I ever got married.

As I watched the girls make complete fools of themselves, it hit me that I should have Jane's bachelorette party at Tonic. Though we hadn't talked about her party or even if she wanted one, I began to plan the whole night out. In my intoxicated state, it didn't get beyond the idea to have the party there.

Once the party vacated the bar and Max was alone, I approached him to ask what he thought about my idea.

"Did that make you jealous?" he asked.

"What?"

"The girls. You know, one of them asked me for my phone number."

"Did you give it to her?"

"Maybe. Would that make you jealous?"

"You probably give your number to anything with a pulse," I jested.

"I haven't given you my number."

"I haven't asked."

There was an awkward silence. He was looking at me, I was

staring at him. Slowly, a smile began to form in the corners of his mouth.

"What?" I asked.

"Nothing."

"It's not nothing. Why are you smiling at me?"

"You haven't moved on."

"Yes, I have." Maybe I hadn't moved on, but I wasn't going to give him the satisfaction. Yet I found myself leaning in closer than I should have and my cheeks might have been a little redder than they usually were.

"No, you haven't," he said. "Because if you did, you wouldn't be blushing."

"I'm not blushing," I said angrily.

He smiled. His grin was beginning to anger me.

"I came over here because I wanted to talk to you about having my sister's bachelorette party here. What do you think?"

"Tell me that you haven't moved on, and I'll tell you what I think."

"You're an asshole," I said. I smirked and walked away.

"What was that all about?" Meredith asked when I joined her on the dance floor.

"What?"

"You and Max. I thought you guys were going to go at it right on the bar."

"He wishes," I replied, throwing Max a dirty look. "I just asked him what he thought about having Jane's bachelorette party here."

"What did he say?"

"He really didn't say anything. He's in a weird mood tonight."

It was half past midnight the next time I spoke to Max. I went up to the bar and asked him for a glass of water.

"What are you slowing down for?" he asked.

"I'm thirsty."

"So have a beer."

"I don't want a beer. I want some water."

Reluctantly, he put a glass on the bar and filled it with water from the bar gun.

"Thanks," I said after I finished the glass. When I got up to walk away, he grabbed my hand.

"What?"

"Tell me you haven't moved on."

"Look, Max." I smiled, feeling in control even though his touch did jumpstart an unexpected reaction in my body. "I don't know what has gotten into you tonight, but yes, I have moved on."

"With who?" he asked, pointing to one of the guys who had bought me a drink earlier. "That guy?"

I looked him straight in his aqua eyes and held his stare. "Do you know how it felt in December when you told me to go home like I was some stupid kid? And then when you told that girl I was interviewing for a job? What happened later that night was your fault."

"I thought you didn't remember," he replied defensively.

"Meredith filled me in," I answered.

"Maybe you should remember me saving your ass that night," he said, and then paused.

We stood in silence, staring at each other while I thought about that night. Shit, I thought, did I really just try to blame him for what happened?

"I know that was a tough night for you," he said, looking directly into my eyes. "Let me make it up to you."

The conversation was intense and filled with emotions I didn't know existed between the two of us. "I . . . ," I began. "I have to pee."

One of the worst things about being drunk is that you have the tendency to tell the truth. At least I do. I didn't want Max to know how I felt about what happened between us. I was thankful for what he did to help me that night, but I also partially blamed him. That was the truth. And the truth was also that I had to pee.

I stumbled away from the bar and motioned to Meredith that I was going to the bathroom. She nodded and continued to bop with a new random. There were lots of randoms that night. I looked around as I entered the girls' bathroom, a subconscious habit I'd formed after Sal, and went in. The bathroom was filled with smoke and half-drunk girls. I fit right in. From my stall I could hear one girl sobbing to another about some stupid bitch who took her boyfriend and how she can't get over him. Another downside of alcohol: drunken rage.

I did what I had to do, washed my hands, checked my face, and left. The girl was still hysterical in the stall, but the door was open and her friend was looking at everyone else, mouthing, "I don't know what to do." That's the mark of a good friend. If someone is willing to spend an evening in a disgusting stall of a bar bathroom while you cry your eyes out, she's a keeper. There was no doubt in my mind that Meredith would do the same for me. I knew I wouldn't think twice about doing it for her.

I wasn't as steady on my feet as I would have liked, but practice makes perfect, and I'd had a lot of practice at maneuvering on heels while drunk. As I passed the hallway that led to the back office, a hand reached out and grabbed me. I was pulled back into the dark hall and pressed up against the wall.

"Tell me you haven't moved on," Max whispered in my ear.

A surge of relief was met with a surge of excitement as my body relaxed in his grasp.

"Show me you're worth sticking around for," I said.

Within a second, his lips were on mine, and just as before, his kiss started off rough and then moved into something more gentle and soft. I kissed him back and raised my left arm to the back of his head and tugged lightly at his hair. I tried to move my right arm, but he kept it pinned against the wall. I bit his lip.

With my wrist still tight in his grip, Max backed up to his office door and unlocked it with one hand. Once inside, he slammed me up against the back of the door and locked it.

CHAPTER TWENTY-SIX

The next time I woke up, I was in a different room, a shared room. There was a small window to my left and outside I could see the sky, a dark evening with stars twinkling brightly. A small TV hung from the ceiling in front of me above a light-brown closet. Two chairs sat vacant at my side. The walls were painted an eggshell white that over time had browned with dust, dirt, and who knows what else. To my right, I could hear someone on the other side of a long curtain that ran the length of my bed. I wondered where my parents were. I wondered why I was in the hospital.

My dad said there had been an accident. From the wounds on my body, it had to have been a pretty serious one. I didn't know how long I'd been in the hospital or what the circumstances of the accident were. I didn't know the extent of my injuries. My mom always smiled when I looked at her, but I could tell she had been crying a lot. It never took long for fresh tears to surface in her eyes, though she was quick to wipe them away. My dad, too, had been crying. He never cried. In my life I had seen him cry only twice, and that was when his parents died. They were distraught over my condition. They looked so frail and old. What had I done to them?

The television in front of the bed on the other side of the curtain was broadcasting the evening news. I listened intently for some clue as to what day it was. No luck.

Jeopardy!'s theme song began when the news ended. My grandfather loved that show. Before he died, we used to have a lot of conversations in the Jeopardy! question-and-answer format. "An

A," I would say to him over the phone. "What is the grade you got on your math test?" he would reply. It was a lot of fun, although it could take a while for him to guess the correct question if I didn't tell him a day or two in advance if I had a test coming up. I missed him a lot. How was it that I could remember him and not the accident? Did I damage my brain?

My roommate began hacking five minutes into the show and it lasted a good ten minutes. She began to moan once her fit ended and called for a nurse. The nurse took her time responding and in that time, the room began to fill with a putrid smell.

Oh my God, I thought, have I lost control of my bowels? It was soon hard to breathe. Though I didn't feel anything amiss below my waist, I wasn't certain that it wasn't me. I couldn't feel any parts of my body with great precision and therefore didn't know what I was capable of.

Two nurses entered the room and my roommate moaned, "I'm so sorry, honey."

"That's quite all right, Cecile," the male nurse replied in a high-pitched voice. "Are you all finished?"

"Yes," she answered. "I'm so sorry."

I heard a bunch of rustling and the smell exploded in intensity. Four feet moved quickly and methodically under the curtain. I stared at the window, willing it to open. I held my breath for as long as I could, but eventually I had to release it and breathe in the stink.

The male nurse peered around the curtain and stole a quick look at me. It was a quick gesture, but in that two-second glance, I pleaded with my eyes for him to open the window. At least, that's what I was trying to do. I lost all hope when he disappeared behind the curtain, but then he looked over again.

"Now, girl." He smiled and walked over to my bed. "I thought you looked at me."

He was a slender man, my height or a little taller, and smelled of expensive cologne. I looked at his hands, imagining where they had just been and praying he would wash them thoroughly before attempting to touch me.

"She's awake, Barney?" Cecile whined in a raspy voice. "Oh, that is so good."

"She is awake," he replied. "She looks like she doesn't know where the heck she is, though. Don't worry, child. You are in good hands here."

Not if you don't wash them, I thought.

"Her parents just stepped out," Cecile continued. "Poor people, sitting by the bed waiting for her to open her eyes, and when she does she closes them right back up again."

"Honey, the important thing is that you keep waking up. Let me go see about getting you some food. Skinny little thing like you must be starving. I'll be right back." Barney smiled and turned to leave, but then turned back to me, leaned in, and whispered, "Sorry about that smell. I'd open the window if I could, but it doesn't open. It should go away soon."

During Double Jeopardy, Barney brought in my dinner, which consisted of chicken noodle soup and Jell-O, a big step up from the ice chips I'd started with. He asked if I wanted him to put the television on. I shrugged my shoulders and nodded my head yes. Reaching across me, he grabbed the long remote with the TV controls and the nurse's call button and switched the television on. He showed me how to adjust the volume, then changed the channel and left it at my side.

"Bon appétit," he said with a smile, and moved to the other side of the curtain. "Stay out of trouble tonight, Cecile," he said. "I heard about you walking the halls at night." Cecile half laughed, half hacked.

I stared at the television while I ate but processed nothing. I was too busy trying to piece together what had happened. Accident, broken leg, cut shoulder, bruising and burns on my face. Obviously I'd been in an automobile of some sort. A car, maybe a taxi. Was I alone? I needed more details.

"Don't worry about the details," my mom said when she and Dad returned that night. Patrick stood solemnly by the bed.

"It's okay," I smiled at him. "You can't hurt me."

He didn't say anything.

"I need to remember something," I said. My voice, though audible was scratchy. It hurt to talk, but I needed information. "When did the accident happen?"

"Saturday morning," my dad answered.

"What time Saturday morning? Where was I going? Who was I with? Was Meredith with me?" When I said the name Meredith, something flashed, but nothing solid.

"The doctor said your memory will come back slowly," my

mom said. Tears rolled down her cheeks. "Your body has been through a lot lately and it needs time to repair itself."

"She had to have been with me," I thought out loud. "Because if she wasn't with me, she would be here in the hospital right now, but she's not. Was she hurt, too? Is she in the hospital? Can I go and see her?"

The tears were pouring down my mother's face. Patrick had turned away from me and was looking out the window. A sick feeling was developing in the pit of my stomach.

"What happened?" I pleaded. "Where is Meredith?"

"She was in the car with you," my father said. "And she was hurt, too."

"Oh my God," I said as water rushed to my eyes. "What happened to her? Is she okay? Why wouldn't they put us in the same room?"

My mom was a sobbing mess. Patrick had moved over to the window. Slowly my dad approached me. He cupped my hands in his, looked me directly in the eyes, and said, "I'm sorry, honey, but she didn't make it."

"What?" I felt like throwing up. "What do you mean?" I cried out. "Daddy, what does that mean?"

"She's dead." He bit his lip and swallowed hard. "She died on the way to the hospital."

"NO!!!" I screamed out. "No, she didn't. Daddy, please tell me she didn't die. Please, Daddy. Tell me she's okay—that she's in another room."

"I'm sorry, Kelly," Dad said. A single tear fell from his left eye. "I wish I could."

"NO!!!" I screamed over and over until I threw up. My mom tried to comfort me, but it was no use.

Either Cecile called the nurse or they heard my cries, because it wasn't long until the night-shift nurse came in with a syringe and injected something into my IV. I wished it was poison.

CHAPTER TWENTY-SEVEN

Up until the last day of finals, I had never slept with two guys in one night. I may have kissed two guys in one night, but never sex. I surely didn't plan it that way. It was just one of those things that happened, and I didn't regret any part of it. Luke, as always, didn't disappoint me at the Crew House. It was a final farewell between friends who'd shared some good times. As for Max, well, let's just say he proved something to me that night in his office, more than once. He was a ten plus.

My mom and dad arrived the following morning and loaded up the car with my remaining stuff. I hugged Molly, Sam, and Meredith goodbye and blew a farewell kiss to Ashwood. It had been an amazing year.

I always felt like a child when I drove in the car with my parents. Sitting in the back with my mom and dad up front, talking about random things: the world, their afternoon, Jane's wedding. It was a good feeling to have every now and then to know that no matter how old I got, I could always feel safe and protected in the company of my parents.

"Did you girls have fun last night?" Mom asked.

I smiled. "Yeah, we did."

"What did you do?"

"There was a party on campus that we went to."

"That's nice," she said. "That reminds me . . ." She trailed off and started talking to my dad about making plans with our neighbors for dinner. I fell asleep in the back seat listening to them talk.

I had two weeks of relaxation before Jane's wedding began to consume every second of my free time. As soon as June first hit, she became psychotic about getting everything together. I told her she still had three months, but she didn't want to hear that. "Besides," she said, "the last month doesn't count."

So there we were, the first weekend in June, stuffing envelopes and sticking stamps. Jane had the bright idea of placing a wax seal on the back of every envelope. I burned my fingers six times before my mother took over for me. In total, one hundred and twenty-five crisp white invitations went out.

"I know a bride is supposed to wear white and everything, but let's be honest," I said as we made our way to the post office. "You have had sex with your fiancé, right?"

"That is kind of a personal question," Jane replied.

"Well, I am your maid of honor."

I wasn't trying to make fun of her. I really wanted to have some quality girl talk with my sister. We had spent so much time talking about the wedding and the plans, but had talked little about ourselves.

"Come on, Jane," I said when she didn't say anything. "You're my older sister. Aren't we supposed to share things like this?"

"You're right," she said, smiling but tensing her grip on the steering wheel. "But if you tell Pete anything I've told you, I will never tell you anything again."

As it turned out, Jane wasn't nearly as innocent or inexperienced as I'd thought she was. She admitted to having four sexual partners, three more than I'd thought. And the more we talked, the more she opened up.

"Sometimes he's too controlling," she said. "I think it would be better if he loosened up a bit. He's too occupied with being amazing."

Pete, not so good in bed? That wasn't hard to believe.

"So what about you?" She turned and looked at me.

"What about me?"

"Have you had sex yet?"

Wow, I thought, how to answer that one? Since she was being honest with me, I decided to be honest with her. "Yes."

"Wow." She looked over at me. "I mean, by now I thought you would have, but you've never had a boyfriend, so I thought maybe not, but you are twenty. So who was he?"

She really thought there was just one.

"This guy named Blake."

"Blake." She repeated the name as if it stunk. "That's an interesting name. When did it happen? Were you guys dating?"

I was the one who'd opened this can of worms, but I'd thought I would be the one getting the information.

"Freshman year, and we were kind of seeing each other. He was a nice guy."

"So what happened? Do you still talk with him?"

"Do you still talk with your other lovers?"

"Two of them, yes," she replied. "They're actually coming to the wedding."

"Well, that is just weird."

"Entering into a physical relationship is a very intimate thing," she said.

I thought about the lack of intimacy Max and I had shared as he pinned me against the door of his office.

"Just because things don't work out romantically doesn't mean they can't work out platonically," she went on.

"Are any of Pete's ex-lovers coming to the wedding?"

"No, he doesn't keep in contact with them."

"Does he know your exes are coming to the wedding?"

"Yes and no," she sighed. "Let's just say I didn't tell him how much of a boyfriend they were—which is why you cannot repeat any of this conversation."

"Why would I say anything to get you in trouble?"

I had successfully managed to get the subject back to her and I escaped divulging anymore personal information. She may have crashed the car if I'd told her I wasn't sure how many guys I had slept with at that point. I guessed the number was somewhere in the area of a dozen, maybe a baker's dozen, definitely not more.

Once we'd finished at the post office—I didn't realize how quickly postage could add up—we picked up Mom and went off to the final dress fitting.

Jane had gone a little crazy on her wedding diet and had lost a lot of weight. Her dress was a size eight, which I was told by the sales associate is the equivalent of a size two in regular clothes. With the alterations complete, the dress fit wonderfully. It looked as though it was made just for her.

I tried on my breezy dress as well. It wasn't bad. It wasn't exactly my style, but it wasn't bad. Dresses in hand, we left the boutique and went out to lunch. Jane ordered a chicken salad. I ordered a burger and fries. We were talking about my new apartment when Mom and Jane looked at me funny. Self-consciously, I felt around my mouth, thinking I had food on my face.

"Are you all right, honey?" Mom asked.

"Yeah, I'm fine," I said. "Why are you looking at me like that?"

I didn't have to wait for her answer because I felt the drip. When I looked down at the napkin on my lap, I saw the crimson drop. My nose was bleeding.

I grabbed the napkin and held it to my nose, leaning my head back.

"Has this ever happened to you before?" Mom asked.

I shook my head no.

"It felt really dry and dusty in the dress shop," I lied.

The truth was that yes, I had had nosebleeds before. This was the third time. I knew the reason for it, and knew it was going to get better over the summer, and that there was nothing I could do about it. I just didn't want my mom to worry.

"Well, maybe you should go see Dr. Fitzpatrick," she said.

"It's fine, Mom." I pinched my nose and thankfully it stopped bleeding.

She gave me her concerned look but let it go, and we resumed our conversation.

Later that night before she left to go home, Jane pulled me aside and got all serious. "Are you sure you're okay?"

"I'm fine, really."

"That nosebleed was pretty serious."

"It's fine."

"And you never had them growing up."

"What are you trying to say?"

"Nothing, but if you're experimenting with things, I think you should take that as a warning."

"Unbelievable." I rolled my eyes. "What exactly is it that you are accusing me of?"

"I'm just trying to tell you to be careful."

"I am careful," I replied bitterly. "I am always careful. Now if you don't mind, I have to go shoot up in the bathroom."

It was wrong of me to snap at Jane like that, but I couldn't have had an indifferent response because she would have known her assumptions were right. And there was absolutely no way I could tell her the truth. I had been honest enough with her for one day. She'd learned I wasn't a virgin. She didn't need to know I was an occasional drug user as well.

I suppose I wouldn't use the term occasional. I was more of a sporadic user. Yes, sporadic. That's how I would have classified myself at that point. Regardless, my mom scheduled an appointment with the doctor, which I "forgot" about, and when they called me, I told them I had to reschedule. That never happened.

CHAPTER TWENTY-EIGHT

The immense joy I felt the day we received the keys to our new apartment was indescribable. The freedom I'd longed for had arrived, and Meredith and I were officially released from the reins of university rules and our parents' scrutiny. The familiarity of home was already there when Meredith and I were back together again. To say that I was excited was an understatement.

Meredith pulled up in her new car, a beautiful white Saab. It was a dealer car, she explained, so they got it for a really good price. It was perfect.

My dad and Patrick slaved away in the blazing August heat unpacking the car and carrying my stuff up three flights of stairs. Dad was happy to hear that Meredith and I planned on staying there through senior year and he wouldn't have to move me again for a while. Meredith's dad got right to work assembling the entertainment center. How he'd been able to take it apart and put it back together so many times since freshman year was incredible to me. It wouldn't have been much good if I'd been in charge of it, but her dad had managed to keep every nut and bolt.

With the furniture in and our parents gone, Meredith and I toasted with champagne. We were juniors in college and had our own apartment on the Hill; we were official. Doing shots at home seemed a little juvenile, so we decided to do them at Tonic instead. We wanted to mark the night with a perfect celebration. Feeling the bubble buzz from the bottle of champagne we'd managed to polish off, we turned the music up high and got ready to hit Main Street, disregarding the unpacked boxes that lined the narrow hall from the living room to our bedrooms.

I was nervous walking into Tonic because I hadn't seen or talked to Max since our office romp in May. Meredith didn't believe me at first when I told her what happened, so I had to go into graphic detail. After I described an egg-shaped birthmark in a private location, she finally believed me and begged me to stop. I didn't, and continued with my dirty play-by-play. She claimed to need a shower when I was finished.

We entered the bar in our finest summer attire: short shorts and tight tank tops. Meredith had accessorized with big hoop earrings and I wore silver studs. Max was surprised to see us, and I think a little nervous as well. It was both our faults, really. We had left things kind of awkward. After we'd finished in his office that night, we both got dressed and walked out in different directions without saying a word. We hadn't spoken the entire time. Instead, we'd let our bodies communicate what we felt inside. I think that's what made it so good.

"My two favorite girls are back," Max said as we approached the bar. "Are you all settled in?"

"Yes, we are," Meredith said, smiling at his unease. "You should come by and check it out sometime."

"Is that an invitation?"

"You don't need an invitation, Max. Mi casa es su casa."

"I'll have to remember that," he grinned. "So, how are you, Kelly?"

"Good," I smiled. "You?"

"Fine."

A couple of seconds of silence passed. If we were in a movie, the crickets would have been cued. The three of us looked around without looking directly at each other.

"Look, Max, we had sex," I blurted out. "And it was great, fantastic, really. It was one of those things that just had to happen and I would be fine with it happening again. But that doesn't mean we have to be all weird with each other now."

Unlike all other forms of alcohol, champagne makes me aggressive. The carbonation must go straight to my head or something, because while I blurt out the truth just as when I drink anything else, I do it in a more forceful and almost angry way.

"All right, then," he exhaled, the awkward moment gone. "So

what can I start you off with tonight?"

And just like that, things between Max and me were right back to normal. There was an undeniable attraction between the two of us and I didn't doubt that we would eventually find ourselves back in his office or in my bed. But in the meantime, it didn't have to be weird. I went to Tonic to relax and enjoy myself, not to feel self-conscious and uneasy.

When the last-call bell rang, we happily threw back the tequila. It was so nice to know we wouldn't have to waste any money on a cab ride home. Just before we left, I clumsily wrote our address on a napkin and handed it over to Max, muttering, "Open invitation." He accepted it with a smile.

Though the sun had been set for hours, it was still humid as we stumbled home that night. The moon illuminated our path and we followed it together until Meredith had to stop and throw up. She said it was starting off with champagne that made her sick. I told her it was because she had no tolerance.

Jane and Pete came over for dinner that Monday night. Being useless in the kitchen, I asked them to pick up some takeout on their way in, their choice. I offered to pay for the meal, but I knew Jane wouldn't let me. Sure enough, she waved my hand away when I offered money. "Think of it as an apartment-warming gift," she said. Their gift was Chinese, not my personal favorite.

"How's the wedding planning coming along?" Meredith asked Jane as we gathered around our small kitchenette set.

"I can't believe we're almost one month out," Jane replied, smiling across the table at Pete.

"How many people are coming?"

"As of right now we have one hundred and sixty-eight."

"That's a lot of people," Meredith said, stuffing her mouth with a spring roll. "I don't think I know that many people."

"You'd be surprised," Jane replied. "I didn't think we knew that many people, either. And those are only the people who have replied. We invited over two hundred and fifty."

"I have the burn marks to prove it," I said. "Speaking of the wedding, we need to discuss your bachelorette party."

Pete sighed.

"Come on, Pete," I said. "Don't tell me your boys don't have an evening planned for you."

"They do," Jane answered. "Two weeks from Saturday."

"Well, that settles it, then," I said. "We'll have yours on the same night."

"We'll see," Pete answered for Jane. "Don't go making any plans yet."

I laughed. "The plans are already made. I just needed a date."

"What do you have planned?" Jane smiled and leaned in for the details.

"Girl stuff." I winked in Pete's direction. "We can't talk about it with him here."

Jane laughed, but Pete didn't find it funny. In fact, for the rest of the evening, he was no longer talkative (not that he was talking much before) and he seemed genuinely annoyed.

I suggested that we walk down to Main Street and get ice cream for dessert, my treat. It was the least I could do since they paid for dinner. Jane and Pete frowned when Meredith lit up a cigarette as we sat on a park bench outside the ice cream shop, watching people as they passed by.

"That's going to kill you if you don't stop," Jane said.

"Something's got to," Meredith smiled. "But thanks for the warning."

Jane smiled affectionately at her. For as much as we annoyed her and Pete, Jane had taken a liking to Meredith.

Jane turned to me. "So what do you have lined up for this year? Any internships or work-study programs?"

"Why do you have to ruin it?" I sighed, spooning the last of my ice cream out of the paper cup.

"Ruin what?"

"Tonight. School doesn't start for another week and a half. Let us enjoy what's left of the summer."

"I'm just saying that senior year is going to be here before you know it, and you're going to need some kind of direction. By the end of summer going into my junior year, I was already sending my résumé out."

"You were?" Meredith asked.

"Yes, that's how I was able to get my internship. That's what led me to getting my current job. If you want a job when you graduate, you're going to have to start looking for one soon."

"Well, that's the difference," I said. "I'm not sure I want a job right away after college."

"No, of course not," Pete said. "You are going to wait until graduation to start looking and then complain when everyone else has a job but you."

"How did you know?" I laughed. "That is exactly what Meredith and I were planning on doing."

"You think it's funny," Pete said, "but at some point you're going to have to grow up."

I didn't get why he was so agitated. We were all having a good time. Besides, how did it affect him one way or the other whether or not I got a job?

We walked back to our apartment in two groups. Meredith and I led the way, joking to each other and catching lightning bugs, while Jane and Pete lagged behind, hand in hand in silence. When we got back to the apartment, Jane went to the bathroom and Meredith plopped down on the couch with another cigarette. Pete approached me and pulled me into the kitchen.

"I know you think you have your family wrapped around your little finger," he said, "but this ditzy 'I don't give a shit about anything' routine doesn't fly with me. If you throw a party for Jane, you need to be respectful of her and of me. No strippers and no drugs."

"No drugs, what is that supposed to mean?"

"You and I both know exactly what it means. She told me about your surprise nosebleed at lunch. She was really worried about you and felt really bad for accusing you of doing drugs."

"Yeah, well, she should have."

"You're saying that you have never done cocaine?"

"Nope."

"I don't believe you."

"You don't have to. You're marrying my sister, not me. And while we're on the subject of that, you need to back down a little, because for as much as you don't like me, I'm still Jane's sister. If my parents knew you were hassling me as much as you do, they wouldn't be so supportive of your union."

"What if your parents knew what kind of daughter you really were?"

My pulse quickened. "They know me," I said. "You don't. And regardless of what I may do, they will always love me. You're the outsider. Remember that."

Jane popped back into view. "Ready to go?"

Pete's fangs retracted and a smile appeared at the corners of his mouth, which was still caked with the froth of anger. Meredith and I walked them out and thanked them for dinner as they got into Pete's car.

"Asshole," I yelled as they drove off. "I really can't stand that guy."

"He's kind of growing on me," Meredith replied as we climbed the stairs back to our apartment. "But he is too serious. I wonder if he's really like that all the time."

"From what Jane says, he is. Even in bed." The words slipped out like a cat through an open door.

"What? She told you about their sex life? Share, please share."

"I can't," I laughed as we headed into the living room. "She would kill me if I told you."

"She doesn't have to know. Please, I don't have a sister to share things like that with. Please."

I gave in. "Fine, but one of these days that line is going to stop working."

Meredith grabbed two cigarettes from the pack in her bag and pulled me over to the couch. "Now, tell me everything."

CHAPTER TWENTY-NINE

In preparation for Jane's bachelorette party, Meredith and I drove to Philadelphia and went back to the King of Condoms. Careful not to go too overboard, we bought novelties for the special evening. My favorites were the penis-shaped lollipops. In total, there would be nine of us: Molly, Sam, Meredith, me, Jane, the two other bridesmaids, and two of Jane's colleagues. I couldn't wait.

We hung pink and white balloons in the corners of our living room and ran pink streamers down the walls. I knew her colors were red and gold, but this wasn't her wedding, it was her bachelorette party. All the guests arrived right on time, which wasn't a surprise since they were Jane's friends, not mine. Pete dropped Jane off on the way to his bachelor party and casually issued me another warning. I ignored him completely.

We began the evening calmly by playing bridal bingo. When that was finished, I passed around plastic flutes of champagne. The second game we played was Kiss and Tell, where Jane had to tell about the first time she and Pete kissed. Then the rest of us told about our best and worst kisses. After that, I filled everyone's flutes for a second time. The key to the party's success was to get everyone drunk, and I had to do so nonchalantly. By playing a game and then drinking and moving on to another game, no one had any idea how much alcohol they were consuming.

When the games were all finished, I brought out the cake. Everyone burst out laughing when the phallic-shaped pastry was unveiled and Jane blushed. I made sure to get a picture before we made her eat the tip. After the cake, I passed out T-shirts, phallic lollipops, and candy necklaces, and told everyone it was time to go. I had to give Jane's friends credit; although they were hesitant at first, they went along with everything.

Somehow we managed to make it to Tonic upright and as a group. I kissed Chris P. on the cheek at the door and ushered everyone to the bar. Max grinned from ear to ear when he saw our party.

"So I hear we have a special occasion on our hands tonight," he said, watching Jane and her friends one at a time as they made their way to the bar.

"We do," I replied. "My sister here is getting married in a couple of weeks."

"Now why would anyone as beautiful as you want to do a crazy thing like that?" he asked. He was such a slut.

"Because I love my fiancé," she replied.

"Well, then, how about a shot for love?"

Max lined up the shots. We all took them in our hands and shouted, "Love!" before throwing them back.

"Let's do another one for marriage," I suggested. Everyone cheered. My mission was a success; they were all drunk. We slammed back our second shots, "Marriage!"

"Isn't a baby carriage next?" Meredith asked.

"Let's not ruin the fun by talking about babies," I answered.

"But babies are cute," Jane said. "I want at least four."

"Enough about babies," I said, rolling my eyes. "Let's go dance."

Jane was fun when she was drunk. She let everything go and allowed herself to get silly. Man, I thought, if only Pete could see her now. But I banished that thought from my brain. I did not want to waste one second of my time thinking about Pete and the stick up his ass. Instead, I took Jane by the hand and twirled her on the dance floor.

"Your sister is hot," Max said when I sat down at the bar for a break.

"I know."

"What's her fiancé like?"

"He's a douchebag."

"You like him that much?"

"Love him."

"You want to go back to my office?"

"Absolutely."

When I resurfaced twenty minutes later, the party was still in progress. Molly and Meredith were outside smoking a cigarette, Sam was flirting with some random, and Jane and her friends were attempting to dance.

"Where did you disappear to?" Jane asked when I bumped up next to her.

"To settle the tab."

"Kelly, this has to be too expensive for you. Let me give you some money."

"Don't worry about it. Max gave me a really good deal."

"I bet he did," Meredith said, rejoining us on the dance floor.

Jane looked at me crossly. "What?"

"Who wants another shot?" I yelled.

Everyone followed me to the bar where Max was standing at his post, observing. He winked at me as the bartender gave us a round of shots. An electric shock pulsed through my body.

Jane refused to take part in any bachelorette-party dares that involved her and a member of the opposite sex. She wouldn't even let a guy dance with her. It amazed me that even in her condition, she was still in control.

Jane and her friends were alarmed when the last-call bell rang and people rushed the bar. Meredith explained the tradition and Jane and her friends happily crowded around for their parting shots. Though we were all pretty drunk and could have done without the tequila, we did it anyway.

Before we left, Jane made it a point to thank Max for tolerating us for the evening. He placed his hand softly on top of hers, told her it was his pleasure, and wished her luck. I told him he was more than welcome to join me back at my apartment after he closed up. He didn't say yes, but he didn't say no.

I told Molly and Sam they could crash at our place, but they decided to go home and called a cab from Tonic. The rest of us staggered back to my apartment together, six pink shirts encircling an immaculate white one. Jane mumbled the songs we'd danced to as we walked. Halfway back to the apartment, she stopped.

"Oh, my God," she said with a smile. "I'm getting married."

"Yes, you are," we said back in unison.

"No, guys," she said. "I am really getting married. Do you hear that, Haysville? I am getting married!"

Her cry was met with a few barking dogs.

"I'm getting married," she repeated before picking up the melody of the last song she'd been singing.

Back at the apartment, the rest of Jane's friends called cabs and left in the same order they'd arrived. Meredith went to change into her pajamas and I helped Jane to the pullout couch.

"Thank you so much for my party," she slurred, falling onto the bed. "I love you so much."

I froze for a second, taken aback because we never said I love you to each other, ever. Sure, we signed our birthday cards and things like that with Love, Jane or Love, Kelly, but we never just came right out and said the words "I love you."

I took the blanket from the back of the couch and spread it over her, turned up the AC the way she liked it, and kissed her on the top of the head. "I love you, too," I whispered. She had already passed out.

Meredith came back out and we shared one last cigarette before she went to bed.

"Did you have a good time tonight?" she asked.

"I did. Did you?"

"I mean with Max."

I smiled. "What are you talking about?"

"Just how exactly did you settle the bill?"

I pulled on the cigarette. "I have no idea what you are talking about."

She laughed as I exhaled the smoke slowly. "I love you, Kel," she smiled.

"I love you, too."

It wasn't weird to say it between Meredith and me. We said it all the time. It may have been a drunken affection, but we didn't mean it any less. Our buzzer rang as I stubbed out my cigarette and Meredith jumped up to answer it.

"I wonder if somebody forgot something."

She picked up the phone, listened, said, "Okay," and buzzed the main door open.

"Who was it?" I asked.

"Not for me," she smiled. "I'm going to bed."

Two minutes later someone knocked on our door. I opened it

to find Max on the other side.

"I hope I'm not disturbing you," he said.

"Not at all."

"Nice place," he said.

"Let me give you the tour." I grabbed his hand. "We can start with my bedroom."

I awoke the following afternoon alone and naked in my bed. The apartment was silent. I looked around my bedroom and was relieved to see Max's shirt in a ball on the floor. Quietly, I made my way to the bathroom and performed a quick makeover; not that it mattered. Max had seen me at my worst and was still interested. Regardless, I washed my face and brushed my teeth. The smell of Tonic was still in my hair and the remnants of the alcohol were escaping through my pores. Maybe Max and I could shower it off together.

On my way to the living room, I stopped back in my room and threw Max's oversized shirt over my head. His smell enveloped me. I breathed it in deeply and was walking back down the hall to the living room when I saw a shirtless Max stumble backwards.

Pete came into view, saying, "Who the fuck are you?"

How did Pete get in?

"Who the fuck am I?" Max asked, steady on his feet again. "Who the fuck are you?"

I interrupted before fists could start to fly. "What the hell do you think you're doing?"

Pete and Max turned and looked at me. Jane was still fast asleep right where I'd tucked her in, oblivious to her raging fiancé.

"What did you do?" Pete demanded, glaring at me. He looked from Max to Jane and back to Max again. "I should have never let you do this."

This could be fun, I thought.

"Did you let him in?" I asked Max.

"He said he was here for Jane. I told him she was still sleeping and he demanded that I let him in."

Pete's head looked like it was ready to explode. Just one little jest, I thought. Then I'll tell him the truth.

"This is my soon-to-be brother-in-law," I said, looking at Max. "Jane's fiancé."

"I see," Max smiled.

"Why the fuck are you smiling?" Pete growled.

"Pete," I said, "this is Horse. You know, as in hung like." I winked. I couldn't help myself. "He was the entertainment last night, and well, I guess Jane didn't get enough of him during the party."

Pete looked like he was going to be sick. He looked around the apartment, processing the room like a crime scene investigator. His eyes darted from the picked-at penis cake on the kitchen table to the penis-shaped lollipops and the pair of pink feathered handcuffs on the floor next to the pullout bed.

"Jane," he hollered, though it came out more like a scream. "Jane, get up." He rushed the bed and shook her violently.

"Careful," I warned.

Pete ignored me. "Jane. Jane, get up."

"What?" Jane whined.

"Get up," Pete demanded.

Jane's eyes squinted open. When she saw Pete, they opened all the way. "Pete," she said with a scratchy voice, "what are you doing here? What time is it?"

"What am I doing here?" he asked. "I came to get my fiancée."

Jane sat up slowly and immediately brought her hand to her head. "Oww. What happened last night?"

"You don't remember?" Pete asked, panicked.

"We drank," Jane half-smiled, "we danced. I had cake. Shots, there were a lot of shots."

"And what about Horse?" Pete demanded.

"What?"

"Horse." Pete turned and looked at Max. Max winked back at him and Pete lunged forward. I thought he was going to kill Max right then and there. I jumped in front of Max before Pete could get to him and told him to relax.

"Nothing happened," I told Pete. I had taken things as far as they could go before lines got crossed, if they hadn't already. "Do you really think Jane would do anything like that?"

Pete recoiled and went back to Jane on the couch. "Do you know this guy?" he asked her.

"Who, Max?"

"I thought his name was Horse."

"That's only what I call him," I said.

"But you said—" Pete said, untrusting.

"I said he was the entertainment last night," I replied. "And for me, he was."

"I don't believe you," Pete snarled.

"Shocker," I replied. "But who's wearing his shirt, tough guy? Jane is still in her clothes from last night."

Pete looked at my shirt and the tension in his shoulders began to dissipate.

"Don't you trust me?" Jane said, making slow movements to get up.

"I do," Pete replied. "But I don't trust her."

Jane looked at Max. I could tell she was trying to process how it was exactly that he'd ended up shirtless in my apartment. Pete didn't give her any time to think.

"Let's go," he said, helping her to her feet.

"I need to go to the bathroom," she said, and she staggered off down the hall.

Pete refused to look at Max or me the entire time Jane was gone. He sat on the pullout with her bag in his lap and his car keys in his hand.

Jane hugged me when she returned to the living room. "Thanks for last night. I had a great time."

Pete ushered her out of the apartment without a word.

"Horse?" Max asked when the door slammed.

"I told you he was a douche bag."

CHAPTER THIRTY

A couple of days after the bachelorette party, Jane and Pete showed up at my apartment. I was sitting out on the balcony enjoying a cigarette and a beer after my afternoon nap when they pulled up out front. They could see me watching them as they approached.

"I think we need to talk," Jane called up to me. "Can we come up?"

"Sure," I replied, stubbing out the cigarette. "The door should be propped."

A couple minutes later, they knocked on my door and I called for them to come in.

"Do you always leave the door propped open downstairs?" Jane asked as they walked in.

"During the day," I said. "That way we don't have to worry about bringing our keys with us if we want to run out real quick."

"That's not very safe," she said.

"It's fine. Everyone does it."

"Can we sit down?"

"Yeah," I shrugged. "Do you want to go outside or stay in here?"

"It's a little muggy out," Jane said. "Why don't we just stay inside. Is that okay, Pete?"

"Sure," he said. He hadn't made eye contact with me.

Jane walked into the living room and sat on the bigger of the two couches. Pete sat next to her.

"So what's up?" I asked, sitting Indian-style on the loveseat.

"I want to talk about what happened last weekend," Jane began. "Pete and I have talked about it a lot, and he's upset with what happened."

"Okay," I replied, though I didn't have much of anything to say.

"We're getting married in less than a month," Jane said, "and I can't have you two at each other's throats."

"Who said we were at each other's throats?" I asked.

"It's no secret that you and Pete don't exactly get along."

"I mess around with him, Jane," I said, speaking as though he wasn't sitting across from me. "I mess around with everyone."

"Well, last weekend you took it a little too far."

"How is that? He's the one who barged into my apartment like a lunatic. Did you talk about his lack of trust in you? Why would he immediately jump to the conclusion that you had done something?"

"You make him nervous," Jane replied. "Isn't that right, Pete?"

"I wouldn't say nervous," Pete said, speaking for the first time. "Agitated is a better word."

"How exactly is it that I agitate you, Pete?" I asked, getting up in search of a cigarette.

"You are extremely self-involved," he replied. "You don't think about anyone but yourself, and you take advantage of the fact that your family loves you so much."

"I don't take anything for granted," I replied.

"Please don't," Jane said just as I was about to light up.

I acquiesced, mainly to show Pete that I wasn't as self-involved as he claimed. I sat back on the couch with the unlit cigarette between my fingers.

"Your behavior is getting out of control," he said.

"What do you know about my behavior?"

"The first time we met, you were hungover. You threw up seconds after our introduction. Then when I met your parents, both you and Meredith were drunk."

"He told me about the vodka in the bottles," Jane said, looking at me with disappointment.

"How do you know we were drunk?" I asked. "Maybe we were just in a good mood."

"Don't insult me," Pete replied.

"Pete's dad was an alcoholic," Jane said, and she patted Pete's knee. "He died of a heart attack seven years ago."

"I'm sorry to hear that." I put the unlit cigarette to my lips. "But I don't see how that has anything to do with me."

"Alcoholics aren't always falling over drunk," Pete said, glaring in my direction but still managing to avoid my eyes. "They find ways to hide their intoxication."

"So now I'm an alcoholic? I hate to break it to you, but I am twenty years old. If you think that of me, then we have a real problem with alcoholism here at Hay U."

"It's not that you drink," Jane said. "It's how you drink. You continue to get yourself in bad situations, and I fear for your safety."

"How much further do you want to push yourself before you do end up getting raped?" Pete asked.

"You told him?" I said to Jane. It was my turn to glare.

"He's my fiancé," Jane replied almost apologetically. "I tell him everything."

I reached over and grabbed the purple lighter off the coffee table.

"I'm your sister," I said, lighting the cigarette and inhaling, "and you made me a promise."

"I'm really worried about you."

"So what does any of this have to do with last weekend?"

"You and Max," Jane answered. "Did you sleep with him?"

"Now see, that is something that I would have told you when I knew you kept your promises. But now I can't trust you."

"You can't trust me?"

"Nope."

"Fine," she replied. "You don't have to tell me. But from the looks of it, something happened. And that's what is weird. He's too old for you. He's too old for me."

"Max and I are friends," I said, watching the ash fall off the end of my cigarette.

"That's what friendship is to you?"

"Sometimes."

"Why are you acting like this, Kelly?"

"Acting like what?"

"Like you don't give a shit what we're saying to you. Like we have no idea what we are talking about and that there is absolutely nothing wrong with the way you are living your life."

I stubbed out my cigarette.

"I'm having fun. Have things gotten out of control from time to time? Sure. Does that mean I have a problem? No. Pete, I am sorry that your dad was an alcoholic. And maybe I shouldn't have gotten you all riled up last weekend when you came to pick up Jane. But you haven't been exactly nice to me. Yes, I was hungover the first time we met. But that was also when you referred to me as a prostitute because I didn't have a career plan mapped out."

"I didn't—" he interrupted.

"Let me finish. And yes, Meredith and I were drinking the night you went home to meet my parents. I'm sorry she threw up. We were just messing around."

"You are always 'just messing around,'" he answered. "That is our point. What if Jane had gotten pulled over that night and the officer smelled alcohol in the car? How would we explain the fact that there were two underage girls drinking in the back seat? Just because it's vodka doesn't mean you can't smell it. The gum and perfume don't do much to disguise it."

"What Pete is trying to say is that you don't think about the consequences of your actions. When you call me to pick you up at a bar at three in the morning because the cops have been called because of a fight, you are putting me at risk."

"Then I won't call you next time."

"There shouldn't be a next time," she replied. "I'm glad you felt comfortable enough to call me. And you know I will always be there for you. But you need to think about the situations you put other people in."

The conversation was painful. I got what they were saying and knew I didn't always make the best decisions, but for them to go on and on was rather unnecessary.

"I'm sorry for the situations I have put you in," I said to Jane. "I am. And I am sorry that you dislike the way I am, Pete."

"He doesn't dislike you," Jane said. "But he had to put up with a lot from his father, and your actions take him back to what he had to deal with."

I thought I'd heard somewhere that when you use the word "but" in the middle of a sentence it negates everything that preceded it. So basically, Jane telling me Pete did not dislike me and following it with a big "but" meant that in actuality, he probably did dislike me a whole lot.

"I will try to be less obnoxious to you, Pete, and more thoughtful to you, Jane." I smiled.

That did the trick. Jane asked Pete if there was anything else he had to say, to which he shook his head no, and she claimed to have gotten everything off her chest. We sat in silence for a couple of minutes before Jane said they should be getting home. I walked them out.

The confrontation and disapproval hung in the air even after they left. It permeated the couch where Jane and Pete had sat with their perfect posture. It stuck around all night and hit Meredith with a warm slap as soon as she walked into the apartment.

"Who died?" she asked, coming through the door.

"My relationship with Jane," I replied. "Let's do some shots."

CHAPTER THIRTY-ONE

I had been intervened, not that it did much good. I continued to drink and smoke and engage in "friendships" with men. Due to our close proximity, Max quickly became a biweekly habit that I thoroughly enjoyed. Not that I could remember much, but I enjoyed all of my evenings. In fact, the enjoyable evenings that I couldn't remember turned into weeks that I couldn't remember.

I asked myself if there was something wrong. Was it normal for life to become such a blur? . . . No, I reasoned, I just knew how to have a good time. My grades were fine, no one was getting hurt, and Meredith and I had been granted the freedom of apartment living by our parents. Responsibility would come at the end of senior year. This was our time to have fun.

We walked the Hay U campus differently as juniors. We had two years' experience. We had clout. The freshmen, easily distinguished by the crimson-and-white lanyards around their necks, looked young and lost. I remembered how big and mature I'd felt freshman year, away from home and free. I'd probably looked just as ridiculous.

The onset of our third year meant that we would begin focusing more on our majors. I was still business undeclared. After numerous conversations with my mom and dad about what I would be good at and what I should pursue, I began the process of elimination. At first I considered finance or accounting, but I hate math and numbers. Then I contemplated information systems, but I'm not a big fan of computers. That really only left me with marketing.

The electives looked pretty interesting. I could choose anything that dealt with marketing, from entertainment to food. I had no idea where that would leave me in terms of employment when I graduated, but I wasn't really concerned with that aspect.

Despite the strain Jane's intervention had put on our relationship, I continued to help with her last-minute wedding plans. It was my assumption that as the wedding date drew closer there would be less to do. I was wrong. Every weekend there was something else that needed to be triple-checked and approved.

One of the last unchecked items on Jane's list was the bridesmaids' luncheon, which was scheduled for the weekend before the wedding at our parents' house. I arrived hungover but disguised it well. Without Inspector Pete there to sniff out the scent of alcohol or vomit, I was in the clear. I drank almost an entire pot of coffee by myself and blamed my headache and haggard appearance on the wonderful joys of menstruation. My plight was met with empathy. Even Jane appeared to understand.

The low-key afternoon passed quickly and quietly. After brunch we formed an assembly line and put together the programs for the church ceremony. When all one hundred programs were completed, we set them in the white-satin-lined baskets that would be placed at the back of the church. Jane thanked us all for being a part of the biggest day of her life and gave us each a gift—pearl earrings and a matching necklace. We oohed and ahhed, praising her taste and agreeing that they would complement the bridesmaids' dresses perfectly. Jane started to cry happy tears.

Jane's friends Gabby and Beth left together and I stayed back to help clean up.

"They are such nice girls," Mom said as she cleared the table. "Are they seeing anyone?"

"Gabby has a boyfriend," Jane answered. "They've been dating for the past six years. She's ready to get married. He's not. You'll meet him at the wedding. And Beth actually just got out of a really long relationship. The guy was a control freak."

"That is such a shame," Mom said, shaking her head. "It must be so hard to find a nice guy these days. I don't envy you girls one bit. I have always prayed that you would both find good, honest men. And in a week, half of my prayers will be answered. Now we just need Kelly to find someone like Pete."

"Kelly is happy single," I replied.

"The key is where you look," Jane said, as if I hadn't said anything. "You can't find a good guy drunk at college parties or in bars. Those guys may be fun, but they're definitely not marriage material."

"You're not looking in bars, are you, Kelly?" Mom asked. "You're not even twenty-one."

"I'm not looking at all," I said.

Jane sighed.

"That's a good attitude to have," Mom said. "Make them look for you, and it will happen when you least expect it."

When I received the invitation to Jane's wedding, which she'd insisted on mailing with the others, I was invited to bring a guest. While Mom said there was no shame in going alone, I refused to consider it. As far as I saw it, I had three viable options for dates.

If I wanted to impress my family and give both my mom and Jane a false sense that I had settled down, Luke would have been perfect. Mom would be sure to fall for his charm and Jane would be relieved to see me with a guy my own age.

Then there was Max. He definitely would have accompanied me if I had asked him to, and would be perfect if I wanted to stir things up a bit. Pete would have been furious, and Jane would have been disappointed. However fun that may have been, it was still Jane and Pete's day, and it would be selfish of me to ruin it. I also didn't want to have to explain Max to my parents. My mom would have been cordial, but the age difference would not have gone over smoothly with Dad.

In the end, I chose option number three: Meredith. There was never really any doubt that she would be my date. She was my best friend. Who else would I want to go with? Besides, everyone knows weddings are great places to meet people and hook up, and nothing would irk Pete more than if I hooked up with one of his friends. I really hoped they weren't as uptight as he was.

On the morning of the wedding, Meredith and I drove to my parents' house, where Jane was getting ready. A delicious spread of fruit, bagels, and pastries was set out on the island in the kitchen. Mom told Jane to eat, but Jane said she was too nervous.

"If you don't eat now," Mom cautioned, "you're going to be starving by the time we get to the church. You don't want your stomach growling on the altar. Worse yet, you don't want to faint."

"Fine," Jane said. She picked at a bagel with her freshly manicured nails.

Christine, Jane's hairstylist, arrived at nine on the dot with a silver case big enough to transport a bomb. She set up in the guest bathroom and went to work on Jane's long black mane. I peeked in after ten minutes and was practically suffocated by the aerosol that hung in the air. A tiara on top of Jane's head was surrounded by loose curls. When Christine was finished, Jane moved on to have her makeup done by Christine's sister and I took a seat.

My hair took half the time that Jane's did. I walked out of the bathroom feeling pretty and happy to breathe fresh air. Meredith got her hair done the same as mine and we did each other's makeup. It was a really fun morning. Knowing that we would be drinking heavily that evening, we made sure to generously sample the breakfast spread.

When the photographer arrived, we followed his direction and posed and smiled. I adjusted Jane's veil as we stood in front of the fireplace and looked in the mirror, positioning the train of her dress to wrap around her on the floor. We posed with Mom, Dad, and Patrick, both inside and out. My cheeks were beginning to get sore from the constant smiling. Mom had to touch up her makeup three times in the first half hour as a result of her tears. As soon as his presence was no longer needed, Patrick disappeared into the basement. While Jane reapplied lipstick, I asked the photographer to snap a couple shots of Meredith and me.

At the church, I performed my maid of honor duties flawlessly. I fluffed my sister's gown, arranged her veil, and held her flowers during the ceremony. Pete's groomsmen were better-looking than I'd imagined them to be, some more than others. I assessed them as Jane and Pete exchanged vows, trying to decide which one I would target.

Three limousines were lined up in front of the church after the ceremony. The guests formed a line from the church doors to the curb and cheered as Jane and Pete exited hand in hand and walked to the first limousine. Pete's mom and stepdad and my mom and dad got in the second car, and both bridal parties jumped into the third. Meredith came along as an honorary bridesmaid.

Patrick was out of his element in the limo with the grown men and women, and I took it upon myself as his older sister to make sure he was comfortable. Pete's mom had arranged for each limo to have a basket with snacks and three bottles of champagne. It didn't take us long to pop the first cork. The champagne flowed as we drove from the church to the park where the pictures were going to be taken.

I told Patrick he could have a glass if he wanted to, and warned him not to go overboard. He laughed and informed me that he was a sophomore in high school and had experience with alcohol. I thought it was cute how mature he was trying to look in front of the groomsmen. I apologized and backed off.

Posing for the pictures was a lot of fun, but it was cold. The groomsmen had pants and jackets to shield them from the September breeze that rushed up the girls' legs every couple of minutes. Jane looked radiant in her white gown with her hair done. She smiled brightly in every picture. Pete did as well, much to my surprise.

The awkwardness and unfamiliarity the bridal parties felt on the way to the park had vanished by the time we rushed back into the warm limousine and headed to the reception. The champagne flowed until there was no more, and Patrick looked like he was either going to be sick or pass out. I hoped for the latter. While Meredith and I eyed up the groomsmen as potential randoms for the evening, I couldn't help but feel as though they were avoiding me. After twenty minutes I caved and allowed the champagne to bring on the confrontation.

"What's the deal?" I asked. "Are you guys married, gay, both?"

They looked at each other and laughed. "No," the one I thought of as Spike because of his pointy hair said with a smile. "We're under strict orders."

"Oh, yeah? And what orders would those be?"

"Not to go near you."

"Why is that?"

"Pete made us promise."

Pete. I should have known.

"What did Pete say?"

"Do you want the truth?" Spike asked.

"Yes, I do," I replied.

"He said you're crazy."

Patrick laughed.

I kicked him with the tip of my shoe. "Do you all plan on listening to him?"

"That depends," Spike said. "Are you crazy?"

"You'll have to wait and see."

When we arrived at the reception hall, we were ushered into a private room where waiters were serving hors d'oeuvres and alcohol. Jane and Pete were in the corner talking to Pete's mom and stepdad. Meredith and I each grabbed a chicken skewer and hit up the bar for a drink. The bartender didn't even look at us twice before giving us our vodka and cranberries. Patrick grabbed four chicken skewers and joined our parents at one of the pub tables that were scattered throughout the room.

Meredith and I had two more cocktails before it was time to move to the ballroom for the bridal party's introductions. I was feeling good at that point and was ready to start dancing. Two by two we lined up outside the hall and waited for our signal to enter. When "Beautiful Day" by U2 began, the line started moving forward. I felt like a rock star when my name was called along with Spike's and we danced our way onto the dance floor. After the parental introductions, the room grew quiet and the music switched over to "At Last" by Etta James. The doors to the hall opened wide and Jane and Pete held hands as they were introduced for the first time as Mr. and Mrs. Collins.

We cleared the dance floor and Pete and Jane danced. I will never forget how gracefully they moved together that night. She was gliding across the floor as if she were walking on air. Her smile hadn't faded all day. If anything, it was brighter. When their song ended, the bridal party was asked to join them. I took Spike by the hand and led him to the dance floor.

"Are you always this forward?" he asked.

"Do you like it?" I replied.

He threw his head back in laughter. "You're something else."

From the corner of my eye I could see Pete watching us. I turned and winked at him. He wasn't going to control my evening.

Halfway through dinner, Pete's best man tapped his glass and delivered his speech. When he was finished, it was my turn.

"I have always wondered what it would be like to have an older brother," I began. "And now I know. You see, Pete has already issued a warning to all of his male guests to steer clear of his new sister-in-law." I turned and winked at him. Everyone laughed, and I continued. "In all seriousness . . ."

I delivered the "you're my best friend" speech to Jane

flawlessly. Jane cried, not that it took much that day, and Pete stood up and gave me a kiss on the forehead—a big step in our relationship. I think he was just relieved that it was over and I hadn't embarrassed him or Jane. While we hadn't exactly gotten along in the months preceding the wedding, that day we did.

I considered myself off duty once the speeches were over, and began to have fun in a controlled manner. Meredith and I convened at the center of the dance floor with all the other bachelorettes in anticipation of the bouquet toss. I found it amusing and rather pathetic how seriously some of the women took it. They watched Jane like a cat about to pounce on a mouse. As soon as the stems left Jane's hands, their primal instincts kicked in and they began pushing, jumping, even clawing their way towards the descending flowers, desperate to grab hold of what they believed to be fate. Meredith joined in on the fun and almost came to blows with a larger woman who boxed her out with enough force to send Meredith flying to the floor. I calmed her down with the suggestion of getting a drink.

"Bitch," Meredith said under her breath as I helped her up. "Did you see what she did to me?"

"No," I smiled, "I was too busy protecting myself. Big girl over there had a friend."

"These women are crazy," she said, straightening out her dress.

"Desperate is more like it."

"Please kill me if I ever get like that. I mean, do they really think that catching a bouquet will make their fat dissolve and turn them into something men find irresistible?"

I shrugged. "I have no idea. Why don't you go over there and ask your best friend?"

"Yeah." Meredith smiled and approached the bar. "She might eat me. Did you see the one who caught it? She needs all the help she can get."

"You never know," I replied. "Maybe she has a boyfriend. Maybe she's already madly in love."

"Not with the way she dove for that thing. She went for that like it was her last chance."

I looked over at the dowdy woman smiling brightly at the white flowers in her hands and wondered how many women actually were the next ones to get married after catching a bouquet. Did it even matter to her, or was she just happy enough having a chance at love, like playing the lottery? Catching the bouquet had given her a ticket, but it didn't mean she was going to win. All it gave her was a chance.

I watched bachelorette number one with interest for the rest of the night. As Meredith suspected, she'd come to the wedding alone—her place card indicated one seat in her party. She talked awkwardly with a couple of men but always returned to the same table with the same group of misfits. I wanted to see how her evening concluded.

Maybe I did, but I don't remember. I don't remember anything that happened after Slick, one of Pete's groomsmen, busted out the shots. That's all I can remember. I woke up in bed with Meredith the next morning to a pounding head and a throbbing ankle.

"What the hell happened?" I asked, looking down at the deep colors that had invaded my ankle over night.

"Hell if I know." Meredith rolled out of bed and clutched her head.

By the time we made it down to brunch, Meredith helping me as I limped, most of the guests had already eaten and gone.

"We need to talk," my mother said in her patented "you're in trouble" voice before I could even sit down at the table.

Jane wouldn't look at me. Pete glared at me and his friend. What was his name? His friend, the guy with the shots, was grinning at me ear to ear. Oh my God, I thought, did I sleep with him?

I turned quickly to Meredith for an answer. She looked from shot guy to me and smiled, whispering, "No. Almost, but no."

From what I could piece together, Meredith, Ralph (the shot guy, a.k.a. Slick), and I did a shot or six too many, and in an attempt to "Get Down, Get Down," I twisted my ankle. I knew those damned heels were too high, but they matched my dress perfectly. Numbed by the alcohol, I didn't feel much pain and continued to bump and grind, yes, grind, with Ralph. Apparently, I'd tried to disrobe him and then myself in the middle of the dance floor.

"An embarrassment" is how my mother described it. "Revolting" was Pete's take, and "disgusting" was Jane's opinion. Sober, the pain from my ankle met the aching in my head, and not only did I feel horrible, but I also felt like a whore.

"Please tell me this doesn't always happen when you go out," my mother asked, afraid of what I might say.

"Mom." I looked her straight in the eyes. "I'm sorry about last night. I guess I let the excitement get to me."

"I'm not the one you have to apologize to," she said, patting my hand to signal that we were okay. "Jane was very ashamed of your behavior."

"I'll sort it out," I promised.

And I did.

I begged Jane for her forgiveness, allowed Pete to berate me, and that was that. It was settled. But somehow I ended up in a worse situation, and no berating will ever make any of it better, ever.

CHAPTER THIRTY-TWO

With Jane's wedding over and done with, my social life and college experience reverted back to normal. My ankle healed quickly from the grinding mishap—it turned out to be a minor twist—and I was back on the dance floor at Tonic in less than two weeks. Jane and Pete left after the post-wedding brunch for a two-week cruise around Europe that started in Barcelona. Pete claimed to be fluent in Spanish and wanted to practice. I wished him luck with that.

Shot guy called me a couple of days after the reception and asked if I wanted to get together. I guess in my drunken stupor I had made the mistake of giving him my real number. I was still unable to remember the reception clearly and could barely remember what he looked like, so I politely declined, thanking him for the invitation, and prayed that he would lose my number. As a last-ditch attempt, he promised he wouldn't tell Pete if we hung out. Again, I declined. I had neither the time nor the desire for a random. I was back at school, which meant I was splitting my time between Luke and Max, neither of whom knew about the other. Not that I claimed to be exclusive with either one of them.

It's hard to explain how I could have spent so much time and physical energy with two men without the need or desire for an emotional bond. Would I have been hurt if Luke turned me away and I saw him holding hands with another girl on campus? Sure. I might have felt the sting of rejection, but I would have gotten over it. I would have gotten over him.

My feelings for Luke didn't extend beyond the bedroom. He was a friend and a good time and regardless of the sex we had, we were never intimate. It was good, but not involved. We never talked about our feelings or our dreams. In fact, we barely spoke at all. The situation with Max, however, was a little more complicated. There may have been a hint of feeling there, but just a hint. Maybe it was the fact that he was older that made me crave his attention. Or maybe it was because he made me work a little harder to get what I wanted. Whatever the case was, I felt more strongly towards Max than I did towards Luke, but I would never have admitted it. That would have made things weird. So Meredith and I continued to go out, black out, and enjoy the men in our lives with no strings attached.

Trying to piece together a night out, or a weekend for that matter, after you black out is a very difficult thing to do. I should know, because at the time of the wedding, I was blacking out almost every weekend. It became sort of like a game, trying to figure out what happened once the alcohol started flowing. It reminded me of the games on television where they cover up a picture of something and reveal it square by square. You see just enough to get an understanding of what the picture is about, but not enough to know exactly what it is. Unlike the television games, though, I was never granted a full reveal. My mind would expose everything except for that center square with all the important details.

I thought I could improve my memory with practice so the alcohol would have less of an effect on my recollections, but I was never able to run a controlled experiment because as my tolerance increased, I drank more. And as I drank more, I remembered less. It was a never-ending conflict and drinking more always took precedence over my memory. I didn't care if I remembered the details as long as I had a good time.

I know, how could I tell if I'd had a good time if I couldn't remember anything about the night before? It was all in the feeling I had when I woke up the morning after, minus the hangover.

Meredith and I worked as a team to piece together our evening ventures, but most of the time we remembered more or less up to the same point. Sometimes we made up what we thought happened based on how we woke up or with whom. Our weekends were a lot more interesting that way.

There was one morning where we woke up together in the same bed with Mardi Gras beads around our necks. Neither one of us remembered getting beads or being at a party that had beads. Thankfully, Molly was there to fill in the details. Although she was the one who'd introduced me to getting blackout drunk, she never seemed to black out. She drank and had fun, but managed to maintain control over herself and her surroundings. According to Molly, that night we'd been lured into going to a party on the Hill after Tonic. She was ready to go home, but Meredith and I insisted.

"How did we get the beads?" I asked, briefly remembering a white house with black leather couches.

She laughed. "Think 'girls gone wild,'" she said.

"How wild?" Meredith asked nervously.

"Your tattoo became quite the conversation piece," Molly answered.

Meredith's hand went instinctively to cup her left breast. "You're joking," she pleaded.

Meredith and I had gotten tattoos when we were in Philadelphia. We'd been talking about it since freshman year, and on a whim we walked into Inked on South. I chose a dancing brown monkey for my right hip because it was cute and made me smile. I didn't want anything too serious or fake, like Asian writing, and refused to get anything near the center of my lower back. I wasn't one of those girls. Meredith went more serious with hers. She had the date of her mother's death from breast cancer tattooed in a curve between two stars under her left breast. She had cried so hard afterwards.

I saw the embarrassment flush to Meredith's face. "Don't worry," I said. "It's not as though half the guys on campus haven't seen it already."

"Like you're one to talk." Meredith laughed and let her arm fall back to her side.

On my second trip to Philadelphia, Meredith and I returned to Inked on South and got matching friendship tattoos on our feet. The symbol looked like a fancy letter L and the tattoo artist said it was the Zibu symbol for friendship. It was perfect and definitely worth the pain, even though it hurt a million times worse than the one on my hip. It may sound silly, but our tattoos brought Meredith and me even closer together. We were bound to each other for life, and that was something I would never regret.

CHAPTER THIRTY-THREE

The freedom of having a means of transportation on campus was even better than Meredith and I had imagined. And although the plan had been for us to pay the insurance, Mr. Short caved when Meredith complained about having to find a job, and he agreed to pay for it until she graduated. Being off the hook for that reduced our expenses to only gas, for which we used our credit cards.

"It's a living expense," I explained to my mom when she complained about the number of gas charges on the credit card statement. It was my card, but it had Mom's name on it, which was yet another area of frustration with Jane. She couldn't believe I had one of Mom's credit cards.

"Do you know how I paid for things when I was in college?" she griped. "I tutored. And if I ran out of money, I tutored some more."

"You had it so rough," I taunted her. "Did you have to walk to school barefoot in the snow, too?"

Mom laughed and Jane turned red with frustration.

"Just wait," she said, turning to Mom. "You created this monster. You're going to have to deal with her."

I smirked at Jane. "It's called love. And I am not a monster."

"Where was that love when I was in college?" Jane asked, turning to Mom.

Mom began to say something, but Jane waved her off and said she didn't want to hear it. It didn't matter what Mom said. Even though she said she loved each of us equally, Jane always insisted she was loved the least. What Jane failed to realize was that our birthing order predisposed us to being treated certain ways by our parents. As much as being the first child had its advantages, it also had its disadvantages. As the first, Jane was subjected to our parents' overprotective neuroses and inexperience. While she was adored and given undivided attention, she was also scrutinized and critiqued, all of which formed her type A personality.

I, on the other hand, was granted a less-controlled childhood because my parents had learned with Jane and relinquished a bit with me. I was allowed to exist and come into my own without much interference. While some second children battle with the shadow cast by their older sibling, I found a way to thrive. And just as I reaped the benefits of coming second, Patrick gained even more by coming third and being the only boy. He does, however, also have to deal with the last-child syndrome, because of which our mother refuses to let him grow up too quickly, if at all. As the middle child, though, the focus was never really on me, regardless of what Jane likes to believe.

Meredith and I drove to campus together every day. We planned our class schedule as we did everything else: together. And on Monday and Wednesday and occasionally Fridays, we met Molly and Sam for lunch.

It was weird being back at school and not living with Sam and Molly. I missed having them around. While our apartment was bigger than theirs, they definitely had the location advantage. Neither of them had cars, so they lived close enough to campus that they could take the shuttle wherever they needed to go. I'd been nervous that we wouldn't be as close when we couldn't see each other every day anymore, but things didn't seem to change at all. In fact, it made hanging out more fun, because we seemed to have more to talk about.

We still pre-gamed before going out. The only thing that changed was the location, depending on our plans for the evening. If it was a Tonic night, we would meet up at our place on Lexington Ave. On the rare occasion that we did anything on or around campus, Meredith and I would go to Molly and Sam's place. Sam joined us when she could, but she was still waitressing a lot at a family restaurant to pay off her school loans and rent. I felt bad watching her get dressed in her ridiculous uniform while we did shots on the couch.

Sam took the bus to and from work every afternoon after class, and every day she came home with another story about how wretched public transportation was—the people smelled, the bus was hot, some guy touched her. Feeling bad, Meredith and I caved and offered to drive her a couple of days a week. As the temperature dropped and winter began to impose itself on the fall, we began driving her almost every day. We drove her to work and she paid for the gas. It was an even exchange.

Driving Sam to and from work gave me an appreciation for my parents and the lifestyle they provided me with. I was thankful that they had found true love when they met and stayed together. I couldn't imagine living a life without the two of them together in one house. Sam said she didn't know any different, that her parents had divorced when she was very young. I wondered if she did remember what it was like when they were together, even if it was only glimpses. According to Sam, her father was dead. She never saw him and he never sent any money. "Once the divorce was finalized," she said one afternoon, "he split. He told my mom he'd never loved her and never wanted children."

What was I supposed to say to that? My parents were in love and they loved their children. Sure, they argued, but at the end of the day they sat together on the couch watching television or reading books. They were comfortable with each other and not afraid to show affection, no matter how uncomfortable it made me. They had something special, something to aspire to. That is, if you were looking for love, which I was not.

Sam wanted a relationship. She wanted to meet someone who was going to sweep her off her feet. She wanted a man, not a sperm donor. I think she believed that finding true love, and not the type of love that her mom seemed to find on a monthly basis, would make all of her problems go away. Sam wanted romance and chivalry. Though she claimed her father was dead, she clearly had daddy issues. And there I was, the product of true love, and I wanted no part of it.

In my opinion, guys ruined everything. No matter how nice or perfect they were, they always messed things up. My life was in a state of perfect equilibrium. I had school, friends, family, and plenty of sex. Simply put, there was neither the room nor the need for a relationship. Unfortunately for Sam, however, her life was anything but balanced.

I don't know why Jane seemed to fall so quickly into the whole love, marriage, and happily-ever-after thing. I couldn't help but wonder whether she and Pete were actually going to live happily ever after, considering his control issues. She was another one without equilibrium. She told me I wouldn't understand until I fell in love. "You'll know," she had said. "Then it will all make sense."

But nothing makes sense anymore, and I honestly doubt that love has the power to make it all right again.

CHAPTER THIRTY-FOUR

Jane returned from her honeymoon with a gorgeous tan and a lot of pictures. "Amazing" was the term she used to describe it, "incredible" was Pete's take. For Jane, it was her first trip outside of the United States, and she was thrilled to get a couple of stamps in her brand-new passport. That may have been more important to her than the cruise itself. Actually, that may have been the only reason she got married—so she could go on an international honeymoon and get her passport stamped.

She insisted on bringing the pictures, which she'd had processed the day after they got back, to our parents' house so we could all see them. Through their narrative slideshow, Jane and Pete gave us a tour of Barcelona, Capri, and a bunch of smaller European cities whose names I forgot as soon as they said them.

"This is Las Ramblas," Pete said, rolling his tongue longer than I thought necessary. "It is a brilliant street in the center of Barcelona where street performers put on all different acts for money."

Who uses the word brilliant to describe a street?

"You should have seen them," Jane smiled. "There was this one guy that was done up like a statue. He painted his face and sprayed his hair, it was amazing. He looked like a piece of marble. I wanted to take a picture, but Pete said we'd have to give him money if I did."

"That's what they're there for," Pete said. "It's only fair. You could have given him a euro."

It became apparent in that moment how much he loved himself, talking about Las Rrramblas and euros. He was so annoying. I stopped listening to his explanations and focused on the pictures, which consisted mainly of Jane posing in front of old buildings or statues. Everything in all the pictures looked so old.

"I don't get it," I said. "Everything looks the same."

"It's the culture, the people," Pete replied, annoyed, as Jane continued flipping through the pictures.

"So, no sicknesses?" I asked when their slideshow concluded.

"Sicknesses?" Jane repeated.

"Yeah, you know how people always get sick on cruises and no one knows where the illness came from."

"No one got sick," Pete sighed. "We had an amazing time."

They had to have, because Jane was glowing with happiness. With the stress of the wedding off her shoulders, she said she was able to let go and really enjoy herself. Pete, though pretentious as usual, appeared more relaxed as well.

Jane's glow, I would come to find out three weeks later, was not from her tan at all. She was pregnant.

Halloween, one of my favorite days of the year, arrived and I was ready to paint the town orange. Numerous parties were being hosted on the Hill and on campus, but Meredith and I were set to go to Tonic. Every year they had a costume contest and the winner won a hundred and fifty dollars.

Freshman year I'd stayed on campus and my suitemates and I dressed up as babies. Angela didn't partake because she didn't worship the devil or any of his holidays. She and Theresa watched a movie in our room instead. Sophomore year, Meredith, Molly, Sam, and I went to a seventies throwback party. Sam styled our hair into beehives. We wore short floral-print dresses and high platform shoes. It was a lot of fun. Junior year, however, Meredith and I were on our own. Sam had to work and Molly had to go home for her grandfather's eighty-fifth birthday party.

In the weeks leading up to Halloween, Meredith and I agonized over our costumes. We wanted ours to be sexy but different. It is a known, and I believe acceptable, fact that women use Halloween to dress as whores—even the uptight ones. In my three years at Hay U, almost every girl I'd seen on campus on Halloween was half-dressed, and some even less than that.

After scouring the racks at the local Halloween stores, Meredith and I came across two bee costumes. They were sexy and really cute, but most importantly, they were a change from the overly abundant and tired nurse, witch, and Playboy bunny costumes.

We put on the fishnet stockings, yellow-and-black striped bodysuits and ruffled skirts, and slid on our black high heels. I helped Meredith with her wings and she helped me attach mine. We did two shots of vodka to warm our bodies for the cold walk to Tonic, positioned our antennas, and set out to win the costume contest.

The mood at Tonic was so fun and cheery that Halloween. Everyone was more than happy to become someone else for the night. Max, sober in his stance behind the bar, was not in costume. He wanted people to know there was still someone in charge.

"You ladies look very sweet," he smiled as we approached the bar. Butterflies still fluttered in my stomach whenever he grinned at me.

"Why, thank you." Meredith winked and handed him her purse. He slid it behind a couple of bottles on the back wall.

"Are you going to enter the contest?" he asked.

"We're thinking about it," I replied. "Do you think we'll win?"

"You have my vote."

"Well, you're biased," Meredith said. She turned and began scanning the crowd. "You know you won't get any if you don't vote for us."

I blushed ever so slightly. Meredith and I talked about Max all the time and it was never weird. It wasn't weird when I was with Max, either. But for some reason, when Meredith alluded to our relationship in front of him, it made me almost bashful.

"So are you saying I shouldn't vote?"

"No, I just want an impartial opinion."

The crowd on the dance floor included the usual variety of doctors, nurses, umpires, witches, and vampires. Some people were so focused on having a unique costume that they hadn't thought about its flexibility or manageability. A guy and his girlfriend, for example, were dressed as a pair of dice. I can't believe it didn't occur to either one of them during the construction of their huge boxes that it would be tough to maneuver a crowded bar wearing them. Some of the couples' costumes were cute, others overdone. There were two outlet-and-plug pairs, a ball and chain, bacon and eggs, and Adam and Eve, who took it a little too far with their interpretation and, in my opinion, needed a little more ivy.

Meredith and I were dancing when a doctor approached and asked Meredith if he could take her pulse. I rolled my eyes. She said yes. Dr. Love told her that her pulse was racing and she needed to get to bed right away. I told him we wanted a second opinion. Another guy buzzed up to us and asked if we had any honey for him. We rolled our eyes and kept dancing.

The costume judging had just begun when the bouncer called Max and told him the police were out front and wanted to come in. Max told him to stall, called us over, and sent us out the back. We'd barely managed to escape down the alley before a squad car pulled around back and blocked the back door.

It was freezing and I was so disappointed we wouldn't be there for the contest.

"We have a more serious problem than that," Meredith said as we walked away from the bar. "I left my purse inside."

"So you'll get it tomorrow," I replied. "If I'm lucky, Max may even bring it over tonight."

"Our keys are in there." Meredith stopped. "We have to go back."

"And say what?" I asked. "Excuse me, Mr. Policeman. I am not twenty-one, but somehow my purse got left behind in the bar you are currently raiding. No, sir, that is not alcohol on my breath."

"So what are we going to do?" Meredith was starting to get a little nervous.

"It's freezing and we have no money or keys."

"Let's call Sam," I suggested.

Meredith shivered. "On what phone?"

"Good point." I thought for a second, smiled, and began walking again.

"Where are we going?"

"To the Main Street diner. There's a payphone there."

"But we don't have any money."

"We'll call collect."

"Sam won't accept a collect call. She probably won't even answer this late."

"That's why I'm going to call Jane."

"Do you think she'll come?"

"I won't give her a choice."

I was thankful when Jane answered the phone and not Pete. She was groggy and confused when the operator asked if she was willing to accept a collect call. It took a couple of seconds for it to process and for her to realize she wasn't dreaming before she accepted the call.

Once the operator had disconnected from the line, I explained the situation. When Jane started asking questions, I told her she was being charged for the call and we were freezing. She told me she would leave right away.

Meredith and I huddled together in the phone booth to keep warm while we waited. We tried to wait in the warm lobby of the diner, but when we claimed to still be waiting for our party after fifteen minutes, they kicked us out. I guess it was suspicious that we didn't want to be seated.

It wasn't too long before Jane's car sped into the parking lot and came to a screeching halt in front of the phone booth.

"She must really be pissed," Meredith said.

"No," I said. My stomach turned. "She's not driving."

"No," Meredith whined. "She sent him."

Pete didn't get out of the car or say anything during the entire ride back to their apartment. I told him our keys were in Tonic, and that all he had to do was swing by there, go in, and ask Max for Meredith's bag.

"I'm not running any errands for you," he barked, keeping his eyes on the road. He drove aggressively and recklessly. Meredith and I knew not to speak.

Jane was sitting on the couch with a cup of herbal tea when we walked through the door. She gave both Meredith and me a good look over and shook her head.

"This is what you go out like? Christ, Kelly, it's almost November."

"Technically it is November," I smiled.

"That's right," Pete said, fighting with his coat to take it off. "Make a joke out of it."

"Pete," Jane said, turning to him, "I've got this."

"You've got this?" he snarled. "You don't have this. She is out of control. You've tried to talk to her, but she doesn't listen. This stops now. You hear me, Jane? No more. I am not doing this again. I don't care where she is or what mess she's gotten herself into."

"Wow," Meredith gasped.

"That's why I called her and not you," I said, glaring at Pete. "I didn't ask for your help, I asked for hers." I turned to Jane. "I'm sorry. I really am. I didn't know who else to call."

"How about your father?" Pete finally wriggled out of his coat and threw it to the ground. "Let's call Detective Rockport and ask him what he thinks about his daughter being at a bar that was raided."

"This is none of your business," I said to Pete.

"Oh, no, that is where you are wrong," he replied. "It is my business. It is very much my business. You see, before, you were my girlfriend's twit of a sister. But now we're married and she is my wife and soon to be the mother of my child, and I refuse to have her driving around God knows where at one o'clock in the morning trying to find you."

I turned to Jane. "You're pregnant?"

She smiled despite the commotion.

"You know, Pete," Meredith slurred, not processing what he'd let slip. "This whole control thing is really unattractive. I can totally see how it affects you in the bedroom."

Jane's smile tightened and her eyes grew wide. We were toast.

He shifted his death glare to her. "Excuse me?"

"You know," she sighed, as if he were asking a ridiculous question. "The reason why you haven't given your wife the big O. Considering which, by the way, you should be happy she still agreed to marry you."

Meredith was rambling a drunken ramble and there was nothing I could do to stop it.

"Is that so." He turned to Jane, who seemed to have stopped breathing altogether.

Jane locked eyes with me, and not in the soft way she had only seconds before. "You told her," she said. "That was confidential."

"Wait." Pete walked towards us. "You talked about me with her?" He said "her" with such revulsion and disgust. "I can't believe this." He shook his head and turned, walked to the bedroom, and slammed the door shut.

"I can't believe you would do that," Jane said. "I trusted you."

"Jane." I had no idea what to say to her.

"Well, that was a real mature way to handle the situation," Meredith said. She sighed and plopped onto the pullout couch Jane had made up for us.

"Don't," Jane said, looking at me. "I have defended you. I have stood up for you. But I am done now. The only person you seem to care about is yourself. What if I had come out and gotten in an accident? What if Pete had gotten in an accident? He's right, this has got to stop. He and I are a family now, and I have to put us first."

I was sobering up really quickly. There would be no blacking out.

"I'm sorry," was all I could say.

"I don't think you are." She shook her head. "Go to sleep. I'll drive you home in the morning."

I didn't wait for the morning. As soon as she was out of sight, I called Max. I gave him directions and waited while Meredith passed out on the bed. From the living room, I could hear Jane and Pete arguing. Pete sounded so angry, and the pitch of Jane's voice climbed higher and higher. She was really upset.

I looked out the window until Max's car pulled up. He flashed his lights twice and I waved down to him. I woke Meredith up, helped her from the bed, and wrote a quick note on the notepad in the kitchen by the phone.

Jane—I am sorry. I will no longer be your problem.

CHAPTER THIRTY-FIVE

Thanksgiving was awkward, to put it mildly. My mom extended the same invitation to Meredith and her father as she had the year before, but they declined. Meredith's dad had come down with the flu at the beginning of November and was still recovering, so Meredith went back to Philadelphia and I went home.

Jane and I hadn't spoken since the Halloween mishap and I wasn't looking forward to our reunion. It was surprising to me that she hadn't called to talk things over like she usually did. I took it to mean that she really had given up on me. It was either that or Pete had forbidden her from contacting me.

When she and Pete arrived just before dinner, I smiled and wished them a happy Thanksgiving. Jane replied with a quick wish in return and Pete walked around me to hug my mom. I'm pretty sure he would have walked straight through me if he could have.

I didn't tell anyone that Jane was pregnant and I acted surprised when she shared the news with everyone over dessert. Mom practically leapt from the table with joy.

"I knew it," she said. "There has been something different about you ever since you got back from your honeymoon. That is such great news. How are you feeling? Oh, Kelly," she said, turning to me, "what do you think about being an aunt?"

"It's great." I mashed a piece of piecrust against my plate with my fork, not looking up.

"It is great," Mom said, too elated to pick up on any of the tension between me, Jane, and Pete. "And Patrick," she continued.

"You are going to be such a wonderful uncle. You can teach the baby how to play soccer and basketball. Oh, I can't believe this. When are you due?"

"June nineteenth," Jane replied, and she looked lovingly at Pete.

I excused myself from the table when they started talking about baby names and began to straighten up in the kitchen.

"Crazy news, huh, kid?" my dad said when he walked in to start the coffee.

"Yeah," I replied.

"Do you want to tell me what's going on?"

"What are you talking about?" I moved to the sink and started washing a pot.

"You're not being yourself tonight," he said. "Is everything okay?"

"I'm fine, Dad," I said, but I fought back tears. "It's just . . . you know . . . woman things."

"Gotcha." He walked over and kissed me on the top of the head. "I can't help you with that. But if anything else was going on, you know you could come to me, right?"

"Right," I said. I swallowed the lump in my throat.

"Good." He turned to leave, but stopped in the doorway. "You two are sisters. You aren't always going to get along. The important thing to remember is the value of family. Life is too short." Then he went back to join everyone in the dining room.

I continued to wash the dishes as the coffee brewed. Things were so tense that even my father had picked up on it. He knew I was lying to him about my girl problems. Over the years I may have used that excuse one too many times with him. He knew more than he let on, but he never got between Jane and me. Instead he gave his advice and left us to work it out. In our adolescence there had been a couple of times when he'd had to physically restrain us from hurting each other, but he never interfered with the emotional stuff. After the last dish was dried and put away, I went to my room and called Meredith. I didn't need Jane when I had a friend like her.

CHAPTER THIRTY-SIX

It was bound to happen sooner or later. I was hoping more for later, but like my mom always said, love happens when you least expect it. Meredith began to have feelings for a guy. At first she tried to pretend she didn't, that he was just another random, but I could see right through her. I was her best friend.

Eli started out as a random, as they all did. We met him at a party at Molly and Sam's apartment after Thanksgiving break. He was a friend of a friend of Molly's and took an immediate liking to Meredith. He made flustered conversation with her and hovered close all night. I found it annoying. Meredith found it endearing. I was happy when Luke appeared and suggested that we go back to my apartment. Somehow Eli managed to tag along. Back at our apartment, we did a couple of shots and smoked a couple of cigarettes out on the balcony. Eli went along happily with everything. He drew the line, however, when Luke suggested doing a couple of lines.

"Nah, man, I'm cool." He shook his head and turned to look at Meredith.

"I'm good, too," she said. Relief surged through Eli's eyes.

I know for a fact that Meredith would have been into doing a line if Eli had said yes. She enjoyed it as much as I did. Since my nosebleed, we'd cut back considerably, only doing it when the time felt right. And after my stressful Thanksgiving with a sister who wasn't talking to me, the time couldn't have been any better.

Eli watched Luke and me in what I can only describe as horror.

When we were finished, Luke cleaned up the table and we said goodnight and disappeared into my bedroom. I hoped Eli would have disappeared by the time I woke up the next morning. Randoms rarely spent the night and if they did, they were always gone first thing in the morning. We had rules. One by one, however, Eli began to break them all. He stayed over that first night and never left. Meredith didn't seem to mind.

I did. He screwed up everything.

It was kind of cute in the beginning. Meredith was acting coy and he did everything he could to impress the both of us. He brought her flowers and cooked us dinner (I never complained about that). But then he started to monopolize her time.

Eli was twenty and didn't have a fake ID, which meant he couldn't go to Tonic, which meant we couldn't go to Tonic. Meredith felt bad and didn't want to go without him, so we returned to campus parties. Together they laughed and danced and had a good time while I watched, the third wheel. Randoms were supposed to be the third wheel, not me.

I was actually looking forward to finals, because surely Eli would have to study, which meant he would be out of the picture, if only temporarily. But I couldn't even escape him then. He and Meredith studied together in our apartment and at the library. They had coffee breaks and snuggle breaks. I didn't know what had gotten into her. It was all becoming rather nauseating.

"Looks like it's just you and me," Molly said after Meredith ditched us for lunch one afternoon.

"What do you mean?"

"I think Meredith is in love."

"No." I shook my head. "He's just a random."

"How many other randoms have stuck around this long?"

"He'll be gone after Christmas break," I said confidently. "She's just having fun with him right now."

"Well, if not, we'll switch apartments," she suggested. "Sam is never around and I'm getting bored."

I laughed at the suggestion, but deep down, I feared that Eli wouldn't be gone by the New Year and that I would have to endure an entire semester of being the odd one out. I couldn't let that happen.

Apart from all the other benefits of having an apartment off campus, like no RAs, we also didn't have to leave for break when the campus shut down. While everyone packed up and was forced out as soon as finals were finished, Meredith and I hung around. There was no need to go home early. In our apartment, we were home.

"Let's go to Tonic," I said once the campus was vacated, "just you and me. I'm in the mood to dance."

"I can't," she said. "Eli is coming over and he can't get in."

"Let me talk to Max," I suggested. "Maybe he'll let him in."

"No chance," Meredith said. "After Halloween he's been really strict. I don't even think he likes it when we go."

The bars on Main Street had been on the evening news after the Halloween raid. That night, several underage students from Hay U had gotten busted and others ended up in the hospital after hopping a four-foot drop behind one of the bars to escape the police. Tonic was one of several bars slapped with hefty fines and strict warnings. Max always took the fine out of the paycheck of the bouncer who was working the door when the bar got raided. Bouncers never lasted long at Tonic, or on Main Street, for that matter.

It wasn't uncommon for Meredith and me to be rejected by the new bouncers before they knew us. This one guy, Rocky, even tried to confiscate our fake IDs. Rocky could tell from the second he looked at the flimsy plastic that Lexis and Carin were fakes. He laughed to himself, put the IDs in his back pocket, and began carding the next people in line, who were of age and had enjoyed watching our rejection.

When Rocky was finished, I asked for Max. When he refused to call him to the front, I whipped out my cell phone and told him I had Max's number and if he didn't call him, I would.

Rocky stood there for a minute and did his best to stare me down, trying to get a read on me and the situation.

"You're new here," I smiled. "I know that because we are not. I don't want to get you in trouble and I am not trying to give you a hard time. All I ask is that you call Max and ask him about taking our IDs and not letting us in. That's all."

Rocky contemplated his options and finally called Max over his radio.

"Who?" I could hear Max yell over the static.

"Lexis and Carin," Rocky shouted.

"Who?" Max yelled again.

"Tell him Kelly is here," I said.

Using my real name cleared up the confusion and Max gave Rocky the go-ahead. "They're fine," he confirmed. "Stamp them and let 'em in."

Reluctantly, Rocky stamped our hands and opened the door. I cleared my throat and pointed to his pocket. "Can we have Carin and Lexis back, please?"

"Don't know why you want 'em," he gruffed. "They're garbage."

"Yeah," Meredith said, snatching her ID from Rocky's fat hands, "we know."

Rocky lasted two months before he was replaced by Chris P.

"When is the last time we went to Tonic?" I asked Meredith.

"Kelly," Meredith sighed.

"Mer," I sighed back. "I know you're having a fun time with Eli, but I want to have fun with you, too. I think he can survive one night without you. Please?" I stared at her with sad eyes and pushed out my lower lip. "Pretty please? I'll buy you any shot you want."

"Fine," Meredith sighed, even louder than before. "Let me call Eli."

Kelly one, Eli none, I thought to myself when she picked up the phone. He was just a random. There was nothing to worry about. In the end, Meredith would always pick me.

CHAPTER THIRTY-SEVEN

I existed in a state of agony for days after learning of Meredith's death. At first, I refused to believe it. I simply told myself that it didn't happen, that she was in Philadelphia with her dad. But no matter how far I pushed it out of my mind, reality always bludgeoned its way back and I would find myself crying uncontrollably.

I'd forget she was gone if I got caught up in conversation or a television show, but that was only temporary. The sinking feeling would return and somehow I would be reminded of my best friend and the fact that I was never going to see her again. Ever.

I was numb from the shock and pain. Nothing anyone could tell me could make me feel any worse. In my misery, I demanded to know the extent of my injuries and what caused them. In a sick way, I guess I wanted to relive every cut and scrape. But no one gave me all the details. They were protecting me from something. I told them they didn't have to protect me from anything, that my heart had already been broken.

Neither Pete nor Jane came to visit. My mom and dad were always there, mostly staying in shifts. I guess someone had to be at home with my brother. When Patrick came to visit, he came with Mom or Dad. I knew Pete wouldn't come. He wasn't my biggest fan, although I wouldn't put it past him to come only to say I told you so. But it hurt that Jane didn't come. I understood that she was still angry and frustrated with me, but I was in the hospital. Didn't that allow me some kind of pardon?

Besides my parents and Patrick, I rarely had any visitors. Molly and Sam came once but I pretended I was asleep. I couldn't face them, even though they might have had information about the accident. I could have asked Molly, like I had done so many times before, to provide me with the details I so desperately needed.

What I was told was that Meredith and I had been in her car. She was driving and I was in the passenger seat. At some time around three in the morning we came to an intersection, again no details such as the street name were provided. The police believe Meredith ran a stop sign and slammed into the passenger side of another vehicle. We'd spun out of control and slid across two front yards before slamming into a tree.

Unrestrained, Meredith went partially through the windshield. She was dead before they reached the hospital with her.

I, according to my mother, was thankfully wearing my seatbelt. The doctor guessed that my shattered ankle was caused by the pressure of my weight coming down on my foot the wrong way as we crashed into the other car. The laceration on my right shoulder was from the seatbelt tearing into my skin when I lurched forward. The airbag that busted my lip also burst when it deployed, and whatever chemicals were inside scalded my skin. When we hit the tree, my head knocked against the window, which caused my brain to swell, but there was no internal bleeding. The worst of my injuries came from a branch that fell through the windshield and punctured my spleen, hence the bandage around my abdomen.

When I asked about the other car and the other driver, my parents shrugged their shoulders and changed the subject.

Did we kill him or her? I wondered. Is that why they don't want to talk about it?

The hospital sent a grief counselor to talk to me after I displayed signs of "deteriorating mental health." My best friend had died in an accident that I survived. How was I supposed to move forward? How was I supposed to be grateful for my life when she no longer had hers?

"I understand that you were involved in an accident with a loved one who didn't make it," the counselor said after introducing himself as Robert Chappell.

I tuned him out.

Robert talked for an hour about survivor's guilt and the havoc it can wreak on a person's life once their body has healed. "Your mental health will take longer to heal than some of the most serious bodily injuries. You need to talk about it." He brought his sermon to a close and gave me his card. "I'll be back tomorrow."

I was in no mood to appreciate his knowledge or false sentiment, even though what he talked about perfectly described how I felt. But I didn't want to find a way past it or to make it better. If Meredith couldn't live, then I didn't want to, either.

Once he was out of the room, tears began to pour down my face, one after the other. My best friend died in an accident with me by her side and I couldn't remember one thing about it. I had no idea what her last words were. Was she happy? Were we laughing? Her smiling face flashed in my mind. I saw her brown curly hair, her freckles, and her perfect white teeth. Suddenly, I couldn't breathe. I reached for the call button and within minutes another syringe was going into my IV and I was floating away on an emotionless tide.

CHAPTER THIRTY-EIGHT

Robert Chappell came back the next day. He began by asking me how I was feeling. Bad question. I looked at him out of the corner of my eye and then turned and stared out the window. I didn't want to talk to him as long as he was going to ask me stupid questions.

"Anger is not uncommon in these situations," he said, as though we were engaged in a normal conversation. "In fact, it is one of the stages of grief. Have you ever heard about the stages of grief?"

The sky was a cold slate and the clouds were sparse. I hadn't been outside in a long time.

"I want to go outside," I replied.

"I don't know how possible that is right now," Robert Chappell replied. "But I can ask the doctor."

By referring to him by his full name in my head and out loud, I kept him distant. There was not and would not be any familiarity between the two of us.

"The first stage is denial. Have you experienced any denial?"

I am denying this conversation.

"Have you told yourself the accident didn't happen? Have you tried to convince yourself that your friend is still alive? If you have, it is perfectly normal behavior. What I want to talk to you about, though, is the pain you may be experiencing."

Pain only began to describe how I felt. Anguish was a little better, torture better than that.

"The only way for you to feel better is to talk about it."

"What if I don't want to feel better?"

"You say that because you are angry," Robert Chappell answered.

I turned to him. "You know what I am angry about?"

"What is that?"

"I have been in the hospital for a long time now, and my bitch of a sister is still too angry with me for something I did to come and visit me. That makes me angry."

"Okay," he said. "Why is she upset with you?"

"I told Mer—"

Saying her name took my breath away. I started again.

"I told someone something that she told me in confidence."

"How did she react when she found out that you'd betrayed her confidence?"

"She told me she was finished dealing with me."

"When was the last time you spoke?"

"I saw her on Christmas."

"You didn't speak?"

"No. Her husband doesn't particularly like me, either."

"Why do you say that?"

"Because he hates me."

"Why?"

"He thinks I drink too much and I'm reckless."

"Do you drink too much?"

"I'm twenty years old."

"That's not an answer."

"I don't drink any more than my friends."

"I see," he said, and began writing something on his notepad.

"So are you going to judge me now, too?"

"I'm not here to judge, Kelly. I am here to help you."

"Whatever."

"Were you drinking the night of the accident?"

"I don't know. Nobody will tell me anything."

"She was," Cecile said from her side of the curtain.

"I'm sorry, but this is a private conversation," Robert Chappell said.

"No," I said loudly. "What do you know, Cecile?"

Cecile and I didn't talk much, despite her best efforts. She was sick and lonely. I was depressed. It wasn't a good combination.

"The doctor was talking to your father about your blood alcohol level. It was twice the legal limit."

"Do you remember consuming large amounts of alcohol that night?" Robert Chappell asked in a lower voice.

"No," I replied. "I don't remember anything."

"Is that common for you, to drink to the point where you don't remember what happened?"

"Sometimes."

"Does it bother you that you don't remember what happened the night of the accident?"

Another stupid question.

"You would think she would be concerned enough to come and see me. If she was in the hospital and we were fighting, I would go and see her. Maybe it's because she's pregnant."

"Oh, dear," Cecile sighed.

"What?" I asked. Robert Chappell rolled his eyes to show his discontent with Cecile's interruptions.

"Oh, nothing," she said. "I forgot to call my granddaughter back."

I didn't remember any mention of a granddaughter.

Great, I thought, the only person who has information for me is losing her mind.

The nurse interrupted our session when she came to take my vitals and administer my feel-good medicine. Whatever they were giving me was good stuff. It made my body almost numb. If only it could do the same to my brain.

"I think this is a good place to pick up tomorrow," Robert Chappell said, and he rose from his seat. "Have a good afternoon, Kelly."

So I was drunk the night of the accident. That wasn't hard to believe. We were out in a car, which meant we didn't go to Tonic. I wondered if Max knew what happened to me. I hadn't asked for my cell phone or any of my personal belongings. I wondered who had them.

"Hey, Cecile," I called through the curtain.

"Yes, dear," she replied.

"What else do you know about the night of the accident?"

"Oh, I don't know," she said. She sounded uncomfortable.

I called the nurse and asked her to move the curtain between Cecile and me. I wanted to talk face to face.

Cecile was a large woman. Her skin was pale and wrinkled and spotted from too much time in the sun. She had dark brown eyes and whiskers on her chin.

"No one is telling me anything," I said. "I'm trying to remember the night of my accident, but it's hard. What other things have you heard about that night?"

"I don't know if I should." She looked cautiously over to the nurse's station as though they were eavesdropping on our conversation.

"Please," I begged. "Anything could help me remember."

"The doctor said you were very drunk and that illegal substances were present."

"Who did he tell that to?"

"Your father. He had just relieved your mother."

"What did he say?"

"He wasn't very happy."

"What else?"

"Your mother and father talked about a girl named Lexis. She was involved in the accident."

"Did they say anything about the other car?" I asked. "Did the other driver make it?"

Cecile tensed. "I'm not sure," she said. "Last I had heard, she was in the hospital on a different floor."

"This hospital?"

"Yes, but I think that's enough information for today. Why don't you try to get some sleep?"

The doctor did say sleep was the best way for my brain to heal. So I asked for something strong to knock me out. He told me I was on enough medication to help.

The truth was, I had no problem falling asleep. The trouble was the nightmares. Every night they repeated, always starting the same, flashing the same vivid sequence through my restless mind. The only variance was when and how I woke up. The first night I had the nightmare was the worst, because I didn't know it wasn't real. I didn't know what to expect, so I allowed my mind to go along for the ride.

Meredith and I were at Tonic, except it wasn't Tonic. It felt more like an underground cave. Max was there but he was older, a lot older. He had wrinkles at the corners of his tired eyes and strands of white hair that were trying to camouflage themselves among his darker locks. I was older, too. Max stood with his back against the wall of bottles, in front of the vodka, observing everything.

"Tell me something good, girls," he sighed.

"You look hot in that shirt," Meredith said, winking at him.

Max managed half of a smile and then looked at me. "How about you, Kel, are you ready to quit your job and liven this place up?"

Job? I had a job? That was when I began to realize it was a dream.

"Don't tempt me."

"What are you waiting for?" he asked, moving in closer. "Anytime you want, the job is yours."

In my dream, I felt the same rush of excitement I always did when Max approached me. For a fleeting moment, I thought it was going to turn into a very, very nice dream.

"When you can offer benefits and a consistent salary, let me know and I'll give my two weeks."

"You wouldn't have to worry about that if you let me take care of you." He refilled my drink.

I was an observer behind the bar watching myself, Meredith, and Max interact. Is that what I was going to look like in a couple of years? Meredith didn't appear to have aged at all. Then I realized, even in my dream state, that Meredith was dead and she was never going to age. My heart ached at the realization, but I didn't want to wake up. I refused. I wanted to see her again, be out with her again.

"So what has you so down tonight?" I saw myself ask Max. "The weekend is just beginning."

Max shrugged his shoulders and had begun to offer an explanation when he was called to the front door.

"You should consider dating him," Meredith said, smiling at me when he walked away. Her smile was so warm, infectious.

"Maybe," I smiled back. "He is sexy in an older, more experienced kind of way."

"Please," Meredith choked on her drink. "I think you may be the more experienced one."

"Shut up."

"Seriously, I bet you could teach him a thing or two, if you haven't already."

"You can teach me anything you want," an overly cologned, slick-haired guy said, taking the stool next to me.

"Sorry," I replied, reaching over and grabbing Meredith's hand. "I'm into chicks."

"That makes two of us." He was eyeing Meredith up and down. "The more the merrier. What are you drinking?"

Meredith decided to have some fun. "Sex on the Beach," she said. "And my girlfriend here is having a Screaming Orgasm."

Slick giggled a childish laugh, like he was looking at a stolen pornographic magazine for the first time. "I'm Carlo."

"Carlos," I replied. "I'm Ginger and this is my friend Candy."

He paused, looking at us, knowing those weren't our real names but obviously deciding it didn't matter. "It's Carlo," he corrected, "no S."

"Well, Carlo no S," Meredith smiled. "It's nice to meet you. But as my friend here told you, we are not into guys."

"One night with me could change that," he grinned.

"You're not thinking of cheating on me?" Max had returned. He placed his hand on my shoulder.

"I would never dream of it, dear." I smiled and winked at Slick.

"Chicks, huh?" he asked, and he slithered away.

"Who was that?" Max asked as he returned to his post behind the bar.

"Just another guy hopeful of converting Meredith and me."

"You two need to be careful with that. One of these days someone is going to call your bluff."

"Who said we're bluffing?" Meredith smiled playfully at Max.

"Trouble," he laughed. "You two are trouble."

As the crowd in Tonic grew, so did the volume. Meredith and I held onto our valuable stools and sat back and observed the expanding crowd before us. The underage girls were easy to spot— holding their drinks anxiously and bopping up and down to the music—so unaware, so clueless. They had no idea what type of creatures were lurking amongst them, waiting for the opportune time to pounce.

No one had told Meredith and me about those men, the ones we'd thought only existed in scary movies but in actuality were clean cut and well dressed, hiding their evil behind soft eyes and free drinks. No, no one had warned us about them. That was a lesson we'd had to learn for ourselves.

"We have to go," Meredith said suddenly, turning to me, panicked.

"What? Why?" I glanced at my watch. It was stuck on two a.m. "Where do we have to go?"

"Home," she said. She looked almost frightened.

"Why?"

"Your sister is waiting," Meredith answered, grabbing her purse.

"Jane? Why is she waiting?"

"I can't tell you," she replied. "We have to go now."

I felt the dream coming to an end but I didn't want to give up Meredith and our fun. I wanted to dance with her, to shoot down guys. I refused to follow her.

"Kelly," she said, pulling at my arm, "we have to go now."

"No, we don't," I insisted. "We can stay."

"I'm going," she said, "with or without you."

"That's not what we do," I said. "We come together and we leave together."

"So why won't you come with me now?"

Suddenly we were in a car. It was hard to see.

"We should have left sooner," Meredith said. She was consumed with fright. "It's going to happen now. I can't stop it."

"What's going to happen?" I asked. Her panic was transferring to me.

"I'm going to die," she said. She turned and looked at me. "You are going to kill me."

"What?" I felt sick. "Nothing like that is going to happen. But you need to look at the road. You're not watching the road."

"It doesn't matter," she replied. "I'm already dead."

"MEREDITH!" I screamed. "Look at the road! You have to watch the road!"

"You're going to kill her, too," Meredith said as two headlights came into view. "Just like you killed me, you are going to kill her."

"Who?" I demanded. "Meredith, watch out!"

Our car collided with another car and I was ejected from the seat. My body was thrown against the windshield and ricocheted hard back against the passenger seat.

A bloody Meredith turned to me. "It's too late," she said. "I'm already dead."

I woke up drenched in sweat with my mother and two nurses hovering over me. My heart could not have been beating any faster.

"Are you all right?" my mom asked. "You were screaming."
I started to cry.

CHAPTER THIRTY-NINE

After Jane's Thanksgiving announcement, my mom found it necessary to supply me with all the information I could possibly need to know about Jane's pregnancy. She had yet to pick up on the fact that we weren't talking.

"Poor thing is sick as a dog," she said. "It must be a girl. Girls make you sick."

"Is that so?" I asked.

"Well, I wasn't half as sick when I was pregnant with Patrick as I was when I was pregnant with both of you."

"I thought you said I was a good pregnancy."

"You were," she answered, "but that doesn't mean I wasn't sick in the beginning. I would have lost so much weight if it wasn't for your father forcing me to eat. He was such a big help. Do you think Pete is helping Jane?"

"Why don't you ask her?"

"I'm sure she wouldn't tell me the truth if he wasn't. Maybe you can ask her next time you talk. Just bring it up in conversation."

"You want me to be your informant?"

"I just want to know she's being taken care of. She's in a fragile state."

"I'm sure she's fine," I lied. "And that Pete is taking great care of her," I lied again. He was the type of guy that would either be extremely helpful or not want anything to do with it. Being the control freak that he was, he was probably hovering over her constantly, even while she was vomiting.

"I just hate to hear how much she's throwing up."

"Yeah, at least when I throw up it's because I had a great time the night before," I blurted out. Big mistake.

"I don't like that, Kelly. How often do you vomit because of your partying?"

"I was just joking, Mom." I forced a chuckle. "I can't tell you the last time I threw up." I could, but I chose not to.

"Good," she exhaled. "It makes me nervous when I hear all those stories about girls your age getting all liquored up. Every year I read about some kid who drank too much and ended up dead. Can you imagine what their parents have to go through? That would just kill me."

"Well, you don't have to worry about that," I assured her. Jane's pregnancy was obviously making her more than a little emotional.

Christmas dinner was just as uncomfortable as Thanksgiving once Jane and Pete arrived. Our mother's attention shifted immediately to Jane's growing belly (she wasn't showing that much) and how she was feeling. Jane thrived on all the attention. For once, the limelight was back on her, and she wasn't going to give it up. Pete, too, enjoyed the focus that was placed on his handiwork (his words, not mine), and smiled like the proud stud he believed himself to be. I listened to the conversations and kept quiet.

My dad confronted me just before we took our seats at the dinner table. "From the looks of it, you and your sister are still at odds," he said.

I shrugged. "You could say that."

"This has been going on for some time now."

"Yes."

"Have you tried to work things out?"

"Not really."

"Well, you should. In the spirit of Christmas and the New Year, let everything that has happened this year go, and start the new year off fresh."

Though it sounded like a good idea, getting Jane alone wouldn't be easy. Pete didn't let her out of his sight for long, especially around me. And technically, I wasn't the one who wasn't talking to her. She was the one who wasn't talking to me. So really, she should have been the one to offer the truce. But it was Christmas, and in the spirit of the holidays, I took my father's advice and approached Jane when Pete went to the bathroom.

Jane was standing by the counter in the kitchen and I slid up next to her and asked quietly if we could talk.

She turned, coldness in her eyes. "About what?"

"About what happened on Halloween."

"The part where you called me collect, drunk at one thirty in the morning asking for a ride? Or when your friend criticized my husband for his performance in the bedroom?"

Yep, she was still angry.

"I said I was sorry."

"I heard what you said." Her cheeks were starting to flush. "But the thing is, I don't believe you. I didn't believe you then and I don't believe you now."

"Jane," I said quietly and calmly, "I don't know what else you want me to do."

"I want you to learn your lesson, to face the consequences of your actions. And the consequence of what you did is losing my trust and my respect. You have to earn it back."

"How?" I was starting to get concerned because Jane's face was changing colors rapidly and perspiration had started forming along her hairline.

"Everything all right?" Pete had snuck up behind us.

"Fine," I hissed over my shoulder.

"No," Jane said faintly, "I don't feel so good."

Pete forced his way between Jane and me and put his arm around her waist.

"Tell me how, Jane," I said as Pete ushered her towards the living room.

"Not now," she panted, right before collapsing into Pete's arms.

The commotion that ensued was filled with hysterics (my mother), anger (Pete), and rational behavior (my father). Pete carried Jane over to the couch as he screamed at me, asking what I'd said to get her so worked up. Mom ran and got a wet washcloth for Jane's forehead. My father stepped in when Mom picked up the phone to call 911. He took the phone from her trembling hands and told her to go get a glass of water for Jane. He then turned to Pete, who was still berating me, and told him to get some pillows from the guest room to prop Jane's feet. Pete began to protest but my father imposed his authority and Pete scampered upstairs.

Jane was awake on the couch, her face as white as the snow that was falling outside. She was shaken. Pete returned in seconds and gently rested Jane's ankles on the pillows. Everyone stood over her, unsure of what to do. I retreated to my bedroom. I had done enough damage for one day.

As planned, Meredith and I both returned to our apartment the afternoon before New Year's Eve. The first thing we did was smoke a cigarette on the balcony. It was freezing outside and the cold metal railing was unforgiving against my skin, but it felt good to be home where I belonged, devoid of judgmental brother-in-laws or angry sisters.

"So, I have decided that I am going to quit smoking as my New Year's resolution," Meredith said, exhaling a long cloud of gray smoke.

I shivered. "Seriously?"

"Yeah," she said. "I don't need to smoke. It's really not good for us. Maybe you should think about quitting, too."

"Wow. Where is this coming from?"

"Nowhere." Meredith stubbed out her cigarette. "I was thinking of resolutions, and quitting smoking seemed like a good one."

I thought about it for a second. Smoking was bad for my health, and if Meredith was going to try to quit, then I guessed that I could, too. "All right." I flicked my butt over the railing. "I'll try, but only if you don't resolve to stop drinking or anything crazy like that."

"I'm not going to give it up," she said. "But I was thinking about cutting back a little."

I stood there in horror as she slid the balcony door open and let the warm air from inside rush out. "What the hell happened to you over Christmas?"

"You know my dad has been sick lately. He doesn't look good at all, and it's because he doesn't take care of himself. He said he got into bad habits when he was young and by the time he realized what he was doing to his body, it was too late to correct them."

"You bought that?"

"I'm serious," Meredith said. She picked up her bag from the floor and walked back to her bedroom. I followed her.

"Mer," I said as she began to unpack her clothes. "You're only in college once. I get the smoking thing, but you can't cut back on your drinking. Who am I going to go out with?"

"I'll still go out with you," she said.

"It won't be the same," I pouted.

I sat in silence on her bed as she pulled clothes from her bag and slid them into her drawers. I watched as she meticulously removed a green-and-brown striped sweater from the bag and unfolded it. Wrapped up neatly under the sleeves and collar of the sweater was a framed picture of her and Eli. She smiled at it briefly before standing it on the dresser next to the picture of us getting our matching tattoos.

"Seriously?" I got up and examined it.

"Jealous?" she asked.

"Not at all." I put it down and went back over to her bed.

"Good," she smiled, "because he's coming back for New Year's."

"You can't be seriously considering ringing in the New Year with him."

"Why not?" she laughed. "He is my boyfriend."

"He is not," I replied, repulsed. "He is a random. Randoms don't become boyfriends."

"He did."

"What are we going to do?" I asked. "He can't get into Tonic and there's no one on campus to throw a party."

"Why don't we have a small party here? I already talked to Molly and Sam, and they're in."

"We're going to Tonic," I insisted. "That was the plan. We are sticking to the plan."

"I'm not going without Eli."

"God, Meredith." I sprang off her bed and stormed out of the room.

"What?" she asked, following me out into the hall between our bedrooms.

"You are becoming one of them and it is making me sick."

"One of who, exactly?" she questioned, on the edge of aggravation.

"One of those girls who ditches her friends for a guy."

"I'm not ditching you," she said. "I suggested having something here so we could all be together."

"He is ruining everything."

"You are ruining things," she said, "not him."

"I'm going to Tonic for New Year's," I said as I walked into my room and slammed the door behind me.

"I don't know why you're being this way," she called through the door. When I didn't respond, I heard her walk away and shut her door.

What just happened? I thought. Meredith and I never fought. Never. Even when we disagreed, we always ended up laughing it off and doing shots. Makeup shots were the best. But there weren't going to be any makeup shots between us that night.

I called Molly to see what she and Sam wanted to do. "You still want to switch apartments?"

"Random still around?"

"Unfortunately."

"Told you."

"Since you know so much, how do I get rid of him?"

"Don't get in their way," she replied.

"What?"

"That is one of the easiest ways to keep him around. If you fight with Meredith, you will just drive her towards him."

"I don't want that."

"Just be patient. Chances are he won't last that long and things will be fine."

"I hope you're right about that. When are you guys coming back?"

"Tomorrow afternoon."

"Do you want to go to Tonic?"

"I thought Mer said you guys were having a party."

"I'm going to Tonic," I said. "Meredith can have a party if she wants to, but I am going to Tonic."

"Is this about Random?" Molly asked.

"Maybe."

"I'm into doing whatever," she said. "And I know Sam is, too. But we are not going to get caught in your little spat. I'll call you when I get back tomorrow."

I hung up with Molly thinking about what she said. I didn't want to push Meredith any closer to Eli. I didn't want to push her away at all, so I decided to apologize for my childish behavior. I still wasn't talking to Jane, and that bothered me, but not as much as fighting with Meredith did. Five minutes of not talking to her made my stomach hurt.

Meredith's door was shut when I walked into the hallway, so I tapped on it, peeked my head in, and asked if we could talk. She was on the phone and told whomever it was that she would call them back.

"I love you, too," she said before hanging up. I told myself it was her father. It had to be. I couldn't tolerate the idea of it being Eli. There was no way they were at that stage yet.

"I miss us," I said.

"We haven't gone anywhere," she said, and she smiled. "We just have a new addition."

"I miss going to Tonic."

"I know," she sighed. "And I miss that, too. But Eli feels bad when I go without him, and I don't think that's really fair. He'll be twenty-one in April. We can go then. I promise."

She was thinking ahead to his birthday? I was about to say something, but I remembered what Molly had said about playing it cool.

"You can go tomorrow night if you want," she said. "I won't be mad."

"Do you want me to stay here?"

She shrugged. "I think it would be fun, but do what you want. I know how much you like to go there."

"I like to go with you." We sounded like a lesbian couple.

"Well, I can't go without Eli."

"Fine." I let out a loud sigh. "We'll have a party here." It pained me to compromise.

"Great." She ran over and hugged me. I got the feeling that our argument upset her just as much as it did me. "It'll be a lot of fun."

Two years in a row I had wanted to go to Tonic for New Year's Eve and two years in a row something prevented me from doing so. Maybe I wasn't meant to ring in the New Year with Max.

Our party turned out to be entertaining; not the best, but not the worst. Molly and Sam came over with some guys that lived in their building and Eli arrived with a couple of his friends. We drank, smoked (Meredith declined, I said it wasn't the New Year yet), and shouted the countdown watching the ball drop in Times Square.

"It must be so amazing there," Meredith said in awe.

"We'll go next year." Eli pulled her in for a kiss.

Molly turned and looked at me. I opened my mouth and inserted my index finger. Molly laughed. I rolled my eyes. I don't know what was worse, ringing in the New Year with strep throat or watching as your best friend was lured away from you. The year was definitely not kicking off the way I wanted it to.

CHAPTER FORTY

I woke up in the hospital one afternoon to find Max sitting in the chair next to my bed watching me.

"Hi," I smiled.

"Hey," he replied.

"How's the weather?" I asked, looking out the window. It felt like forever since I had been outside and I was craving the fresh air. When it was clear, I imagined myself having lunch on a blanket in the sun. When it was raining, I yearned to feel the cold drops land on my head. I wanted to be out of bed, out of that room, out of the hospital.

"It's cold." He looked at me with soft eyes. "You would freeze." I was always cold and he knew that. "I would have come sooner, but I didn't know."

"How did you find out?"

"Molly came to see me. She thought I would want to know. I've tried to call you but it went straight to your voicemail. Now it says your mailbox is full."

"I don't know where my phone is."

"How are you doing?" he asked. And unlike with everyone else, his question didn't feel rhetorical. He cared to know how I was feeling and I wanted to tell him.

"You didn't happen to sneak in a shot for me, did you?"

"Kelly," he said. He took my hand. As he moved closer to me, I caught a whiff of his scent and began to cry. Max was safe. He was home for me in that displaced world.

Without asking him to, Max got up and curled up next to me in bed. Though I couldn't see her through the privacy curtain, I could sense Cecile straining to hear what was going on. Max stretched out his right arm and placed it gingerly around my head. His body snuggled up tightly against mine and it felt so good, so right.

"She's dead," I sobbed.

"I know." He kissed me gently on the side of my head.

Together we lay in bed. Max held me silently while I cried myself to sleep in his sound embrace, lulled by the familiarity of his touch and smell.

I could have slept like that forever. But as soon as my father entered the room Max jumped out of my bed and stood at attention. My father stared him down, from head to toe and back again.

"Dad," I said, sitting up as best I could, "this is Max. He's a . . . ugh . . . friend of mine from Hay U."

It was obvious that Max was well out of college and uncomfortable in my father's presence.

I smiled at Max. "Max, this is my dad."

My father extended his hand towards Max. "Detective Rockport."

Max shook his hand. "Nice to meet you, sir."

I was thankful when the nurse came in to administer my medication, breaking the awkward silence.

"I was just coming in to check on you," my father said, keeping his eyes on Max. "I'm going to grab a quick bite with your mother in the cafeteria and then we'll be back."

"Oh, is she here, too?" I asked, wondering why she hadn't come up with him.

"No," Dad said. His eyes darted from Max to the window. "She's on her way. We'll see you in a little bit." He nodded at Max, "Max," and then disappeared behind the curtain.

"Can you bring me a piece of pie?" Cecile asked my father. She was on a restricted diet which didn't allow sweets. Dad laughed and told her he wouldn't be responsible for her getting sick even though my mother had already snuck her snacks a couple of times.

"I haven't slept like that in a while," I said, smiling at Max, who had pulled the chair close to the bed.

"Glad I could help." He smiled back at me.

Something hit me when I looked into his eyes, and it wasn't the usual lust. In fact, for the first time ever since knowing Max, I had not one sexual thought in my mind. Yet there was something pulling at my stomach, at my heart, at my mind.

"What?" he asked.

"Nothing." I shook my head. "I am just really happy to see you."

"Me too," he said. "I thought something was up when I didn't hear from you. I went by your place a couple of times. Then I thought maybe you finally got tired of me."

I laughed a little. "How could I ever get sick of Horse?"

It was weird. My parents had known me my entire life and loved me more than anyone else in the world, yet I felt more comfortable and more at peace with Max there by my side than I did with them.

"Can I ask you something?" I asked.

"Sure."

"Do you know what happened the night of the accident? Because I don't remember anything. Did we come in to Tonic?"

"For a little bit, yes."

"Did we have a good time?"

"From what I could tell," he answered. "But you didn't stay very long."

"Do you know why not?"

"Eli was having a party. You weren't very happy about that."

I tried to process the information to see if I could get any sort of flashback or tidbit of recollection.

"What was I wearing?"

Max chuckled to himself and I realized how ridiculous it was asking a grown man to remember that.

"Sorry," I smiled. "I'm just trying to remember something."

"Don't you have the clothes here with you?"

"They had to cut them off of me," I said. "My mom threw what was left out."

"Oh." He turned white for an instant. "Sorry."

"Don't be," I replied. "Can you please try to remember what I was wearing, or anything descriptive about that night?"

"Okay, give me a second to think."

During the silence that ensued, Cecile turned her television on but kept the volume low.

"You came in right after happy hour," he said, looking at the floor while he racked his brain. I didn't say anything for fear of interrupting.

"You were wearing your jean skirt with black tights underneath," he said with a wry smile. "I remember that because you told me you weren't wearing any underwear."

Cecile gasped. Max's eyes grew wide and he stopped talking. As I waved her off, I had a quick vision of me in my tights, skirt, and black heels. I had a beat in my head, but no lyrics.

"Was I wearing my off-the-shoulder black sweater?" I asked excitedly, as part of the evening began to come into focus.

Max thought for a moment. "Yes," he chuckled. "You told me you weren't wearing a bra, either."

Cecile sucked her teeth three times in a row.

"What else happened?" I asked, eager for another flash.

"You sat at the bar for a while. Meredith only did one shot because she said she had to drive to the party. You rolled your eyes and did two in a row." That sounded about right. "You got her to dance for a little bit but when some guy tried to dance with the two of you, she sat back at the bar. You danced for a little bit with the guy. I didn't appreciate that."

"Sorry."

"It's okay. You got bored with him pretty quickly and came back to the bar, too. Meredith said she wanted to go and you said you wanted to stay. I had never seen you two bicker like that before."

"Do you know what the party was for?" I wanted to avoid the topic of discontent between Meredith and me.

"I want to say Eli's roommate, but I'm not sure. You should ask Molly."

"Were she and Sam at Tonic, too?"

"No." He shook his head. "Meredith said they were going to meet you guys at the party."

I was concentrating on Max's every word and willing my mind to remember something so hard that my brain began to ache. "What else happened?"

"I don't know," he said, looking apologetically into my eyes. "You asked for another shot, I went back to the office for a couple of minutes, and you were gone by the time I came back out."

"I didn't join you in the office?"

"I wish you had."

"What time was that?"

"I have no idea."

"And that was it? You never heard from us again?"

"No. Trust me, if I had known what was going to happen I would have never let you leave."

"But Meredith wasn't drunk when we left Tonic?"

"Not at all."

"Was I?"

"You were feeling good, but I've seen you much worse."

"And she was happy, Meredith?"

"Yeah," Max replied. "She was."

I wanted to know, in the hours leading up to Meredith's death, how she was feeling. I needed to know she was enjoying herself, because it would have killed me to know that her last moments weren't fun.

Having part of the night put together was a big step towards getting back some semblance of what happened. Knowing that Molly and Sam held the key to the rest of the night was huge.

Max didn't stay long after he'd recounted everything that he knew. Without my father in the room and with the curtain pulled, he leaned in and kissed me on the lips before he left.

"Call me when you get out of here," he said. "I'll come and take care of you."

I kissed him back gently and felt the urge to beg him to stay. Instead, I watched sadly as he left.

Things between Max and me had progressed a little more towards the serious side after New Year's. I began to feel bad when I spent time with Luke or fantasized about anyone other than Max. That being said, I wasn't too quick to give Luke up, and I didn't have any plans to do so.

I knew I'd be on my own for Valentine's Day, because Meredith and Eli had been talking about their plans since January. He was taking her to an authentic French restaurant twenty minutes outside of Haysville and then to a movie of her choice.

"Authentic just means expensive, not good," I told her.

"What do you know about French restaurants?" she asked.

"What do you?" I returned. "You know they probably won't have French fries."

Meredith started laughing and I couldn't hate on her plans with Eli anymore. After all, it was Valentine's Day. I had to cut her some slack. He was entitled to have her to himself for at least one day.

Then she asked the pretentious question. "What are you going to do?"

In all fairness, it was only pretentious because she had a boyfriend and I didn't.

"What do you think?" I answered. "Molly and I are going to Tonic. Who knows, maybe Cupid will strike us."

"Maybe he already has," she giggled.

"What are you talking about?"

"When are you going to stop pretending you don't care about Max?"

"I never said I didn't care about him."

"You act as though he's just another random, and in your words, randoms don't last that long."

"Things are great the way they are," I said, defending my position. "There is no reason to screw them up."

"You're in love," she smiled, sliding a slinky black dress over her shoulders. "Everyone can see it except for you."

Tonic was packed by the time Molly and I arrived on Valentine's Day. There were no stools left at the bar and none of the tables in the back were available so we were forced to stand, crammed in the corner against the bar. Max was running around helping the bartenders. He didn't notice us until about an hour after we had arrived.

"What can I get you?" he asked quickly, no friendly banter or Valentine's Day wishes.

"Happy Valentine's Day to you too, Scrooge," Molly said, making a face at him.

"Sorry," he replied, "but we're slammed tonight. Do you want a drink or not?"

Molly ordered from the specials menu for us. "Two Cupid's Cocktails."

"Okay." Max turned and walked away. He reappeared five minutes later with two martini glasses filled with red liquid and garnished with three maraschino cherries. "Enjoy."

I didn't see Max much at all that night and was feeling rather dejected. Molly had found a really good-looking random who passed all of her tests, so she allowed him to go home with her. I didn't want to get in the way of her romance so I didn't protest when she said they were ready to leave. The line was six people deep to get to the bar where Max was, so I left without saying goodbye.

Molly, Random, and I grabbed a cab and they dropped me off in front of my apartment. She felt bad for bailing on me and didn't want me to walk home alone. I jumped out of the cab as soon as it pulled up along the curb, thanked Molly and the random, and trudged up the stairs to my apartment, alone and bitter. I wouldn't say I was sad, because that would mean I had feelings about having a man in my life, which I didn't. I was bitter because everyone was going to get to have sex that night except for me.

I changed into my Hay U sweats and plopped in front of the television with a tub of mint chocolate chip ice cream. Of course, all that was on were romantic comedies and love stories. I settled on a Lifetime Original Movie about a teacher who was seduced by her student. I was allowed some sort of guilty pleasure on Valentine's Day.

It was after three when my phone rang. I had drifted off to sleep and what was left of the ice cream had melted into a green pool at the bottom of the carton with floating black specs. I contemplated not answering the phone, but when I saw the caller, I changed my mind.

"I hope you weren't planning on sleeping alone tonight," Max said.

"I'm not decent," I replied stubbornly.

"That's never been a problem before."

"I look disgusting," I replied. "And I just ate half a gallon of ice cream."

"Let me up," he said.

"You're here?" I got up and ran to the window and peered down.

"Of course," he smiled up at me. "The only question is, do you want to be my Valentine or not?"

I ran to the door and buzzed him in. I could hear him climbing the steps rapidly, at least two at a time. When I opened the door, he presented me with three sunflowers. I wanted to cry. What's happening to me? I thought. I wasn't one to get sentimental or emotional.

"Happy Valentine's Day," he smiled.

Pushing my feelings to the back of my mind, I wrapped my

arms around his neck and jumped up, wrapping my legs around his waist. For me, Valentine's Day was not about love or mushy feelings. It was about sex, and that is exactly what I planned on having.

CHAPTER FORTY-ONE

My dad appeared content and almost relieved to see that Max was gone when he returned after dinner with my mom. Though there were no signs of Max, Dad looked around thoroughly before he relaxed.

"Your father tells me you had a male visitor," Mom smiled, sensing my father's preoccupation.

"Yeah, Max. He's a good friend of mine."

"Your father says he looks older."

"How old is older?" I smiled.

"How did you meet him?"

Interesting question, I thought. How did I want to describe the circumstances of that relationship?

"We met on Main Street one night," I answered.

"What does he do?"

"He manages a place called Tonic." By not categorizing the type of place, I wasn't lying. Being deceitful, maybe. "He's a good guy," I felt the need to add.

She searched for more information. "Is it serious?"

"Max and I are just friends," I answered.

"It didn't look like you were just friends," my father said.

"He was really good friends with Meredith, too." I choked up, hating my father for making me say her name.

"All right." My mom shot my father a look. "Are you hungry?"

I shook my head. "Not really. I forgot to order dinner."

Staying in the hospital was sort of like staying in a hotel; a budget hotel, but a hotel nonetheless. I slept in a bed that wasn't mine, had the sheets changed when they got dirty, and ordered room service every day. Though the selection of meals wasn't awful, it was repetitive, and I'd begun to lose interest in eating altogether.

"You have to eat something," my mom said. "You need your strength."

Of all the things I needed, strength was not one of them.

"You know what I need," I said, "is my cell phone. Have you seen it?"

My mother looked over at my father.

"It's in the closet," he replied. "Who do you need to call?"

I told a white lie. "No one. I just wanted to check my messages and see who called. Max said my mailbox was full. Who knows, maybe Jane even called to check on her only sister who's in the hospital."

Mom straightened in her chair and Dad walked over to the closet.

"It was beeping a lot that first night," he said, rummaging roughly through a plastic bag. "I think the battery died after a while."

"Would it be too much to ask you to go to my apartment and get the charger for me? It's plugged in next to my bed."

My mom's eyes darted in my father's direction. He had retrieved my phone and tried to turn it on. When it didn't power up, he placed it back in the bag and closed the closet door. So much for checking my voicemail. "We need to talk about your apartment," he said.

"What about it?"

"Your mother and I don't think it would be such a good idea for you to go back there alone. Meredith's father has already moved her stuff out."

"What?" The sound of her name sent chills down my spine. "When did he do that? Why did he do that? What if there were things I wanted?"

"He wanted to get her and her belongings back to Philadelphia," Dad answered.

"Poor man," my mother said. Tears streamed down her cheeks. "He has been through so much."

"I can live there by myself or with Molly," I said, clinging to the hope that I could stay in the apartment, that I could hold on to Meredith somehow.

"It's not just that," my mom replied. "We are concerned about your behavior and how you ended up in the accident."

"Oh, so it's my fault?" I snapped. "The whole thing is my fault?"

"No one is saying that," she said, placing a hand on my knee. I jerked it away from her. "But we talked with Pete, and he agrees that bringing you home might be the best thing for everyone."

"Pete." I spat his name as though it were dirt. "You talked to Pete about me? The asshole can't come visit me, but he can talk all the shit about me that he wants. What exactly did Pete say, and since when did you begin consulting him on me?"

"Kelly," my father interrupted in a stern voice. "That kind of language will not be tolerated."

I cowered slightly.

"We have been very understanding of your situation and what happened up until this point. Our first concern was to make sure you were okay. When we heard you were in an accident, all we wanted to know was whether or not you were all right. When they told us that one of the two passengers had died en route to the hospital, it almost killed us."

Being a detective, my father was awarded special privileges when it came to sensitive information.

"But at some point we have to address your blood alcohol level the night of the accident."

They knew. I knew they knew, but it was still surprising to hear my father talk about it.

I dropped my head back onto the pillow and closed my eyes tightly. Why did Max have to leave? Couldn't he have rescued me? Maybe I could move in with him.

"So, what, am I going to move back home with you and Mom?"

"You already have," Mom said. She smiled uncomfortably.

"What?" I yelled. Cecile ruffled her blankets on the other side of the curtain.

"Your father had a talk with the landlord, and he agreed to terminate the lease because of the circumstances."

"That easily?"

"He didn't think it would be that difficult to find other tenants," my dad replied.

"Just like that, I'm out. What about my stuff?"

"Your father and Patrick took care of it."

I didn't even want to think about the things my father and brother had discovered moving me out of my apartment. I had condoms in my nightstand and dresser, pictures, thongs, all things that men you are related to should never come in contact with. I shook the image of my father and brother packing my underwear from my mind.

"What about school?" I asked.

"You'll be able to go back once you have healed."

"There are only two months left in the year."

"Your teachers have been very understanding. You can complete the work from home and online if you feel up to it."

"What if I don't?" My head was beginning to pound.

"We didn't discuss that."

"Why didn't you tell me any of this before?"

"You need your strength," my mom repeated. "There is no sense in getting all worked up about little details."

"This is my life!" I cried out. "My best friend is dead and now you are taking me from everything I love and bringing me back home. That all may be little details to you, but they are pretty big things to me."

"Damn it, Kelly." My father's tone made me catch my breath. "You are not the only one affected by the accident. You are not the only one who was involved. Your—"

"Ray," my mother interrupted with a sharp tone of her own. My father stopped talking immediately and backed down. "Kelly," Mom said, turning to me, "we have all been through a lot, and we are not trying to do anything to upset you. But the fact of the matter is that you and Meredith were both intoxicated at the time of the accident. From what Pete told us, your behavior has been immature and lacking in good judgment for a while now. The worst thing that we can do as your parents is to throw you back into the exact environment that caused this mess."

I decided it would be best if I stopped speaking. They had already broken my lease and moved me out. Meredith's dad had taken any fragments of her from my life. Pete had ratted me out. With the exception of Max coming to see me, it was an awful day.

"Congratulations," I heard as the doctor came through on his evening rounds. He was on no particular schedule. Sometimes I saw him at five thirty, other times as late as ten. It didn't matter much to me, since I wasn't going anywhere. "Looks like you'll get to go home tomorrow."

"Really?" I sat up, giving him my full attention for once.

"Yes, really," he smiled. "You seem to be managing the pain a little better, and your wounds are healing nicely. You'll have to stay in that cast for a while, but after that you should be good as new."

Good as new. Can anything ever be as good as new? Sure, the scar on my stomach would fade, the laceration on my shoulder would heal, and my ankle would mend, but I wasn't going to be good as new, not even close. My body may have been able to repair itself and fool the rest of the world into believing it was better, but I would always know. I would always carry in my mind and in my heart the knowledge that the world had lost one amazing person and that it was partly, if not all, my fault.

CHAPTER FORTY-TWO

In all the movies I have ever seen that take place in hospitals, the roommates always find a way to connect and enrich each other's lives, especially when there is a considerable age gap between them. That didn't happen with Cecile and me. I had a chance, in the beginning. When I first came to, she felt bad for me and my parents. She offered words of encouragement when she heard me struggling and an open ear if I needed to talk, but that all changed when Robert Chappell began coming to our room.

She learned things about me that she didn't like. She learned what kind of person I really was. Cecile's conversations with me became less frequent as my sessions progressed. And after Max's description of how I'd behaved when I saw him the night of the accident, she shut down altogether. Maybe she'd thought I was someone I wasn't. She didn't even congratulate me when I got the news about being released. Maybe she was just jealous.

Robert Chappell came to see me first thing in the morning on the day of my release. He was delighted to see the smile on my face when he walked in. I think he thought I'd had a breakthrough.

"I hear you're leaving us today, Kelly," he said as he assumed his position in the seat by the bed and adjusted the tablet on his lap.

"Yes, sir," I replied. "My parents should be here soon to pick me up."

"Have they talked to you about going home?"

"Have they talked to you about me going home?"

"We have discussed it, yes."

"And what do you think about it?" I asked.

"I think that it's vital for you to be around loved ones during this upcoming time of healing."

"Do you speak like that all the time?" I asked, feeling perkier than I had in a long time.

"Speak like what?" He repositioned himself slightly.

"Vital and upcoming time of healing," I said, glancing at his left hand. No wedding band there; I wasn't surprised.

"You seem to be deflecting the situation," he said with a hint of attitude.

I rolled my eyes. "I am not deflecting anything. I'm going home to live with my parents," I said. "There's not much I can do about it."

"Does that anger you?"

"You must think I'm an angry person, Robert Chappell."

He paused and looked up from his notes at me.

"I think you are angry right now," he said. "Despite your games and attempts to mask your emotions, I can see what's going on."

"Oh, yeah?" I taunted him. "And what exactly is going on?"

"I'm worried for you, Kelly. I am worried that you are not feeling your emotions."

"Isn't that all you can do with emotions?" My sarcasm was coming back to me. It may have been a bad time for Robert Chappell, but it was perfect for me.

"You know what I mean," he sighed.

"I'm going home today." I looked out the window with a smile, knowing that the fresh air was awaiting my return. "That's what I'm feeling today. I am happy today because I am leaving."

"I believe it would be in your best interest if you sought a professional outlet once you got settled in back home."

"What," I feigned injury, "you don't want to see me as an outpatient?"

"You live too far," he replied, unsure as to whether or not I was joking. He didn't know what was going on at all. Robert Chappell was a joke. "However, I have requested that you come back at least once after you have been home a couple of days to talk to me."

Robert Chappell wrapped up his spiel on the stages of grief and self-destructive behavior before handing me his card and wishing me luck.

The morning nurse was my next visitor, announcing that she would be coordinating my discharge. I didn't listen to anything she had to say. Once she left I sat back and watched the television. I caught the tail end of the weather and smiled when the meteorologist declared it a cool but sunny day.

I got dressed on my own after asking the nurse to get my clothes for me. It was hard to maneuver my pants around my cast, but my mom had the insight to only bring sweatpants for me to wear in the hospital. I was getting used to the infringements on my mobility and learning how to cope. Showering still required assistance, as would going up and down stairs. But other than that, I felt pretty self-sufficient.

Mom arrived not long after the doctor signed off on me one last time. She was happy to see me dressed and ready to go.

"How are you feeling?" she asked. I could tell she felt bad for the route our discussion had taken the previous evening.

"Ready to get out of here," I smiled. "Can we go?"

"Absolutely." She returned the smile. It had been a while since I'd seen that smile. "Your father is pulling the car up."

"What took you so long to get here?" I asked as she helped me into the wheelchair.

"Your father and I had some last-minute errands to run."

Because I was leaving, Mom pulled back the privacy curtain. Cecile had often complained that the only view she had was of the nurse's station, and Mom wanted her to be able to see out the window.

"Goodbye, Cecile," I said, waving from the wheelchair like Miss America. "Take care of yourself."

She frowned. "You take care of yourself."

"Here you go, Cecile," my mom said, placing a Hostess dessert cake on her tray. "It was nice talking with you."

"You too, dear," Cecile said, smiling warmly at Mom. "Good luck with everything."

"Thank you, Cecile," Mom replied, and with that, we were out of the room of my captivity. I felt so high, so elated.

"What was all that about?" I asked Mom.

"All of what?"

"Why did she wish you well with everything when I'm the one who was injured?"

"She probably meant it for both of us."

I didn't buy it, but I also didn't want to put any more thought into it. As my mom wheeled me down the long white hall, I looked down at the cast on my foot and the plastic bag of belongings on my lap. I had experienced a serious auto accident and survived. Moving back home with my parents shouldn't be that difficult, right?

With each ding of the elevator as it descended the floors to the lobby, my smile grew larger and larger. When the doors opened, I felt, only for a second, that I had the strength to get up and run through the lobby and out of the revolving door, cast and all.

"Here we are," Mom said, tapping my shoulder. "It'll be so nice to be back at home."

"It will," I said. I offered no debate as to the definition of home. "The first thing I want to—"

My sentence was cut short as a familiar figure came through the door. My heart started to pound and I felt a tremor begin in my hands.

"Pete. What a surprise," my mom said, sounding weary but not genuinely surprised.

He didn't respond at first, and instead glowered down at me.

"What a surprise, indeed," I said, matching his glare. "Are you just coming now to wish me well, Judas?"

"Kelly," Mom said.

"Where is your turncoat wife? Is she too ashamed to come and visit her only sister in the hospital? And what?" I pointed to the bouquet of flowers in his hand. "Are those for me?"

"You stupid, stupid little girl," he snarled at me.

"Pete, I don't think this is the time," my mother said with a shaky voice.

"No," he replied, "I think it is the perfect time."

"The perfect time for what?" I began to feel uncomfortable.

"I didn't come to see you," he replied. "I could care less how your progress is. I have been here every day for the past three weeks, watching as my baby girl fights for her life because of a decision that you made. You made me fight with my wife. You made me fight with her, and she almost died. I almost didn't get the chance to tell her that I was sorry and that I loved her because of you."

"I don't understand," I thought out loud. Jane was hurt?

"How could someone as small-minded and self-absorbed as you

possibly understand? I'll tell you this." He was frothing at the mouth. "If my daughter dies, I will never forgive you. If anything happens to Jane, I will never forgive you."

My heart stopped. "Jane's here? Why didn't you tell me?" I turned to my mom, regretting all of the nasty things I had thought about her.

"You needed your strength," my mom replied, her default answer.

"What happened?" I asked.

"You!" Pete yelled, loud enough to quiet the private conversations around us. "You happened. And because of you, your sister is in the hospital and your best friend is dead. Whose lives are you going to turn upside down next?"

"I have to see her."

"No, you don't," Pete growled. "You don't have to see her. You don't have to talk to her. In fact, I would prefer it if you didn't even think about her."

"She's my sister," I said.

"And she is my wife," he shot back. "As her husband, I forbid you to see her or the baby at all."

"Jane had the baby?"

Pete laughed a psycho-killer laugh. "She didn't have the baby. She had a car accident and the baby had to be delivered."

I looked to my mom for some explanation, but she stood as still as a statue. "What happened?"

"I can't do this." Pete shook his head violently, tightening his grip on the bouquet in his hand.

"Please," I begged, unsure whether I was ready for the truth or not. "Please tell me what happened."

"Jane was hit by a drunk driver," my mom finally said. "The impact was so forceful that it sent her into premature labor."

"A drunk driver?"

"Stop sugar-coating it," Pete hissed towards my mother. "Your sister was hit by you and your dead friend."

CHAPTER FORTY-THREE

Any happiness I had about leaving the hospital came to an abrupt end after my confrontation with Pete in the lobby. I wanted to lurch at him and beat him with my cast for the way he spoke about Meredith, but at the same time I understood his anger. My sister's injury hit me just as hard as the way Pete had said, "you and your dead friend." A fully charged shock raced through my body. There were no attempts to disguise Pete's contempt for me. He didn't care how brutal he came off. I couldn't blame him.

We were silent on the ride home from the hospital, during which I did a lot of thinking. I hadn't realized that my mom and dad were commuting every day to be with both Jane and me. Jane . . . I had put her in the hospital.

After learning that my sister was the other driver and she was in intensive care, things started to make more sense. My parents had split their time so one of them could be with each of us throughout the day. Cecile's negative reaction to me had to mean that she knew about Jane. That's why she had wished my mom luck with everything. I knew Mom was crying a lot, even after I woke up. And Jane—I'd thought such nasty things about why she hadn't come to visit me. I hadn't even asked once if there was something wrong with her. What was wrong with me?

It wasn't long before my tears found their familiar paths down my cheeks. I sniffled as quietly as I could, not wanting my parents to notice. My mother, still shaken from Pete's outburst, appeared too deep in thought to notice anything. My father looked back in the rearview mirror every so often. When he did, I closed my eyes.

There were no signs of life as we pulled up the driveway at my parents' house. The bare trees cowered in front and the grass was brittle and brown. I preferred it that way.

When Dad shut the car off, Mom commented on how quick the ride had seemed. She was the first one out and opened my door, helping me steady myself on one foot. Seeing that we would be able to make it into the house without his assistance, my father grabbed my bag and hustled to open the front door.

The house seemed to have grown larger in my absence. The kitchen was enormous, the living room massive, and the dining room yearning for a feast. But there would be no feast, no celebration. My homecoming was not a joyous occasion and would not be marked with any salutation.

"Are you hungry?" Mom asked.

"No," I said, hobbling to the stairs. "I think I'm going to lie down."

"I think that's a good idea."

I smiled weakly and turned back to face the staircase. One at a time I climbed each step, holding onto the railing. My breath became shorter each time I pulled myself up. Sweat trickled between my breasts, down the small of my back, and inside my cast. My leg would definitely be itching later.

The pain in my body crept to my nerve endings as I inched up the stairs and was overpowering by the time I made it to the top. I endured and dragged myself the four feet down the hall to my bedroom.

I pushed the door open with too much force, causing it to hit the doorjamb with a loud thud. Mom called up to make sure I was all right. I reassured her and entered the room, closing the door softly behind me. To my surprise, my father had set up my room like my bedroom in my apartment. My bed was in the corner away from the window (I hate it when the sun shines on my face in the morning) and my pictures sat on top of my dresser with my jewelry box and my perfume. I closed my eyes tight, trying to convince myself I was back on Lexington Ave. That it was all a horrible nightmare. But when I opened my eyes, I wasn't back in my white room with green carpet. Instead, peach walls and cream carpeting surrounded me. The view from the window wasn't a cluttered city street, but rather a dead lawn and the doghouse that had been empty since Misty died when I was a sophomore in high school.

The depression took hold of me before I even felt it coming, and all I wanted to do was die. I fell onto my bed and cried myself to sleep.

I'm not sure what time it was when my mom came to check on me, but the dark night sky had replaced the gloomy afternoon. She brought my painkillers and the antidepressant that had been prescribed for me just in case I needed them. She rationalized that it was a long and emotional day and that it probably couldn't hurt. I said "whatever," swallowed the pills like a psych patient in a mental ward, and went back to sleep.

I slept off and on the entire first week that I was home. My parents didn't pressure me to do anything, and my plan was to think as little as possible. I ate the minimum, took my pills, and slept the maximum. Molly and Sam called the house and asked if they could come and visit. I told my mom I didn't think that would be such a good idea. She rejected them for me.

Mom told me Jane had to leave the hospital without the baby. Marnie, who they'd named after one of Pete's grandmothers, was fighting to stay alive. No one said out loud that the odds were stacked against her fragile two-pound frame. I asked if I could go and see her. Mom said it wasn't a good idea. She said we had to respect Jane and Pete's wishes.

"Jane doesn't want me to see the baby either?" I asked.

"She is still upset," my mother replied. "She needs some time. Once Marnie is out of the hospital, things should get better."

"Do you think Jane will talk to me?"

"I'm not sure that is a good idea right now."

"Does she hate me?"

"You're her sister."

"Does she hate me?"

"She's angry, Kelly." Mom gave me a look that signified that we should stop talking about Jane. "Why don't you try and get some rest?"

All I had been doing was resting. Yet that was her answer whenever things got awkward or uncomfortable: I needed my rest. But I didn't need rest. What I needed were answers. My mind was plagued with questions about the accident and that night. I had yet to have another glimmer of memory since Max visited me.

The plastic bag from the hospital was still in the corner of my closet where I'd thrown it the day I got home. It was a reminder of the accident and I didn't want to see it. I also hadn't had the nerve to go through it and see what it contained. But I needed my cell phone, so I had to go through it.

I pulled out random articles one by one until I found my phone, which was still nestled in its pink rubber case. I pressed the button that turned it on and held it for a couple of seconds. Nothing. It hadn't magically charged in the closet like I'd hoped it would, and I had no idea where my dad had put my charger when he packed up my apartment. I staggered back to my bed and felt along the outlet on the wall. Just as it had been plugged in at the apartment, my charger jutted out from the wall there in my bedroom at home. My eyes filled with tears at my dad's thoughtfulness.

I fished the cord from the base of the charger up the wall and tried to plug it into my phone. As it so often did, the case protruded just enough over the part where the end of the charger went in to prevent it from charging correctly. Knowing that hadn't changed brought a smile to my face. The case that had caused me so much frustration was actually a calming factor for once. I placed the black wire on the bed next to me and pulled the rubber from the top of the phone and slid it off the bottom.

The phone was caked with a dark substance that blended against its slick black background. I chipped away at it with my fingernail and caught my breath when it began to flake away. My heart stopped as tiny specks of red fell to the carpet. I looked inside the case. It was blood.

I was in the bathroom within seconds heaving into the toilet. My appetite had yet to return, so thankfully there wasn't much to purge. Normally the sight of blood doesn't elicit any response from me. But seeing my own blood and knowing there was a slight possibility that it was Meredith's made my stomach explode. The phone had been wiped down, I could tell. The hidden evidence, however, was left behind.

Hearing the commotion, my mother came running up the stairs to my side. She hadn't left me once since the day I came home from the hospital.

"There's blood," I sobbed into the toilet when she asked me what was wrong.

"Blood?" her voice was panicked. "Where? Are you vomiting blood? Ray!" she screamed down to my father.

"No," I said, shaking my head, "on my phone. There is blood on my phone." I dry heaved.

My father made the same frantic dash up the stairs and joined us in the bathroom. "What is it?"

"Her phone," my mom said. "Go get it."

He returned to the bathroom with a solemn look of understanding. "I'll wash it for you," he said.

"I don't want it," I replied, staring into the disturbed water.

My mom patted my back. "We'll get you a new one."

She sat with me until I felt strong enough to stand and certain I wasn't going to vomit again. Then she ushered me back to my bed and took away all traces of my phone and the hospital bag. The next morning when I woke up there was a box on my nightstand. In it was a new, fancy phone. Phones were easily replaced. Best friends were not.

The phone turned on easily and indicated immediately that I had messages waiting. I wasted no time in checking each one. The first call had come in on the night of the accident from Molly.

"Kel," she said in her impatient tone, "We're here. Where are you two? You better not be off with Max. Call me."

The second message was from a more discontented Molly. "Seriously, if you two don't get here soon, we are leaving. This place is gross."

We must have arrived before she left, because there was no third message from her. The time on her second call was eleven thirty-seven p.m. I began a mental timeline of the evening, starting with Tonic and continuing to the party around midnight.

The third message I listened to was the hardest. It was Meredith, and she wasn't happy.

"Kelly," she said, panicked. My skin prickled with goose bumps at the sound of her voice. "Where are you? Eli said you stormed out when I went to the bathroom. You win. I'm in the car, but I don't know which way you went. Call me please." The time stamp on the message was one fifty-two am. We'd had an argument and I left. Where did I go?

The next message was from Jane at two o'clock on the dot. "Kelly," she sighed, "I'm on my way. I picked up the phone in the kitchen when you called. Please call me and let me know where to pick you up. I'm headed down to Main Street right now."

Something happened. I knew that much. Something happened

and I got angry and left the party. Between one fifty and two, I'd called Jane. From her message, I assumed that I got Pete on the phone and he refused to let me talk to Jane. Whatever I said must have worried her enough to ignore his protests (he had to have put up a fight) and leave in search of me. The thought of her climbing into the car at such a late hour with her protruding belly made me shudder.

I listened sadly as the next message began to play. It was Meredith again, more panicked than her previous call. "Kel," she said, sounding as though she was about to cry, "where are you? I'm sorry. I should have left with you right away. I'm driving down . . . what the hell is this street called? Trinston Ave!" She rejoiced to find some type of landmark. "Do you know where that is? Because I sure as hell don't. I am going to keep calling you until you . . . hey," she whistled. "Hey, sexy lady, do you want a ride?"

I heard my voice, distant in the background. "Are you talking to me? I don't get into cars with strangers whose boyfriends are assholes."

"We'll talk about that later. Please get in the car," she begged.

I'd had a fight with Eli. There was no shocker there.

"Fine, but I am not going to sleep with you." The anger in my voice had relented.

"Come on, baby," Meredith laughed. Hearing her infectious laugh brought a smile to my face and tears to my eyes. I would never hear that laugh again. "I'll show you a good time."

A car door opened and closed and the call disconnected. I saved the message.

The remainder of the messages had come in after the accident took place. The first was from Pete, panicked that it was after three and he hadn't heard from Jane.

The tone of the messages from that point on escalated in concern and disbelief before turning to sadness and sympathy. I stopped listening after the fifth acquaintance called with yet another apology. I appreciated their thoughts, but I wasn't interested. I deserved no one's remorse or pity. The calls from earlier in the night made it clear. I was the reason for the accident. I caused two of the people I loved most in the world to leave their comfortable surroundings and brought them out into the late night, leading them to disaster. I was a murderer.

CHAPTER FORTY-FOUR

The sun was shining brightly into my room as I awoke from yet another restless night. Armed with the incriminating voicemails from the day before, my subconscious had unleashed a fury of nightmares. Meredith and Jane interchanged places, laughing one minute and crying the next.

In one particularly horrible segment, I dreamed that Jane went into labor and I had to drive her to the hospital because no one else was around. It began harmlessly enough with me helping her into the car, making sure we had her overnight bag and video camera. But as I backed out of the driveway, I lost control of the car. Jane screamed as the car swerved from left to right. I tried to brake but couldn't. I tried to put the car in park, but it wouldn't shift gears. Jane accused me of being drunk. I swore I wasn't. Meredith appeared in the back seat laughing hysterically. The other drivers on the road were swerving to avoid hitting us, blaring their horns and shouting their disapproval.

Everything I tried failed. Meredith told me to give up and enjoy the ride. Jane told me the baby was coming. I turned to reassure her but she was gone, replaced by a pool of blood. Meredith was gone too and I was alone, driving into a truck head-on. I screamed and closed my eyes as tightly as I could as the headlights drew closer and the automobiles collided.

I awoke to my father picking me up off the floor. My mother, white as a ghost, was by his side. My scream was real; everything else was not.

"I have to see Jane," I said hoarsely.

"We'll see," my mother answered. "Try and go back to sleep for now."

I slept restlessly for the remainder of the night. Sitting up in bed, I squinted until my eyes adjusted. It made no sense how the sun could shine so brightly in a world filled with such tragedy and loss. Nothing made much sense to me.

My father had left for work by the time I made it down to the kitchen but my mom was happy to see me so early and offered to make me breakfast. The first two weeks that I was home, I barely left my bedroom. However, I slowly began to force myself out of the room for at least two meals a day. I was anything but consistent. I didn't feel the need to eat at regular intervals nor did I really want to see anyone. But things had changed after I listened to my messages. There were calls that needed to be made to get the answers to the questions that lingered in my mind. Starting with a solid breakfast couldn't hurt.

Molly was the first person on my list. She held the key to my memory of the party. I was ready to unlock that door. I dialed her number just after lunch. The butterflies in my stomach were flapping violently enough to break free and take over my entire body. She answered on the third ring.

"Kelly?" She sounded happy to have me calling.

"Hey, Mol," I replied.

"Oh my God," she sighed. "How are you? I have been thinking about you. Sam and I both have. Did your mom tell you we called? That we came to the hospital?"

"Yeah," I answered. "Sorry I haven't called you sooner."

"Don't be," she said. I could almost see her shaking her head. "So how are you?"

"Not great." A lump found its way into my throat. I will not cry, I will not cry, I thought.

"Did you get everything from your apartment? I helped your parents pack. I have a box here for you when you're ready for it. I didn't think they needed to see everything you kept in that place." She laughed lightly, unsure as to whether it was all right to laugh with me.

"Thanks," I replied, trying to keep lightness in my voice. It came out more like a sigh. "So, what's been going on with you guys?"

"Same old thing," she answered, returning to a more serious tone. "Sam's working. I'm not."

"Have you been to Tonic?"

"Not much, but Max said he went to see you. I think he misses you."

I smiled. "Listen, I was wondering if you could do me a favor."

"Sure," Molly replied, sounding eager to help. "What do you need?"

"I need you to tell me what happened the night of the accident, at the party."

Molly was silent for a while.

"Are you still there?"

"Yeah," she stuttered. "Nothing really happened that night."

"I know I got into a fight with Meredith."

"How do you know that?"

"She left a message on my cell phone."

"Oh."

"So what happened?"

"Why do you want to do this now?" Molly asked. "Why don't you wait a little longer?"

"It's been killing me not knowing, Mol. Please, I have to know why we were in the car. Please?"

"Fine," she sighed. "You weren't happy about hanging out with Eli and his friends that night, but we all promised Mer we would go. You two agreed to stop at Tonic for a little while first. I waited until Sam got home from work and then we were supposed to meet you at Eli's friend's place. It was somewhere past the Hill. When Sam and I got there, you and Meredith weren't."

"I got those messages, too," I interjected.

She laughed. "The place was such a dump. We were about to leave when the two of you came bouncing in, singing 'Old Apartment.'"

"I thought I wasn't happy."

"You were drunk," Molly answered. "Anyway, we all started drinking then and the party started to get crowded. More people showed up than Eli and his friends wanted and they started to panic. Instead of handling it like they should have and asking a couple of people to leave, they kicked everyone out, including the randoms we were talking to.

"That really seemed to bother you, and you kept complaining to

Eli that he was killing your action. He told you he had plenty of friends for you. You pointed at his friends and then practically laughed in his face. You should have seen how angry he got, Kel. Even Meredith couldn't believe it."

"So what happened?"

"I'm not sure what he said. He claimed not to have said anything, but all of a sudden you picked up a bottle and threw it against the wall by his head and started screaming at him. You said he called you a whore."

"Did he?"

"I don't know," she answered. "Meredith tried to calm you down, but you wouldn't listen to her. You said she had to pick between him and you. Sam and I asked you if you wanted us to take you home, but you demanded that Meredith take you."

Come together, leave together, I thought.

"Meredith said she was too drunk to drive. You pouted and told her if she didn't drive you that you would walk and never speak to her again. But we were off campus and you had no idea where we were, so she thought you were kidding. We all did. Sam and I asked you one last time before we left if you wanted to come with us, but you refused to leave without Meredith.

"I called your cell when we got back to our place and you didn't answer, so I called Meredith. When I asked her how you were doing, she panicked. She said you were gone and that she thought you went with us. She said she had to go and find you. That was the last time I talked to her."

"Why didn't Eli go with her? Why did he let her leave alone?"

"He said she was out the door before he could stop her. He tried." Molly grew quiet.

"What?"

"He is having a really hard time with this," she said. "He blames himself for letting her go."

I didn't say anything. She didn't need to tell me about blame.

"When did you talk to him?"

"At the funeral."

My heart exploded. I missed her funeral. How could I not have thought about that?

"When was that?"

"A couple of days after the accident."

"How was Mr. Short?"

"Not good," Molly replied with a long exhalation. "He didn't really talk to anyone."

"I bet he hates me," I thought aloud. "Eli probably hates me too. Do you hate me?"

"What?" Molly sounded surprised. "Why would I hate you?"

"Because I killed our friend."

"Kel, you didn't kill her."

"It's my fault she was in the car."

"It was an accident. I don't hate you. No one does."

If only I could believe her. Mr. Short and Eli definitely hated me, as well as Pete. My only hope was that there was room in Jane's heart for forgiveness.

Molly and I spoke a little while longer about menial things before I told her I had to go take my medicine. She didn't ask for details and I didn't give her any. In reality, I had to go so I could call Jane.

Jane's cell phone went unanswered when I called. I decided not to leave a message. Instead, I called information and asked for the number to the hospital. I called the hospital and asked for the neonatal intensive care unit where Jane had been spending all of her time, praying that Pete would not be there.

Thankfully, she accepted the call. I was half expecting the nurse who answered the phone to come back and say Jane was busy.

My sister picked up the phone, her voice groggy and tired. "Hello?"

"Please don't hang up," I said. I had hoped to speak with courage and determination, but my words came out no louder than a whisper.

"Kelly?" she said with disbelief.

"Yes," I answered.

"How are you?"

The question threw me off. Of all of the reactions I'd imagined, her inquiring about me was not one of them.

"I . . . ugh . . . I'm okay. How are you? How is Marnie?"

"We're doing all right. She's a fighter," Jane said with the strength I'd hoped would be in my own voice.

"Can I come see you? Her?"

She inhaled and exhaled slowly while I waited with bated breath.

"I don't think you should," she finally answered. My heart sank.

"Jane, I am so sorry. I really want to see you. I want to meet Marnie."

"I promised Pete I wouldn't let you visit," she stated without emotion. "It's too soon."

"You know that Meredith died?" The words seemed to blurt themselves out of my mouth.

"Yes," she replied. "I was sorry to hear about that."

"I can't lose you both." The tears surfaced and my throat choked up.

"You haven't lost me," Jane replied.

"It feels like I have," I said. "You haven't called and now you won't let me see you. I know that this is all my fault, but you have to forgive me."

I transformed into a babbling, sobbing mess.

"I'm sorry, Kelly, but I have more important things going on right now that I need to focus on. I should get back to Marnie."

"I love you," I replied.

"I have to go," she said, and she hung up the phone.

I'd never told her I loved her on the phone before, and yet the words were spoken. I needed her to realize what she meant to me and how sorry I was. She couldn't hate me if she told me she loved me, but she hadn't, so what did that mean?

CHAPTER FORTY-FIVE

When my mom insisted that I go see Robert Chappell to talk about how I was feeling and about my violent dreams, I didn't object. It was the perfect excuse to get a ride to the hospital and a way to see Jane. Sure, she was cold on the phone, but I doubted she would be like that in person.

The neonatal intensive care unit was like nothing I had ever seen before. All the machines, beds, and equipment that were present on the other floors were there, but shrunken considerably. Small beds were occupied by the tiniest of babies everywhere I looked. I didn't know babies could be so tiny outside of the womb. It was a lot busier than I expected, too. Monitors were beeping, nurses bustling from baby to baby. It was surreal.

Known as the NICU for short, the unit catered to the sickest of babies. IV lines no thicker than fishing wire ran from their infinitesimally small hands to clear liquid bags that provided nourishment. Some of the babies had plastic tubes as slender as the IV lines running from their noses. They were so frail. It made me feel silly for ever complaining about getting needles.

The nurse on duty pointed me to where Jane sat hunched over a plastic case. As I approached, I saw that her hand was inside the case and she was caressing Marnie's little arm. She was watching her baby so intently that she didn't notice me until I spoke.

"So this is the little diva who made you so sick?" I asked with a weak smile, sliding a chair over close to her.

Jane jumped at the sound of my voice.

"What are you doing here?" she asked.

"I had to see you . . . the baby."

"If Pete finds you here . . ." She looked past me to the entrance of the unit.

"I've missed you," I said. I'd resolved in the car ride over to be completely honest and to hold nothing back. I didn't have anything else left to lose.

"You need to go," she said. She turned her attention back to Marnie.

"How is she doing?"

"She's getting stronger every day."

"And you?"

"I just want to bring my baby home."

"I'm sorry, Jane. I am so sorry. If I could change places with you and Meredith so I was the only one hurt, I would. I wouldn't even think about it."

"Do you think that would make everything better?" She turned to me with a stern glare yet spoke very softly. It was important to keep quiet in the NICU.

"I do," I answered.

"So instead of trying to get my daughter better, I would be grieving my sister? She would still be growing inside me, but you would be dead. Mom and Dad would be grieving their daughter? I don't see how that would make anything better, except maybe for you."

"I'm just saying—" Fresh tears fell from my eyes. "You wouldn't be in the hospital. You would be having a baby shower and waiting for Marnie to arrive. Meredith would be with Eli and her dad, finishing up another year of college."

"And what, your life doesn't mean anything?"

"It's not worth all of this." I shook my head. "No."

"You've never valued your life." She looked up at me. "That is the problem with you, Kelly. You never realized how great your life was. You just took it for granted. You thought nothing bad could happen to you, so you lived recklessly. Every time you escaped a situation unscathed, you chalked it up to being lucky without learning your lesson. Maybe now you will."

Jane spoke directly but with very little emotion. I wanted her to yell at me, to scream at me. It was the least I deserved.

"Pete hates me," I replied.

"He's angry, yes."

"No, he hates me."

"He's too occupied with Marnie to put any thought into you," she replied.

"Do you hate me, too?"

"All of my love and emotion is going to this little girl right here," she said. "I am not going to waste an ounce of energy anywhere else. She needs me. Besides, what do you want me to say to you? I told you so? What good would come of that?"

"I thought maybe if you yelled at me that we could move past this and I would feel better. But all I feel is worse."

"You should," she said. "You can't fix this one with an apology. Not even to yourself."

"I know," I said. I hung my head. "I've tried."

I looked around at the tiny beds, feeling my heart break a little more with each baby. Some were awake, most were asleep. Some even had their eyes taped shut. My attention was diverted to a couple of special beds spread out across the room.

"Is that . . ." I pointed to what appeared to be a tanning bed for a baby. "Are those . . . ?"

Jane followed my stare. "Kind of," she said, "but these babies need it. It's not the senseless frying you do."

"Oh."

"Is Mom here?" Jane asked.

"She's in the chapel. She thinks I'm meeting with the counselor."

"You should go see him," she replied. "I don't want Pete coming in and seeing you here."

"When can I come back?"

"I don't think you should."

Tears began to flow from my eyes. "Jane, please. I need you."

"I need time, Kelly. I think we all do."

"Can you at least tell me what happened that night? Then I'll go. I promise."

She sighed. "You don't remember anything?"

"Not really."

"You sounded pretty drunk."

"Yeah, so I've been told. Why did you come to get me if we still weren't talking? I thought you were finished with me."

"You sounded scared. You were crying hysterically, talking

about how some guy called you a whore and how Meredith chose him. I've never heard you like that before. This time was different."

"I wish you would have let me be," I sighed.

"You can't look back, Kel. What's done is done, and nothing you do or say will change that."

I couldn't help but wonder if Jane's attitude on the situation would have been different if she had lost Marnie. If I hadn't lost Meredith, would I have been as remorseful as I was?

I played the what-if game a lot in the days following my visit with Jane and Marnie, and never came out ahead. In fact, one particular scenario kept creeping into my mind when the pain got to be too much. What if I had died instead of Meredith? What if Jane hadn't come to get me? What if I had hooked up with one of Eli's gross friends? What if I'd killed myself? Would I feel better then? Come together, leave together . . . Live together, die together.

CHAPTER FORTY-SIX

The piercing noise of the saw the doctor used to cut the cast off my leg brought vivid flashbacks of the accident and the Jaws of Life that were used to extricate me and Meredith from the car. I closed my eyes and prayed for the strength to get the images out of my head.

When he cracked the cast open, the cool air hit my leg and shocked it back to life. My skin was dry and scaly and disgusting. The pen I'd lost while trying to scratch an unreachable itch was found. It wasn't the first one the doctor had come across. "You'd be amazed at what I've found," he smiled. I felt freed from the weight that had been dragging me down. I was ready to walk unhindered.

I looked down at my foot and wiggled my toes to make sure everything still functioned correctly. All five moved on command. My tattoo was still there, a reminder of the friendship I had lost.

"You are going to notice some weakness," the doctor said. My eyes remained fixed on the black ink on my foot. "You may even have some pain." I tuned him out completely.

The first thing I did when I got home was take a shower. It had been such a pain to wrap my cast in plastic and tape it off at the top to keep moisture out that I'd begun to limit my bathing. I wasn't seeing anyone or making any plans, so hygiene had become less important to me.

My mom asked me what was wrong on the way home from the doctor's office. She'd thought I would be happier to have the cast off. I told her I was. She didn't buy it. I stared at my foot the entire way home, thinking of my tattoo and of Meredith. I felt hollow.

Everything I did once the cast was off felt foreign. I had forgotten what walking normally felt like. Climbing the stairs was a breeze. Once I was in the bathroom, I took off my clothes, turned the water on in the shower, and stepped in. When the water came shooting out of the showerhead, I let it hit me directly in the face.

I stood motionless in the shower, allowing the water to beat down on my head and run down my back. Slowly I began to wash my hair, unable to appreciate the aroma of the shampoo, despite how long it had been since I'd last done this. I washed my skin over and over again, hoping to somehow dissolve like the soap in my hand. When there was nothing else left for me to do, I turned the faucet all the way to the right. It took a second, but the water turned ice cold and sent a chill down my body. Finally, some degree of feeling. I stood there until I began to tremble and could no longer take the cold. I turned the water off and exited the shower and the bathroom.

I stood in front of the closet looking at the clothes hanging in the same way they had in my apartment. Unsure of what to wear and not wanting to think about it, I grabbed the darkest clothes I had.

Once dressed, I asked my mom if I could borrow her car to run an errand. When she asked me what I needed, I shrugged and told her I just wanted to get out and be alone. She nodded as though she understood and told me to drive carefully.

I made a left out of our development, drove three miles and picked up the highway. I followed the interstate forty miles to Philadelphia, to the cemetery where Molly said Meredith was buried. I knew where to find her. I had been there with Meredith to visit her mother once.

It took some time, but eventually I found it. The dirt was still fresh on top of the earth. I fell into a ball and cried. It was cold for spring, yet I was numb. Both my mind and my body stopped feeling anything except pain. Time had managed to move so quickly while standing still at the same time. I read the epitaph, Only the Good Die Young, and smiled. I wasn't any good, but she was the best.

Sitting on the cold, hard earth in front of my best friend's granite tombstone, my hopes of everything being a bad joke vanished. It wasn't real until that moment, the permanence of it, and I only had myself to blame.

I couldn't imagine what Meredith's dad had gone through burying his only daughter, especially after losing his wife. Standing there with what little family he had left beside him, shaking the hands of people he'd never met.

I know that if I was there, they would have all stared at me, all of them. They would have forced smiles and condolences while they secretly blamed me. Murderer, they would have thought. And they would have been right. I wouldn't have been able to face Mr. Short, to look him in the eye. Though no one knew for sure what happened, I would have been the one to blame. I was the survivor. Molly said there were a lot of people there for Meredith, and that made me happy.

"It wasn't supposed to happen this way," I said out loud. "This wasn't supposed to happen at all. I think that's why my mind has yet to accept it. I pray every night that I will go to sleep and wake up in our apartment, ready for school as though nothing happened. But I can never seem to fall asleep. And when I do manage to drift off, I awake in a cold sweat, barely able to catch my breath. I watch in the dark as the last digit on my alarm clock changes. One to a two, to a three, to a four.

"I wish that I didn't exist. I wish I was the one who died and you were still living and loving Eli. I haven't seen him yet, not that he would talk to me. I miss you, Mer. I miss everything we used to do, everything we planned to do. I don't know what to do with myself and I keep thinking how you would know what to do, but then I realize you aren't here. I wish I wasn't here."

I stayed with Meredith until the sun went down and the cemetery grew dark. My eyes were empty and I was hoarse from talking in the cold. It was time to go, but I couldn't leave. My mom had called several times and I knew if I didn't get back to her soon she would start to panic.

I got off the ground and dusted myself off, and promised Meredith that I would be back soon, that I would come back a lot. I started the car and called my mom back once the car had heated up and the chatter in my chin was gone.

Mom was panicked and I reassured her that everything was fine. I told her I would be back within the hour. I glanced back at the fresh mound of dirt at the end of the row as I drove out of the cemetery and put the radio on. Playing on the first station was "Old Apartment" by the Barenaked Ladies. That was our song, and the words had never rung so true.

Only memories, fading memories
Blending into dull tableaux
I want them back
I want them back

I shook my head, looked up at the sky, and smiled. "I want them back, too," I said. "I want them back."

EPILOGUE

It was hot, even in the shade under the tent. The president of Hay U looked uncomfortable in his suit as he addressed our class. Molly sat on my right playing with her phone and Sam sat next to her. When he finished, Sarah Clay, the valedictorian, took over.

"I want to start by congratulating you on entering the adult world," she began, echoing the speech the president had delivered to us four years earlier. "You are no longer children. Now take a look at the person on your left."

Everyone started to giggle. Everyone but me. Instead, I looked out onto the lawn where my parents sat with Patrick and Jane. In the distance I could see Pete walking slowly behind Marnie as she wobbled in front of him.

"Take a look at the person on your right," Sarah continued, bringing my attention back to the stage. "You were not the one out of three. Congratulations!"

The tent erupted in whistles and applause. I began to cry.

ABOUT THE AUTHOR

A.K. Mills is a graduate of St. Joseph's University in Philadelphia. The Parts I Remember is her debut novel. To learn more, visit www.byakmills.com.